Eye on You- The Mississippi Queen

by Joe Hamilton

Dedication

I would like to dedicate this book to my son Dean, who laughs at my jokes.

High praise for *Eye on You - Rock You Like a Hurricane*

"This is a really, really good book. It's totally amazing. Dozens of people tell me that. Believe me. Other than me, Joe Hamilton has the best words."

"The author says his motivation in writing this book is to help reduce children's hunger. One question, what is the charity supposed to do with a bunch of books?"

"I thought this was about the Scorpions hit song...Bummer."

I took "Rock You Like a Hurricane" on my last cruise. I was never more frightened. Not because of the book, but the ship almost capsized from a hurricane."

<u>This is the third book in a series.</u>

Book 1   *Murder in Biloxi* takes place from November 1978 to April of 1979 and deals with police corruption and murder. Gabriel Ross, having fallen into the job of Private Detective, muddles his way through to capture the bad guy and win the girl while staying clear of the Dixie Mafia.

Book 2   *Rock You Like a Hurricane* takes place from November 1982 to March 1983 and tells the story of Gabriel's hunt to find a madman who has been abducting teenage girls, while also trying to solve a 14-year-old missing person case.

Book 3   *The Mississippi Queen* takes place in July of 1979 and challenges Gabriel and his team to foil a blackmail scheme while trying to not start a race war.

Notes on this book

The title of this book comes from the famous steamboat *Mississippi Queen*, which delighted passengers traveling the Mississippi River for decades. It has nothing to do with the hit song by the group Mountain, as some have suggested.

IMBD# 978-0-9939999-2-5

Thank you to my editor- *QuestionMark*

Table of Contents

Prologue

It was well after dark when Willy Parnell shuffled across a deserted Hiller Park. A sliver of a moon hung in the night sky like a shiny fingernail, doing little to illuminate his path. Large oak and pine trees, dating back to the Civil War, stood sentry as Willy made his way to his apartment.

He was thinking about his two granddaughters. They'd enjoyed a wonderful day at Biloxi Beach making *Muppet* sand castles. The cool Gulf waters proved to be the perfect relief from July's hot Mississippi sun. The girls kept him busy by constantly running in the surf and washing away their suntan lotion. Cicely was obsessed with Miss Piggy and had her nasal voice down pat. Miriam, on the other hand, was a die-hard Cookie Monster Fan. Whenever the girls came to his apartment, he always made sure there was a plate of chocolate chip cookies available. Willy loved his granddaughters very much.

The only sound in the park were the crickets, no doubt even they, were complaining about the heat. He thought about his younger days working on the docks. *I'd be able to run through the park with a grandchild on each shoulder. That was another lifetime.* Willy stopped briefly at a lamppost to catch his breath. He reached down and tapped the pill container in his trouser pocket to reassure himself.

Ever since Ruth, his wife of forty years, passed of throat cancer he had tried his best to fill in his life with his daughter's children. When playing with the kids, his mind would usually drift back to the early days. *Ruth, you were one wonderful woman. I knows you lookin down at me now. I just know you're proud of our daughter and the kids.*

Thinking of Ruth gave him a touch of sadness. One of his most vivid memories was when their daughter Justyne announced her decision to marry Morgan, one of the whitest men to ever to walk the earth. He knew enough to keep his reservations to himself. You have to let your children chose their own path in life. Ruth for her part hadn't had a judgmental bone in her body and heartily welcomed the big-eared, redheaded, investment advisor into the family. The girls inherited what Ruth liked to call, the best of both with a smooth coffee color complexion.

Willy's apartment bordered the park where he often took the kids after meeting them at school. Because he was near, inexpensive, and loved the kids so much, Willy had become the before and after school caregiver, along with his other duties of cookie baker, grade two art aficionado, and number one storyteller. Normally he liked to walk home before nightfall, but Justyne had insisted that he stay for the fresh catfish meal. After putting the twins to bed with yet another story, he thanked his daughter and son-in-law and headed across the park to his apartment.

He looked up at the lamppost and saw that the light was burned out. *What's the point of having street lights when they don't bother to replace them? They could spend some of our tax dollars so an old guy could see where he's going.* His musings were interrupted by the sound of a twig snapping behind him. He turned around only to find an empty path. When he turned back, he was startled by two men who appeared out of the shadows and blocked his path. They were tough looking, punks.

"Help you men with something?" asked Willy, his face breaking into an uneasy smile.

"Maybe we help you old man, you having hard time? Eh? Don't it look like he having struggle?," said one thug to the other in a heavy Eastern European accent. Willy thought they sounded like guys he used to work with on the docks.

"Struggling….yeah," replied the second thug.

Willy looked from one man to another. In the dark, it was hard to make out their features. They appeared to be in their late twenties and were dressed in jeans and dark t-shirts. Both were white with hard features, including muscular, drawn-back shoulders, and strong jawlines. They both had short hair like the fuzz on a tennis ball. One of them moved closer.

Stay calm, they probably just want my wallet. He could smell last night's dinner off the one who was now a few inches from his face. *Something with garlic.* Willy turned away and looked at the guy's partner, a slack-jawed punk who seemed to have a permanent sneer wallpapered across his face.

"Thank you, but I'll be fine, I don't live far."

"Yeah?" asked the one with the breath. *The leader.* "Maybe you want help. I think Nigger Man needs help."

"Yeah. Help," came the reply from the punk with a sneer. Willy felt hands on his back shoving him forward towards the trees. He stumbled briefly before catching himself by grasping onto an oak tree. *No point in trying to outrun these two, so I'm gonna have to teach them not to mess with...,* his thought was interrupted by sneering man pushing him again towards a small clump of trees.

"Why don't we show him shortcut?" said the guy with the breath.

"Shortcut, yeah."

"Listen I don't want any trouble. Do you want money?" Willy pulled his billfold from his pant pocket, but the leader slapped it out of his hands and pushed him further towards the trees. They took turns pushing Willy until the old man tripped over a tree root and fell over backward.

"Help!" Willy yelled out weakly.

As he was struggling to get to his feet, garlic breath kicked him in the face, knocking him back to the ground, causing a searing pain in between his eyes. His nose began to bleed.

"Shut up, Nigger."

"Yeah, shut up Coon," added his partner.

Willy absorbed the trauma, swallowing the pain, then kicked his way slowly back to the surface. "If you don't want money, what do you want?" Willy was conscious of his heavy breathing and the pleading sound of his voice.

The response was another kick, this time to the kidneys. Since talking wasn't working, Willy just lay down and suffered through their repetitive kicks to most of his body. Ten seconds passed, then twenty and thirty. Every blow sent ripples of pain throughout his whole body. He felt his chest tightening. He struggled to sit up and reach for the pills in his pocket. The thugs laughed as he fell back to the ground. All he could manage were the words, "Please."

On another day, he could have taught these punks a lesson. Willy didn't last long. His last thoughts were of Miss Piggie and the Cookie Monster.

Chapter 1

July 9th, 1979. It was the kind of day where your ice cream cone would melt all over your hand. Where young kids would spend hours jumping into the cool waters of the Mississippi. Gabriel looked up at the wall calendar. A young couple huddled together in a horse-drawn sleigh making their way across a snow-covered field. A subtle message from Mom in Detroit on his last birthday. Here he was feeling like a snowman in a sauna, and it now seemed like a cruel joke. It had been nine consecutive days of thermostats stuck in the mid-nineties. Mercifully his little one-room office, which was originally meant to be a janitor's closet, had a little twelve-inch fan.

The *Biloxi Herald* screamed out headlines about the war in Vietnam, which was now spilling over into neighboring countries like a drunk who couldn't hold his liquor. The Shah of Iran had been overthrown, and the Arab world was in chaos causing gas prices to rise to unheard of levels. Domestically, Jimmy Carter's popularity as President was dropping as unemployment rose. People were now looking to a fresh wave of conservatism and a new face. Ronald Regan with his supply-side economics was garnering a lot of press coverage in his run for the White House.

Locally, Gabriel's notoriety in solving the case of the corrupt sheriff was now yesterday's news. It had been 3 months since William Cooper was arrested, and given immunity and relocation in return for testimony against the really bad guys. Updates from the ongoing trials were now banished to the back pages. It had also been six long weeks since Jacqueline Cooper, the Sheriff's former wife and Gabriel's lover, decided that Biloxi and Gabriel were not what she wanted. With little notice, had she left to live with her parents in Chicago.

Gabriel was debating buying a kiddy pool and stripping down to his boxers in front of the fan when a man walked into the Eye on You Detective Agency.

Gabriel was a little disappointed to learn that the lawyer in front of him was actually named Lawrence O'Brien. The man was the splitting image of Wally Cox, the aging actor who played Mr. Peepers. Tall, thin, and bespectacled, he had thinning brown hair combed over to hide his bald spot. It wasn't just his physical appearance, the guy also had a distinctively soft voice with a faint lisp that made him sound more than a little creepy.

"So let me get this right," said Gabriel, recapping what Peepers had told him so far. "You work for someone, who you won't name, and this person is interested in hiring me to make a problem go away?"

"In a nutshell, that is correct sir." Peepers was wearing a gray pinstripe suit and had his legs neatly crossed, knee over knee.

"Well great, I specialize in making problems go away." Gabriel's orange tabby companion Bourbon jumped up on the desk, startling Peepers. Gabriel felt that Bourbon had a keen sense of judgment about people, and he was sure the fruity way the man was crossing his legs wasn't winning any points. "Well, listen Peep….I mean Mr. O'Brien, are you going to elaborate on this problem or are we supposed to guess?"

"We?" Peepers looked around at the small one-room office. The *Eye on You Detective Agency's* main, and only office, was housed on the 8th floor of a downtown Biloxi office tower.

"Just a figure of speech, although I do rely on Bourbon, my feline associate here, to tell me which cases to take. My guess is that he currently thinks you'd better get to the point before he decides to scratch your eyes out."

"Alright." Peepers said, acting a little put out. "That business with Sheriff Cooper a while ago was remarkable. The individual I represent was very impressed with your persistence with that case, and your discretion after the Sheriff was arrested. You declined most interviews. Others would have jumped at the chance to blow their own horn."

Gabriel said thank you, but didn't feel the compliment was fully deserved. He had been so new in the detective game, he just didn't know how to exploit the publicity. Looking back at it now, saying nothing somehow seemed to have worked in his favor judging by the recent uptick in new customers. Gabriel made a circular motion with his hand gesturing Peepers to continue.

"My employer has found himself in a bit of a pickle. He has somehow been photographed in a compromising position by someone. The individual is threatening to go public if my client doesn't pay them a million dollars."

"A million dollars? That doesn't sound like a pickle, Mr. O'Brien...more like a cucumber. What outcome is this client looking for?"

"He wants the retrieval of the pictures and the negatives, without any of this made public or reported to the authorities."

"Why? Like ... why not just go to the cops? They're the experts. Even if I'm successful in getting these pictures back, the people doing this would just do it again to someone else."

"My employer doesn't care about that. He has recently suffered a catastrophic event with his wife dying in a car accident. He has no wish to have his family's reputation sullied by having this matter played out on television. He is insisting on your complete discretion and no police."

"Not a very neighborly attitude." At this point, Bourbon lifted a hind leg and started to lick his privates. Peepers stared at the cat until Bourbon suddenly looked up and caught him staring. Gabriel couldn't think of a better gesture of disdain. He guessed that Peepers wasn't cutting it on the Bourbon scale. "So if I take the case when do I find out who the client is?"

Peepers reached down and put a black attaché case on his lap. Using a key attached to his pants by a chain, he unlocked both of the clasps. He extracted a sheet of paper and handed it to Gabriel. "If you're hired, then you must agree to the terms outlined in this memorandum."

Gabriel took the document and gave it a quick read, "As a Private Detective and owner of the *Eye on You Detective Agency*, I am bound by my own agreement to respect a client's confidences. So none of this is necessary."

"As I said, Mr. Ross, you need to agree to my employer's terms."

Gabriel took a few minutes to re-read the text. It threatened to sue him for damages specified to be no less than one million dollars if, in the pursuit of the case, Gabriel happened to let slip or cause to be disclosed to the press or to any police authority, the details of the case. *Good luck. I have a suitcase of dirty clothes, an old Volkswagon bug, and this wonderful cat.* "I don't think this is going to work for me, Mr. O'Brien," Gabriel said, picking up Bourbon and putting him on the floor.

"That's unfortunate Mr. Ross. I have been authorized to pay you a $5,000 retainer plus an additional $5,000 upon satisfactory completion of the matter."

Ten grand just for scaring away a couple of punks with a camera? Gabriel looked over the agreement again. He had no doubt that Ben O'Shea, his silent partner and a Biloxi Police Detective, would just throw Peepers out the eighth story window. If Gabriel were to take the case, he would have to keep all of the details away from Ben. Gabriel looked at the little office and did the math. Some new furniture, equipment, air conditioning and maybe an associate. This one case could add up to a hundred employee reference checks and insurance claims. He might even be able to convince Ben to move into a new location. He grabbed his pen and with one final look at Peepers, signed the document. "Now your turn, who's the client?"

"The client would like to interview you before agreeing to hire you."

"That's fine. I'd like to meet the person willing to let these scumbags continue to do this."

"Fine, I will set it up for tomorrow afternoon, at 2 p.m. Congressman Emmett Rogers will receive you at his country estate in Tylertown.

Chapter 2

Gabriel had heard of Congressman Emmett Rogers but learned a great deal more by going to the *Herald* and looking him up in the newspaper archives. Rogers was elected by a significant margin to the 4th Congressional District, which comprised the Gulf coast and areas directly north right up to Hattiesburg. He also knew that the two-term Congressman was one of the Republican Party's rising young stars. The few times that Gabriel had heard him speak on television, the man came across as the bright, fresh-faced, charismatic personality that Republicans were looking for.

Sitting in the archives, Gabriel remembered something about Congressman Rogers' wife and her accident. It took him only a few minutes to find the story. It had gained front page headlines back in June. The picture showed a new model Mercedes sedan doing an imitation of an accordion. An accordion parked up against an old oak tree. There were tires and various debris scattered all around the wreck, items thrown by the collision. The reporter explained that Esther Rogers, wife of Congressman Emmett Rogers, was pronounced dead at the scene of a head-on collision on Snake Road in Walthall County. The County Sheriff, Larry Mitchum, suggested that wet pavement and excessive speed might have contributed to Mrs. Rogers losing control of the car. "The car must have been traveling at over sixty miles an hour when it hit that tree," said the Sheriff. Mrs. Rogers had been returning from a social event in Gulfport. In addition to her husband Congressman Rogers, she is survived by her two children.

There was a follow-up story on page three detailing Mrs. Rogers' community involvement and her husband's political achievements, with a grainy picture of Esther Rogers at her husband's side during an early campaign rally. From the picture, they looked like an odd match. He was tall, slim and handsome while she seemed older, frumpy and dressed in dowdy clothes. *Someone comfortable in the shadow of her husband.* Gabriel turned back to the front page and looked at the car wreck again, and a thought came into his mind.

Gabriel went to the pay phone in the front lobby and popped a dime. It only took a moment before he was connected to the Sheriff.

"Hello Sheriff Mitchum, my name is Gabriel Ross, I'm a Private Detective in Biloxi. I'm doing some checking on an accident that took place in early June of this year up on Snake Road." When there was no response, Gabriel prompted with, "You know, the one involving Congressman's Rogers' wife?"

A few more seconds went by before the Sheriff spoke, 'What ya'll say your name was?"

"Gabriel Ross." When there was no response, he sheepishly coughed and added "A Private Detective in Biloxi."

"What's yar interest in this case?"

"I might be doing some confidential work for the Congressman, and I have a couple of questions that don't appear to be covered in any of the news reports."

"Are you saying that the Congressman has hired you to look into his wife's accident?"

Gabriel felt the mud sliding beneath his feet. One simple conversation and he had already raised suspicions. He wasn't even technically working the case. He decided to ignore the question and plow on regardless. "Deputy Mitchum, I was wondering if there was any indication of alcohol found during the autopsy?"

There was another pause, and Gabriel was about to hang up fearing he had taken things too far when Mitchum responded. "I don't know what road you're traveling on, but I suggest you might have taken a wrong turn, Mr. Ross. I would have thought you would know that the State of Mississippi does not do autopsies on traffic accidents."

"What about in the case of a suspicious accident?"

"The only thing suspicious are these questions you're asking. The only time our medical examiner will ask for an autopsy would be if it was in the public interest to do so. Now I suggest you not waste anyone else's time."

Gabriel started to ask another question but realized he was talking to the dial tone.

Unbowed by the call, Gabriel was able to uncover numerous other references to Congressman Rogers in the archives. He was the kind of man that cameras liked to follow. Many of his campaign speeches espoused what the Republican Party called "family values," a key plank of the Party's platform suggesting the sanctity of the traditional family. This would include strong opposition to pre-marital sex, women working outside the home, feminism, abortion, pornography, common law marriage and, of course, same-sex relationships. As Gabriel read through the text of Rogers' speeches, he wondered how such a man could have gotten himself elected along the Gulf Coast. One of the first things Gabriel had learned about his new home was that the state of Mississippi had two major groups. Those up north, near the state capital that made the laws, and those down south that ignored them. The legislators up north, probably influenced by their Presbyterian or Baptist upbringing, enacted all kinds of laws dealing with illegal gambling, illegal drinking, prostitution and various other sins. The people along the coast were more akin to a Mediterranean culture, probably from the influence of Europeans such as Croatians, and the French from Louisiana. These people were primarily Roman Catholics and were just about okay with most things provided no one got hurt. For that reason, illegal gambling continued to thrive along Biloxi's beach strip.

One of the articles he found showed a picture of Emmett Rogers together with his two kids. A boy aged twelve, and a daughter aged ten. The Congressman's wife had been the heir to a timber fortune up north, so before his wife's death, he literally had a million dollar family. Gabriel wondered if the indiscretion had happened after his wife had died. It was hard to imagine a successful man like Rogers risking everything for an affair.

Gabriel felt the need for company, so he went back to the pay phone and called Rachel Henderson. He had met the young nurse on a previous case, and they had been hanging out together for the past couple of weeks.

While Rachel was being paged, Gabriel thought back to Jacqueline. He'd had something pretty good with Jacqueline Cooper up until she left to go live with her parents. She was one of Gabriel's first clients, and he successfully proved that her husband William was cheating on her. It was a traumatic time for her, not only was her marriage over but the man she had loved turned out to be a crook. When confronted by Jacqueline, Sheriff Cooper was unwilling to let his wife go, and crazily decided kidnapping her made perfect sense. Then, when she wasn't willing to resume her duty as his spouse, he decided that burying her alive would also make sense. If it hadn't been for Gabriel, Ben O'Shea and an FBI agent named Wil Graham, he would have succeeded in making sure that she never lived long enough to leave him. Through all of these events, Jacqueline and Gabriel became romantically involved. Gabriel knew that Jacqueline would always be grateful to him for saving her life. However he had read in *Psychology Today* that couples who got together to support each other during times of crisis often broke up once the crisis was over. Jacqueline had stayed at his apartment for a few months while the story and court trial unfolded. A few months later she'd announced that she needed space and that she was leaving.

"Hello, Nurse Rachel Henderson, may I help you?" The sound of Rachel's voice brought him out of his remembrance.

"Do you have a band-aid?" Gabriel asked trying to disguise his voice.

"Band-Aid?" she answered, a little flustered.

"Yes, it's Gabriel, I scraped my knee falling for you."

"Ah, that's cute and a more than a little sucky."

"I can't help it, I'm feeling a little lonely and was hoping we could hang out tonight," Gabriel said, preparing to beg.

"Well, I was going to study for my law class this evening. You can come over and help me study I guess."

"Hmm, not exactly what I had in mind. How about I swing by and we can grab a bite?" After a great deal of begging, they settled on 6 p.m. that evening. Gabriel knew just the spot to take her.

Gabriel's next call was to Ben O'Shea, his business partner. Ben had been the driving force in starting the Eye on You Detective Agency, as a type of retirement plan for when he called it quits with the Biloxi PD. While Ben was involved in business decisions, they had decided to keep this a secret. Occasionally Ben had been able to refer customers to the Agency, a practice that if made public, would most likely lead to his dismissal.

Ben had found that there were situations where the local police had either given up or were not nimble enough, to get at the truth. One example was the significant limitation put on police forces around procedure. Ben had gotten on the wrong side of his boss on some occasions for being a cowboy and not following the rules. During the Sheriff Cooper case, Gabriel had learned valuable information by having a listening device placed in the ribbon surrounding the Sheriff's hat, something that the Biloxi PD would never have been able to do.

Ben answered after a couple of rings and recognized Gabriel's voice right away. Gabriel had rehearsed this part a few times and launched right into it. "Hi Ben, do you have time for coffee?"

"What's up Gabriel?" Ben answered, cutting right to the point.

"Does this mean you're too busy for coffee?"

"Shitfuck, I'm just busy. Did you read the *Herald* this morning?"

"No, I was just about to, but I had an appointment. What's up?"

"A black man was found beaten to death in the park. All signs look like it was racially motivated," replied a clearly stressed Ben. When Gabriel didn't respond Ben said, "Fuckshit, you know I could use a second pair of eyes on this. The Mayor and the Police Chief have already had a meeting, and we've been told to wrap this up quick."

"Want to meet me at the Café in a half hour?

Chapter 3

Ben was already seated in their usual booth at the back of the Friendship Café when Gabriel arrived. Tweedy, their regular waitress, gave him a big smile and showed Gabriel to the table, giving him a breakfast menu. Gabriel checked his watch and saw it was too early for dinner and just accepted a coffee. Ben, on the other hand, ordered a coffee with a side order of eggs and bacon, white toast and grits.

"No breakfast this morning?" Gabriel asked, putting a copy of the *Herald* in front of them. "I had breakfast, but I guess it didn't take. With all that's going on, I'm not sure when I'll get another chance to eat."

Gabriel noticed that his partner had put on a few pounds. Ben was tall, in his mid-forties with streaks of gray invading his dark hair. His complexion today seemed pasty, likely the result of too many meals on the run and not enough sunshine. Ben liked wearing bright clothes to offset what he called his boring personality. Today he wore a striped green and white shirt with a tartan tie.

"Heard from Jackie?" asked Ben.

"I called her last week, but she was out. So far no callback."

Ben gave Gabriel a sympathetic look. "Just give her time Gabriel. Jackie's been through a lot."

It had been forty-one days, but who's counting? When they were together, Gabriel had thought their relationship was like pieces of a puzzle that were meant to fit together. Since she left, he'd had spoken to her on the phone a few times. He had called a dozen more times, but the response from her parents was consistent. "She's not home right now, but I'll leave her a message." Her mother, a French Canadian, who like Jacqueline, wore her emotions on her sleeve, seemed sympathetic. She had told him that crap people say, "If you really love someone, let them go...." Over the past year, he had come to hate that expression. He felt the same about people telling him to give her more time. He kept telling himself that he needed to move on. Gabriel quickly changed the topic, trying to avoid more thoughts of Jacqueline. "So what's in the file?"

"Just some pictures from the crime scene last night. I would be in a serious pickle if the Chief ever found out I was showing you these."

"That's odd, you're the second person to use that expression today."

"That so, who was the first?"

Gabriel realized too late that he had potentially ventured into verbal quicksand. "Just a new client that I signed up, we can talk about it later." Gabriel realized that Ben received all of the bank statements. He would surely notice the $5,000 retainer going into the account.

Ben fixed him with a speculative look. "Great, we could use some cash in the account. How are the employment checks coming?"

Gabriel wanted to say he hated the routine. Since opening the agency, most of his days were consumed with checking up on employees who liked to embellish their resumes. "I'm getting through them, I can usually turn them around in a day." With the country slipping into a recession the competition for what few jobs there were, was intense. More and more companies were looking to hire investigation firms to do their legwork. "The fax machine rings a couple of times a day with new checks. So are you going to show me the file or what?"

Instead of handing him the file Ben pointed to the newspaper, "Did you read the piece?"

"Not much there, they make it sound like a mugging gone bad."

Ben shook his head. "I don't think so." He handed the file folder over to Gabriel. There was an 8 by 10, black and white headshot of a Negro man lying next to a tree. Gabriel was momentarily taken aback by the savagery. Even in black and white, Gabriel could see that the man had been brutally beaten. Distinguishing the man's features was hard. Whoever did this had hit him repeatedly in the face.

"The paper said the old guy's name was Willy Parnell. Is he in the system?" Gabriel took a sip of his coffee.

"Clean as a whistle. He lived alone in a one-bedroom apartment near the Hiller Park, you know the one off Creek Road?" Gabriel nodded and Ben continued reading from a small spiral notebook. "Time of death was placed around 9:30 p.m. give or take. He was coming back from having dinner with his daughter and her family."

"A robbery?"

"Nope, we found his wallet nearby, full of cash, credit cards. Plus he was still wearing his watch and his wedding ring."

"Old men usually don't get murdered," Gabriel said, stating the obvious. "What's the motive?"

Ben's answer was to show Gabriel the next picture. "I think we're supposed to believe it's this." The next photo showed a close-up of a scrap of paper with the words "Dye Nigger" scrawled in blue pen. "This was found about six feet from the body under a little pile of stones."

"Bad speller. Do the press know about this?"

"Not as of now, but it won't take long for word to get out, then we'll have folks marching in the street. We already had a cover your ass, bullshit firestorm this morning."

Gabriel nodded understanding. "Have there been any other incidences of racially motivated crimes in the area?"

"Nothing that I know of, but to be sure my team is checking with the Sheriff." Ben worked for the Biloxi Police Department while the Sheriff was responsible for crimes within all of Harrison County.

Gabriel looked at the picture again, holding it away from Tweedy who was back with Ben's meal. When she left, Gabriel said, "I'm struck by the excessive violence. It looks personal."

"We're just getting started, but it seems like Willy was just a nice old man who retired from working on the docks. He lost his wife to cancer a couple of years ago."

"If this was racially motivated it would be hard to believe that there haven't been other cases. Do you have the official cause of death yet?"

"I won't get the coroner's report for a while yet. If I had to guess, the guy's ticker couldn't take the beating. There was a prescription of nitro tablets in his pocket."

Gabriel nodded and picked up the original photo. "It looks like there's scratches and bruising are on both sides of the face. You could be looking for more than one perp."

Ben looked at the photo and then nodded his head. "That's helpful Gabriel." After putting the pictures back in the file, "You said you wanted to run something by me. This new case?"

Here it is, decision time. "I'll be honest with you Ben, at least as far as I can. I accepted a case this morning, but I had to sign a document that said that if I tell any details of the case to the police or the press, then the client has the right to sue us for a million bucks."

Ben choked on a piece of bacon. Once he recovered, he alternated between looking at Gabriel and gobbling his breakfast. He started to say something a couple of times then corrected himself, his expression changing from surprise to disbelief before finally landing on comprehension. "Is the client famous?"

"You could say that. If I tell you, what are you going to do?"

"I'm not sure I want to know. I wouldn't be able to help anyway, blackmail is a federal crime. I'm just a local cop." Ben paused for a moment while munching on a piece of toast. "Assuming the document you signed is enforceable, and that somehow word got out, then it's goodbye to my retirement plan. We lose the Agency and everything else we own. Why did you take the case?"

"Let's just say there were 10,000 reasons."

Ben whistled, "That's a lot of money Gabriel." He stared at Gabriel, weighing how much he wanted to know.

Gabriel cut things short, "Congressman Emmett Rogers."

"What! Oh my God! Are you serious?" Ben gasped. His back stiffened, his mouth agape in shock, "That guy might be President one day! Okay, okay....don't tell me another word about this. I don't want to know." His expression changed again, becoming deadly serious, "Be very careful Gabriel, these are serious people, and I'm not talking about the blackmailers."

Chapter 4

Rachel lived in Gulfport in an apartment on Jones Avenue. She answered Gabriel's knock right away, and he was pleased to see that she had already changed from her nurse's uniform into a colorful summer dress. She greeted him with a hug and a peck on the cheek. "You look beautiful," commented Gabriel.

"Thank you, I don't get to wear dresses very much, but it's been so hot lately."

Gabriel had already seen the inside of her apartment, so he said, "Are you ready?"

"You said you knew just the place, I hope I've dressed appropriately."

"You're perfect. Have you ever been to Angelo's Eatery up on Highway 90?"

"Oh Italian food, I love Italian food. No, but I've heard of it, I think it is one of Gulfport's most famous."

The two left the building holding hands like high school sweethearts. On the way to the restaurant they talked about her work in the hospital which comprised mainly on greeting visitors at the reception desk and cleaning up after the patients, many of whom were unable to look after themselves.

As soon as they got in the car, Rachel lit up a cigarette, opening the car window.

"I thought you were going to quit? asked Gabriel, putting the car in gear.

"Yeah...well, I tried but school and work ....it's been really stressful lately."

Gabriel gave her a look that suggested she was making excuses for continuing her bad habit.

"Trying to quit also makes me irritable."

"How so?" he asked, pulling into traffic.

"Like if you don't change the subject, I'm going to stab you in the fucking neck," Rachel smiled.

"Okay then, how is Mr. Dermody these days?" Alex Dermody was a former reporter for the *Herald*, who had been paralyzed after a car accident. Originally Dermody's accident was thought to have been caused by drinking and driving. When Gabriel had confirmed that the reporter was not a drinker, it had prompted him to look into Dermody's recent news stories, and more specifically, who might have had a motive. Gabriel's investigation led him to uncover a conspiracy involving one of the Sheriff's deputies and the disappearance of numerous teenage girls. While the deputy suffered for his crimes in a hail of gunfire, the real architect behind the scheme disappeared. The similarity between Mrs. Rogers' accident and Dermody's accident had occurred to Gabriel.

Meanwhile, Dermody had become a permanent resident of Gulf Oaks Psychiatric Hospital. Despite his complete paralysis, he was able to impart an important clue to Rachel.

"I think he winked at me the other day. I told him a funny story, and well, he can't laugh, but somehow I think he liked it."

"What was the story?"

"Well, you see there was a visitor who asked the Hospital Director about the criterion he uses to decide whether someone should be institutionalized." Rachel dropped her voice a couple of octaves, apparently mimicking a man. 'We fill up a bathtub, then offer a teaspoon, a teacup or a bucket to the patient and ask them to empty the bathtub.' 'Oh, I understand,' said the visitor, 'A normal person would use the bucket because it's bigger than the spoon or teacup.' 'No,' said the Director, 'a normal person would pull the plug.' Then the director asked him if he would like a bed near the window."

"Hah, that's pretty good. That's not really how they do it, is it?" Rachel gave Gabriel a smart-ass look. "Do you really think Dermody understood that?"

"Probably not. But it is much more fun thinking that he might. Sometimes I lie awake at night thinking of things I can say to him."

"You are a very kind person Rachel."

"Thanks, Gabriel, I appreciate that you think that. A lot of those patients at the hospital are so sad, any little thing I can do to make a difference is worth it, even if some don't understand."

Gabriel pulled the car into Angelo's parking lot which was more than half full, not bad for a weeknight. The receptionist who greeted them asked if they wanted a table in the smoking or non-smoking section. Gabriel turned to Rachel and said, "Extra Smoking?"

Rachel laughed and told the receptionist that non-smoking would be fine. The waitress showed them to a table at the back. The table was covered with a red checkered linen tablecloth and a burning candle mounted in an old Chianti bottle. The restaurant's décor was unique with a huge stone fireplace bordered by two large oak trees growing right through the ceiling. The windows offered a great view of the coast.

"This is a really cool place Gabriel." Rachel was clearly impressed as she sat down at the table near the fireplace.

"The building was destroyed by Hurricane Camille. The place was leveled, but the owner Angelo Xidis had it rebuilt using steel and glass."

"Aren't you the little historian," Rachel said with amazement.

"Arnie Sims, the super at my apartment building, told me that the owner is very secretive about his recipes. He won't even let his staff know what he puts into his spaghetti sauce. The place has become a bit of a landmark. The big sign outside, *We Feed the People,* has become an icon."

Once the waitress came by to collect their order, Rachel asked, "So anything new on Sheriff Cooper's court case?"

"As you know he made a deal with the District Attorney and now that he's finished testifying, he's in the witness relocation program. The trial of those implicated will drag on for most of the year. It's all being kept hush hush, but I heard from Ben that he apparently gave enough evidence on the mob here and in New Orleans to put them away for a long time."

"What about the missing girls?"

"He's claiming that this was all the work of one of his Deputies and his brother Boone Cooper. The deputy's dead, and Boone Cooper suspiciously took off, just before he was about to be arrested. The Sheriff testified that he knew nothing about what happened to the girls, or this guy the papers dubbed the Mardi Gras killer. He let slip one small thing that is worth pursuing, though."

"What's that?"

"When the DA hammered him about the killer's whereabouts, Cooper apparently said something about that boat having already sailed. Might just be a figure of speech, but it was said in such a way that the authorities think he was giving them a clue."

"All those poor families. Not knowing what happened to their daughters must be tearing them apart."

"None of the girls have ever been found nor have any bodies been recovered. If they're dead, then the idea of the killer having a boat makes sense. The Gulf is pretty deep. But it could also be that they've been sold off into a white slavery ring."

"Are you still involved in the investigation?"

"No, I believe the FBI is setting up a task force. I would help if they wanted me to, but I have lots of other cases."

"Like what?"

"We're getting into areas that are confidential, but I can say I'm doing some preliminary work on a blackmail scheme. Other than that, there are all the routine employee reference checks."

"Blackmail? Someone famous?" Rachel munched on a breadstick.

Gabriel just shrugged. "I can't talk about it."

"Sounds exciting."

"You're making it sound more glamorous than it is. Believe me, your job is just as interesting."

Rachel rolled her eyes in response, "Did you see the story in the paper about that poor man who died in the park yesterday?"

"Yes, pretty horrible."

"The paper didn't give a motive, so I guess it must have been a mugging."

'I think there's more to it that will come out in the next few days. It might even be racially motivated." Gabriel lowered his voice.

"Really?"

Gabriel once again shrugged his shoulders as if to suggest that he might know something but couldn't say.

Rachel had a pensive look for a moment before saying that her law professor had told a funny story in class the other day. She was taking a law class at night to give her more perspective before committing to a career. "Want to hear it? It's kind of related."

Gabriel nodded, and she continued. "First off what makes this funny is my law professor Mr. Brant is the only black professor in the school. Anyway, the story goes that a black man walked into a restaurant, and a white man yelled out, 'COLOREDS AREN'T ALLOWED IN HERE!'" Once again Rachel mimicked a deep South accent. "So the professor said to the man, 'When I was born, I was black, when I'm cold, I'm black, when I'm sick, I'm black, when I die, I'll be black. But when you were born you were pink, when you're cold you're blue, when you're sick you're green, when you die, you'll be purple. Yet you have the nerve to call me colored?'"

They both laughed over the story which was interrupted by the waitress bringing Chianti, fresh warm bread and a platter of Angelo's Spaghetti with the secret sauce. The two of them dug in like two people stranded on a deserted island off the coast of Italy.

As they devoured the food, Gabriel couldn't help wonder about Willy Parnell and why he had to die.

Chapter 5

The next day Gabriel was having a late breakfast, reading that morning's paper. As he took a sip of his coffee, details of last night's dinner with Rachel came into focus. Great company, fantastic food, and judging by his headache, maybe a little too much Chianti. They had ended up at the front door of her apartment, giggling and laughing like two teenagers. He kissed her, she kissed him back. This went on for a few minutes before she invited him in for a nightcap.

That's when he said he was tired. She gave him a funny look and said fine, she had to study for her law test anyway. Thinking back on it, he was at a loss to explain what must have come off as pretty weird. His thoughts about last night were interrupted by a knock on the apartment door. When he opened the door, he found the smiling face of the building's superintendent, Arnie Sims. Sims was a tall black man in his senior years, with a mottled complexion and a wide smile. "Good morning Gabriel. My, my, you're looking like ten miles of bad road this morning. Your coffee maker working?"

"Come on in Arnie," said Gabriel, leading the way to a small kitchen where he poured a cup of coffee for his friend.

As they sat down at the small table, "Going to be hotter than blue blazes today," commented Arnie.

"Last night I saw a bunch of people sleeping on their balconies. I have to get some air conditioning."

"I hear ya. You should get yourself one of those window units." Arnie took a long sip of his coffee, "Gabriel, you never did explain what happened that caused Jacqueline to leave town."

Gabriel looked at his friend, "I don't really know. The court case against her husband had wrapped up. Things settled down. Maybe she had been operating on adrenaline. I think she started thinking seriously about what she wanted. She missed her family up north, but it's more than that. I wish I could say it was something I did, then I could apologize, but I honestly don't think that's it."

"You still calling her?"

"I'm developing a pretty good relationship with her mother. We were talking about exchanging recipes the last time I called. Jacqueline's apparently working hard and taking classes at the college. Her mother always ends the call saying she'll get a message to her."

"Do you think Jacqueline's Mom might be able to tell you what her daughter's feeling?"

"I've asked, and she has politely declined to speculate, or maybe to violate her confidentiality."

"So she hasn't told you to stop calling," the older man said after taking a sip from his coffee. "So there's still a chance?"

"I don't know."

Arnie nodded to show his understanding.

The two of them slipped into an easy conversation about the relative merits of home ownership versus living in an apartment.

After he had left, Gabriel picked up the *Daily Herald* and Dana Lorimer's headline blazed across the front page, *"Racial Prejudice Suspected in Weekend Death."* Gabriel wasn't surprised, it was going to come out sooner or later.

*****

Later that morning at the office, Gabriel had the window open, the blinds pulled down and the cheap fan working at full speed, and he was still dripping with sweat. He was trying to gather his thoughts before his meeting with the Congressman. He first reviewed the scant details he had noted from his initial meeting with Mr. Peepers.

–Caught in compromising position

-Threat to go public

-Want a million dollars for pictures & negatives

- No publicity, no police.

-Accomplice?

He then compared it to the notes he made when reading up about Congressman Rogers.

—- Elected to two terms as Congressman for 4th District

— Republican Rising Star

— Bright, fresh-faced, charismatic

- A strong proponent of Family Values

-Two kids and a spouse who recently died in an accident.

Gabriel sat back and contemplated the Congressman's situation. Most likely some hot twenty-something intern with blonde shoulder length hair and heaving breasts. She likely volunteered to work late, flashed a little skin, maybe joined him for a late night drink before getting him to take her to an out of the way hotel room where an accomplice was set up with a camera. Then comes the demand for money along with compromising pictures that might just find its way to the press, or for that matter to Mrs. Rogers. The congressman certainly wouldn't have been the first, or the last guy, to fall for this. The key would be to lean on the chick until she gave up her partner.

Bourbon jumped up on his desk which gave him an idea. He picked up the phone and dialed a familiar number. A young woman answered almost immediately.

"Gulf Oaks Psychiatric Hospital, Nurse Henderson speaking."

"If I were a cat, I would spend all nine lives with you."

"That's corny. You say that, but you wouldn't even come in for a nightcap." Gabriel tried to gauge Rachel's mood based on her tone. He decided it was somewhere between playful and put out.

"I know. I called to apologize and to beg you for another chance. I had a great time last night and, well I would like our first time to be memorable."

"What would be memorable?"

"You know."

"You can't even say it, can you?"

"Jeopardy."

"You said that was what you and Jacqueline used to call it when you had sex. You think about her a lot, don't you?"

"Uh, no, well sometimes, but not when I'm with you."

"So if we had had sex last night, and I'm not saying we would have, why wouldn't it have been memorable?"

Gabriel felt that sinking feeling again, "Only because … I was a little tired, and I want to be at my best." He decided to try to shift tactics. "How can I make it up to you?"

"Well, there is a way..."

"I'll do anything."

"Anything?"

"Well, almost anything."

She let out a sigh of frustration. "My boss at the hospital invited me to have dinner with her and her husband on Wednesday night, and she told me to bring a date."

"I thought you didn't like your boss."

"I don't, but I need to get serious about my career. I think she wants to see whether I would be a good fit for management."

"…and you want me to come with you and impress her with all your wonderful attributes, laugh at your corny jokes … that type of thing?"

"Exactly!"

Chapter 6

When Ben had first moved from Rhode Island to Biloxi, he found it very difficult to get used to Mississippi's summer heat and humidity. People from Biloxi called the heat waves "training grounds for down below." Sitting in his bachelor apartment Ben thought the saying aptly described what his day was going to be like. He poured himself a second cup of coffee and looked at the headlines in the *Daily Herald.*

Racial Prejudice Suspected in Weekend Death.

By Dana Lorimer

An unnamed but reliable source in the Biloxi Police Department told this reporter that Willy Parnell might have been the victim of a hate crime. "Evidence found close to the body would indicate that the victim might have been targeted because of his race," said the source.

Willy Parnell's body was discovered at the base of an oak tree in the park early on Sunday morning. Robbery had already been ruled out as a motive by local police. Mr. Parnell had been severely beaten and might have succumbed to a heart attack. Police recovered a bottle of heart medicine in his pocket. The 64-year-old resident of Biloxi was returning from having dinner with his family and walking home through the park. Officials in the Biloxi PD have declined comment, although Chief of Police Bernard

Willis said that resolving this case was a top priority. In
a statement released by Mayor Baxter, he urged
citizens to stay calm and let the police investigation
take place.

Ben put the paper down in disgust. He wasn't surprised that someone had spoken to a reporter. That type of thing regularly happened despite the Chief's threats. Relationships get built between members of the force and the press. He could just picture the Chief railing about the disloyalty of cops talking about confidential matters to the press. He had heard the speech on more than one occasion. "Would you put your life in the hands of someone who would risk your safety by revealing confidential information to the press?"

*****

After arriving at the Police Station, Ben was advised that the Chief had called an all hands on deck meeting to discuss the case. Ben decided to check in with Chief Willis before the meeting. The Chief was a political appointee of the Mayor's, and as such could sometimes be influenced by shifting political winds. Ben and his boss had clashed on some occasions, usually over what Ben thought was political butt covering.

Ben stuck his head in Willis' office. The white man was in his early sixties. If he were one inch taller, he would be round. A copy of the *Herald* was open on his desk. "Any idea?" asked Ben pointing to the story and deciding to get right to the heart of the matter.

"No, and I'm pretty pissed about it."

"You're pissed?" Willis stood up and flung his stapler against the wall. "THE COCKSUCKER HAS TO BE SOMEONE ON YOUR TEAM. Now, this fucking reporter is going to get everyone all riled up," Ben felt like commenting that the leak was going to get out anyway, but didn't want the blowback. "Now I have all this fucking vandalism downtown," the Chief continued. When Ben didn't comment, Willis continued on, "Here, check it out, there's racist graffiti painted all over the place. This is tourist season O'Shea. This kind of thing makes us look like a bunch of crazies." Willis was getting red in the face.

Ben got up and closed the office door and sat back down before looking at some Polaroids. They showed walls spray painted with "Long live the Klan," "All Niggers must dye," and "White Power." Ben handed the photos back to Willis, who was looking at him spoiling for a fight.

"Well?" Willis finally said in a tone that indicated he was on edge and a comment away from blowing up.

"These pictures were taken, when, this morning? Since the story just came out, I can't see how this could have anything to do with the newspaper story, or someone leaking anything to the press. I bet this graffiti was done by the same shitheads that killed Willy. Look at the way the word die is spelled. It's the same people."

Willis, who was standing over Ben, looked at the pictures again, "Why do you say people, you weren't singing that tune yesterday when we were talking to the Mayor."

"If you look at the lacerations on the old guy's face, you'll see that the bruises are on both sides of his face. It's not conclusive, but a pretty good bet that we're looking for more than one perp. Then they went on a painting spree." Ben paused for a moment before adding, "They're working mighty hard to convince us that this was a hate crime."

Willis sat back down at his desk and fixed Ben with a steely-eyed look, "If it wasn't a mugging, and wasn't a hate crime despite what they wrote on that note, what the fuck was it, smart guy?"

"I didn't say it wasn't a hate crime. I just don't think we should get locked on to one theory at this point."

Willis shook his head in a clear sign of dismissal, "We'd better get to the briefing room."

There were a dozen detectives sitting in cheap metal folding chairs when Willis and Ben walked in. The volume of conversation was pretty high, so Willis took charge right away. "Shut the fuck up everybody and grab a seat." Ben took a seat at the back while Willis remained standing at the front of the room. "We've got a lot to cover off, but before we do I want each of you to look at the people beside you, in front of you and behind you and call them a no good fucking butthole of a traitor."

This brought the volume up in the room which Willis squelched by yelling, "Shut the fuck up now. I don't know which one of you is slamming that slut Dana Lorimer in exchange for inside information, but I promise you this, I'm going to find out, and when I do, you won't be able to fuck anything anymore."

Laughter erupted until Willis began reviewing what was known about the victim and the crime scene, the nitro, and wallet recovered at the scene before ending up talking about what was written on the piece of paper and spray painted on the walls around town. "I have already had my ass reamed by the Mayor, who thinks all the blacks are going to be out on the streets rioting. I've assured him that we are going to put this fucking case to bed yester-fucking day. Now any questions?" Willis always asked for questions, but he didn't want any questions. Everyone knew to just go along rather than being ridiculed for asking something stupid.

"Detective O'Shea is heading up this investigation. O'Shea, what the fuck are you wearing?"

Everyone looked over at Ben, who sat there wearing a blue sear-sucker with a yellow shirt and lime tie. "Just trying to add a little class to the place." This broke everyone up, and Willis once again told everyone to shut the fuck up.

"Do you have anything you want to add Chuckles?"

It was a bit that had been played out numerous times since Willis became the boss. It was funny mainly because it happened on a regular basis and the detectives had come to anticipate it. Ben stood up and greeted his fellow detectives. "The investigation is just getting underway, but we've already started doing a few things. Burnside, you were going to check with the Sheriff's people about other cases of racial crimes."

A youthful-looking man wearing an expensive lightweight sports jacket stood up. "I spoke to Deputy Murdock yesterday as instructed. The dude left a message early this morning to say that no incidents have been reported."

"Thank you. I'll be interviewing the vic's family later this morning to see if there might be a motive that we're missing." Ben offered.

A middle-aged man sitting on the other side of the room called out. "Detective Chuckles, with this graffiti looking like it was done by the same perp, aren't we wasting time chasing down other motives?"

"Good question Harry, and it's Mr. Chuckles, please. This just happened on Sunday night. As you no doubt know from experience, since you're just about as old as time itself, the first step is to gather all the information you can, then when that's complete, you start narrowing down theories of what happened until you find the answer. It's possible that there might be another motive, and the punks just want to throw us off by making it look like a racial thing." Ben took a quick glance at Willis, who seemed to be frittering around impatiently.

"I realize that there are big issues involved here but regardless, the perps might be counting on us doing just that," added Willis.

When no one else said anything. Willis yelled at Ben from the front of the room, "What the fuck else are you doing to move this along?"

"Quigley and Robbins are going out to the site again. Maybe in daylight, they might find something we missed. Then they're going to the graffiti sites to do a canvas. Someone could have seen the artist. Lawson and Munroe will be doing a canvass of the neighborhood and people in the park to see if anyone might have seen anything, and like I said I'm going to take Burnside with me to interview the family."

No one else said anything and Ben silently counted to ten under his breath. If he made it to ten without a sharp comment from Willis, then he would be alright.

"Okay shit-heads those working with Chuckles on this, let's get this fucking thing resolved. Those of you who are not on this case can focus on getting some of the other fucking cases resolved. I won't have our percentage closed rate go down because you people sit around navel gazing with your thumbs up your arses."

The meeting broke up and the detectives started filing out. "You have to love the guy, always so eloquent," Harry mentioned as he walked by Ben.

*****

On the way over to meet Willy's daughter, Ben had a chance to discuss the case with Burnside. When Chief Willis first brought up assigning the new detective to Ben, it was met with resistance. Ben had developed a reputation as a solid police detective, but one who would never receive a Mr. Congeniality award as an easy going partner. His protests were met with a "Shut the fuck up and treat the guy like your first partner treated you."

Ben thought back to his first day with a gold shield up in Providence. He had no sooner arrived in the squad room when his Lieutenant told him to head down to the city morgue to compare a picture of a wanted black felon, to a body that had been found near the rail yards. He arrived at the morgue and after a short wait was ushered into a room with a body lying under a white sheet. The attendant checked the toe tag to make sure that he had the right body. When the attendant gestured for Ben to remove the sheet, he stared at the face of a black man. All of a sudden the corpse opened his eyes and said, "Hiya Ben. I'm your new partner!" Thinking back on it, Ben could still remember the sound of laughter coming from his squad mates as they came into the morgue and introduced themselves.

Burnside and Ben had been partners for almost a month and so far Ben would give the kid a mixed report card. There seemed to be some smarts, the guy asked good questions, but there was something missing. The kid didn't have the respect for the job that Ben was expecting. "So what do you think about this case, Burnside?"

"You said someone might have had a motive, and the whole racial thing might be a smokescreen. But I guess I'm not sure I buy it."

"What do you mean?" asked Ben, turning onto the daughter's street.

"Well, it was a little old man. He's harmless. Who would want to kill a 64-year old guy? I kind of think losers beating up a black guy is more believable."

"You from around here Burnside?"

"I was born up in Tylertown, which is about a couple of hours northwest."

"Where do you come down on the whole race issue?"

"The Chief said to me when I first came on board that I needed to be careful with the coloreds. He said they commit most of the crimes."

Ben thought about that for a minute, "Ever wonder why there are no black police officers on the force? Roughly about 20% of the population of Biloxi is black, but on a police force with over a hundred officers, there isn't one black person."

Burnside took a moment before replying. "Most likely because the black community doesn't trust the cops, so they don't apply."

Ben nodded his head and parked the cruiser in front of Justyne Armstrong's apartment building. He had never considered himself to be racist. He'd grown up near Boston, and Biloxi was his adopted home. The fact that he had no black friends was more of a function of him being a loner. He wondered if when he first met Gabriel, six months ago, whether he would have set him up in business if he had been black. Ben didn't like the answer he came up with, so he did his best to put the issue out of his mind.

The knock on Armstrong's door was answered by a little girl who Ben figured was somewhere north of five but south of ten. She took one wide-eyed look at the two policemen and slammed the door. Ben knocked again, and the door was answered by another little girl who looked remarkably like the first girl but was wearing a different outfit. When this little girl tried to slam the door, she found that Ben had wedged his foot in the doorway. He bent down to eye level with her, "It's okay, we're police officers." The girl just stared at him, her brown eyes as wide as a pair of giant marbles. Ben finally stood up, pushed the door open, and stepped into the apartment.

The little girl looked up at him and said, "Ah-ha, Oh-NOOOO." She exclaimed in a kind of dramatic, nasally sing-song way of speaking. "Are you here to see Meeeee?"

"Er. We're here to see your Momma."

The little girl turned her back to them and yelled out, "Ah-Ha Mommyyyyyy, there are some little piggies at the door!" Her Sesame Street imitation of Miss Piggy was bang on. At this point, she looked at the other little girl and then as if on cue, they both started screaming, "Helpppppp, piggies at the door."

This brought their mother running from one of the back bedrooms. Ben looked over at Burnside, who was trying to stifle a laugh.

"I'm so sorry, I was on the phone talking to my husband and didn't hear you knock. Girls, I want you to apologize to these men."

"Sorry men," they said in unison. One girl added a couple of snorts.

"Go to your room girls and stay there," said their mother sternly. Ben presumed she was Willy's daughter. She was a tall, attractive black woman who looked to be in her early forties. He could tell that she was doing her best to hold things together, but the sniffling and watery eyes suggested otherwise.

"I'm sure they'll have wonderful careers in the entertainment business," said Ben, introducing himself and showing his credentials. "And this," he said reaching out into the hall to retrieve his partner, "is Detective Burnside."

"My name is Justyne Armstrong. My husband Morgan had a meeting, but here's his card. He said he would be happy to meet with you if you had any questions for him." Ben pocketed the card. "Won't you have a seat in the living room? I just put on a pot of coffee. Would you join me?"

"Sure, thanks, Ma'am," said Burnside as the detectives sat down on the couch.

"Really those two girls," Justyne said softly. "Morgan and I haven't told them about what happened yet. I was waiting until he got home tonight. It's going to be very hard, they worshiped their grandfather," she said, tearing up. Ben thought that Justyne was about to fall apart.

"Maybe Detective Burnside would help out and get that coffee for you," Ben said, gesturing to his partner with a nod.

"I can't believe that someone would hurt him like that, he was such a nice man. He would literally give the poor the shirt off his back."

Ben pulled out his notebook, "We're very sorry for your loss, Ma'am, maybe it will help to talk a bit more about him."

"He was sixty-four. Mom passed a few years back of throat cancer, that's when I really noticed him getting old. He seemed to age ten years when she died. I offered to have him live with us. My husband Morgan would have been fine with it, but Dad wanted his privacy. Still, he was over here all the time, reading stories to the kids, helping them with their school work." Ben reached into his pocket and pulled out a handkerchief and gave it to her. She immediately used it to wipe the tears from her eyes.

"Hope you don't mind, but I poured us each a cup, and I found this plate of cookies on the counter," said Burnside, returning from the kitchen.

"No, not at all. I was leaving them out to serve you." Justyne said, starting to cry again. In between sobs, she explained that her Dad had made the cookies and brought them over for the girls. Ben was just about to bite into one when he put it back on the plate.

Burnside got up from the couch and examined a picture of the girls with their parents and grandfather down at the beach.

"Is this a recent picture?" he asked. Justyne nodded. Burnside went over to Ben and showed him the picture. With his back turned towards Justyne, he used his finger to point to the husband and mouthed the word Caucasian.

Ben made a note to kick his ass when they got out of there. "You were talking about your Dad, did he have any hobbies, things he liked to do?" Ben asked.

"No hobbies really, I know he liked to read and keep up with the news of the day. He didn't have a lot of friends. Most of the guys he worked with were younger, or they moved on. He was in the War and got a postcard every once in a while. Other than coming here, and going to church, I think that was his life."

"Where did he work?"

"He worked as a longshoreman until 1970. There was a big hurricane and the business closed down."

"Was he alright financially?"

"I think he had a bit of money, he wouldn't talk to me about that kind of stuff. He was a little old fashioned that way I guess. Morgan would know more, they talked investments sometimes.

Most of anything that Dad had, came from life insurance that paid out after Mom passed. Why are you asking all these questions?"

Burnside jumped in at that point, speaking in an officious tone. "When investigating a crime, you need to gather all of the relevant information on the victim before narrowing things down to a particular theory of the crime."

Ben rolled his eyes. "We found a bottle of nitroglycerine pills in his coat pocket. Was your Dad having health problems?"

"He had back problems. Most likely from the kind of work he used to do. When Mom passed, Dad seemed to lose interest in things and ended up suffering a heart attack. It was minor, he kept the pills around just in case."

"Who knew he had heart problems?" asked Burnside, taking a big bite of a second cookie. "These cookies are great."

"Other than his family.....just his Doctor, I think, it's not something you brag about."

A gruff voice belonging to one of the girls came from one of the bedrooms. "I smell cookies."

"I think you might have a cookie monster problem," said Ben, getting up from the sofa and taking the plate of cookies away from Burnside. "I hope you don't mind, but I have a fondness for cookie monsters." Ben walked down the hallway and knocked on the bedroom door. "I have a special cookie delivery for the Cookie Monster and Miss Piggy." He heard more snorting and snickering from behind the door. When there was no answer, he knocked again before opening the door to an empty room. "Ah, I must have the wrong address. These chocolate chip cookies must be for someone else."

"Leave the cookies on the bed," said a gruff voice from under the bed.

"Are you bringing presents for moi?" came the voice of Miss Piggy in the closet.

"I usually get a tip when I make deliveries," said Ben.

There was more snickering and snorting coming from the girls as Ben left the room.

When he returned to the living room, Justyne thanked him and commented that he had made the girl's day. Her eyes started to tear up again, and Ben asked if the family was religious.

"We're Southern Baptists, but I don't feel particularly religious at the moment."

"I wonder if your minister might be of help in trying to explain what happened to your father, to the girls." Justyne nodded and wiped away the tears. Ben took a long sip of his coffee and then asked, "Did your Dad know his neighbors well? Can you think of anyone we should speak to?"

"No, he pretty much kept to himself. Oh, there's a couple of old biddies who live on the same floor as Dad. Uh…Maven and Mabel. He used to say they were always flirting with him, offering to cook for him. I think he stayed away from them. He said all they wanted was sex."

Ben smiled. "Have you noticed anyone in the park that might have been acting suspiciously?"

"I'm not really sure what that means, but I did see a couple of guys hanging out in front of my building. They weren't doing anything, just smoking so it's probably nothing. It kind of stuck with me because of the way they looked at me. It was creepy. I heard one say something as I walked by but it was in some other language. Anyway, I walked quickly to the car and drove away. I looked back in the rearview mirror, and they were both watching me."

Ben looked over at Burnside and wondered if it hadn't been just a case of an attractive woman being checked out by a couple of pervs. "What did they look like?"

"I only saw them briefly, but they were white, and both had jeans and black t-shirts. One had a black jacket. Oh, and they both had brush cuts like they were soldiers."

There was an Air Force base in town, "Would you be able to recognize them again Justyne?" asked Ben.

"Maybe... I don't know. You don't think any of this is related do you, Detective?"

"Probably not, but you never know. We're just getting started," replied Ben, closing his notebook indicating that he had finished his questions.

"Do you have any suspects Detectives?"

"Not at the present time," replied Burnside.

"It was suggested in the *Herald* that Dad was killed because he was black. Is that true?"

"It might be. Have you or your husband ever been threatened?"

"You probably noticed that Morgan's white, or as dad used to say, extra white," she said, looking at Burnside. "I don't believe we've ever received anything resembling a threat. I know the girls might have trouble when they get older, but maybe by that time, Mississippi will be different."

"I think with their personalities you shouldn't have to worry. Good luck with the conversation tonight. I don't envy you." Ben got up to leave. Burnside was still eating his cookie. "Are you coming, Detective?"

Ben finally dragged him out of there, and they walked back to the car. "So Detective, what do you think our next steps should be?" Ben asked, deciding to suppress his annoyance with his young partner.

"I hope the people canvassing the neighbors come up with something, because other than the cookies, that was a waste of time."

"Maybe so, but I think we need to go meet a couple of old biddies."

Chapter 7

The drive to Brookhaven took almost two and a half hours. It seemed like a lifetime ago that Gabriel had bought his aging VW bug from a second-hand car lot in Detroit. Since moving to Biloxi, he had often regretted the decision not to spring for air conditioning. The salesman had said running the air conditioning would transform the little car's engine into nothing more powerful than a sewing machine. Days like today, with temperatures well into the nineties, made Gabriel want to take up sewing.

As he traveled Highway 98 west of Hattiesburg, his thoughts were bouncing around like Mexican jumping beans. From thinking about the Congressman, his mind would go to why Jacqueline hadn't returned his call. He tried to think about Rachel and Wednesday night, only to have his thoughts hijacked by an imaginary call he could make to Jacqueline's parents. *"I'm only calling to see if she's ok."* If he got her father, the mathematics professor, the response might sound like, *"Why don't you look at this logically, Mr. Ross? What can you deduce from the number of unreturned calls? What would you say about the probability as the number of unreturned calls increases?"*

On the other hand, if the call were answered by her Mom she would respond in an emotional manner. She would probably say something like give her space, give her time.

He tried to think about the case only to find that he his mind would shift back to the hypothetical conversation he was having with her mother. *"So where is Jacqueline working? What is she taking in college? Does she speak about me at all? Is she seeing someone else? If so, is he taller than me? Should I have offered to dump the agency, desert Ben and follow her to Chicago?*

Gabriel tried to blank out his thoughts by turning on the radio. He scrolled through a dozen religious stations before finding one playing a song by a group called Mountain, they were singing about a Cajun girl from Vicksburg. At the top of the hour, the station switched to news reporting. The newscaster covered a landmark ruling by the US Supreme Court limiting federal aid for abortions. The reporter went to the local congressman for comment. It was kind of surreal to hear the smooth and southern-tinged voice of Emmett Rogers, "I fully support the ruling and I call on all citizens of the great state of Mississippi to rejoice and give thanks. Just recently I have been personally reminded about the preciousness of life. To think that there are people who would so callously put an end to God's gift is a black mark on our great state. It is my hope that come next year, we will have a Republican President who will return our country to the family values that have made the United States the greatest nation in the world."

Gabriel turned the radio off when he saw a large water tower announcing his arrival at Tylertown. Numerous billboards threatening eternal damnation to those who have abortions led the way into downtown. He thought it funny that the signs were positioned next to ones promoting an upcoming gun show.

When he reached downtown, Gabriel felt like he had gone back in time. Brick and clapboard retail shops bordered the main street and made him think of a Norman Rockwell drawing. Many of the shops flew the red, white and blue flag of Mississippi that featured the Confederate battle flag prominently in the top left. He remembered something about the town being a central railway hub for the Confederacy during the Civil War. As he drove down the street, there were numerous people out shopping. Many stood and stared as the VW rumbled by noisily.

When he got to the outer edge of town, Gabriel found the Rogers estate. He pulled into a circular drive leading to a majestic white antebellum mansion with large white pillars. In the lane sat a blue Mercedes 200e, a twin of the one the late Mrs. Rogers had driven into a tree. An older black gentleman wearing a colorful vest and white shirt under a black jacket appeared out of nowhere and ran down the stairs from the house. *A strange choice for the temperature* thought Gabriel.

"Are you Mr. Ross suh?" inquired the older man.

"I sure am," Gabriel turned off the ignition, and the car's engine did its normal sputter and shake before letting out a final gasp. "Sorry, the Mercedes is in the shop," Gabriel smiled.

The man grinned and introduced himself as Charlie. With white-gloved hands, he opened the driver's door which of course opened with its usual creak, prompting a shared laugh.

"Maybe while you're in conversing with Congressman Rogers, I'll just squirt a little oil on that door."

"Thank you, Charlie that would be nice of you." Gabriel extended a hand which the black man tentatively shook.

Charlie led the way up the stairs and held a large wooden door open for Gabriel. "The Congressman has instructed me to have you wait for him in the foyer. Y'all, please make yourself comfortable. I'll be right back with some sweet tea for you."

"Thank you again," said Gabriel as the older man disappeared through a doorway. Gabriel took a seat on a red velvet bench and admired the huge circular staircase and the ornate plaster ceilings. He got up to examine a beautiful tapestry which hung on one of the walls. A small plaque proclaimed that it was made by the local Choctaw Indian tribe. On other walls, there were paintings of somber looking military men, many in civil war dress. Part way up the staircase he saw a beautiful painting of the congressman holding his two kids.

As he was admiring the painting, Charlie returned with a glass of tea. "How long have you worked for Mr. Rogers?"

"You mean Congressman Rogers?" he asked, correcting Gabriel. "I've worked for the Congressman ever since he married Mrs. Rogers. Before that, I worked for her family for as long as I can remember. I reckon most of that time I worked for her father, Mr. Zeke Burnside. There is a painting of him over here," he pointed out one of the paintings Gabriel had noticed earlier. "He was a Colonel during the Second World War. Before and after the war he owned a timber business."

"A sad thing that happened to Mrs. Rogers," Gabriel commented, returning his gaze from the painting to Charlie.

"Yes, Mr. Ross suh, that was a tragedy. The children took it pretty hard." Gabriel thought it was interesting that he hadn't said anything about how devastating this must have been for the Congressman.

"Are the children in summer school?"

"The Congressman has arranged for them to go to camp for the summer."

"I noticed the painting of the congressman and the kids by the staircase. Was it done locally?"

"Yes, it was commissioned a couple of years ago. A local artist."

"Is there a similar painting of Mrs. Ross?" Gabriel asked. He thought he saw Charlie give a quick wince.

"There's no paintings or photos of the missus here. She was frightfully shy and didn't enjoy having that done."

"I noticed that she didn't appear in many of the campaign photos and wondered why. I guess that explains it."

"Mrs. Rogers was a little self-conscious about her looks..." Charlie looked like he was going to say more, but a door to the right opened, and a young dark haired man joined them. He flashed a scowl at Charlie who quickly reminded Gabriel that he had some maintenance to attend to.

The newcomer was dressed in a light blue sear-sucker suit with an open collar white satin shirt. Gabriel guessed his age to be mid to late twenties. Once Charlie had left, the man's glare was replaced by a smarmy smile as he introduced himself as Ashley Loewen III, the congressman's senior aide. After they had shaken hands, Loewen directed Gabriel to the bench and sat beside him.

"The Congressman is just finishing a critically important conference call with some of the staff in Washington. He should only be a few more minutes."

Maybe it was the look he'd given Charlie or the way he said he was the "senior" aide, or the way that he was the third edition, or just the way he showed off his perfect teeth when he smiled, Gabriel didn't know, but he took an immediate dislike to Mr. Ashley Loewen III.

"I thought we could cover a few things that might be inappropriate to discuss with the Congressman."

"Sure, fire away Ash." The guy had striking blue eyes that matched his jacket. The term pretty jumped into Gabriel's mind.

Ashley's facial expression changed chameleon-like, reflecting a somber look. "As I'm sure you're aware, the Congressman recently lost his wife in a horrific car accident." Ashley shook his head in sorrow. "Of course, he wants to keep up appearances and project an image of strength, so since his wife's accident is not related to what you're here to discuss, I suggest you not get into that."

"Thanks for the advice Ash," Gabriel answered *I'll ask him whatever the I want, pretty boy.*

"Very good, I'm glad we understand each other. Have you any questions about the confidentiality agreement that you signed with Mr. O'Brien?

Yeah, is Wally Cox still appearing on Hollywood Squares?
"No, it's pretty straightforward," Gabriel said, gesturing as if he was locking his mouth with an imaginary key.

"Great, then I'm sure the Congressman will be along shortly. The three of us can go into his study. Want another sweet tea?"

"No thanks, Ashton." *But something tells me I might need a shot of bourbon.*

Chapter 8

"So Burnside, what's your story?" asked Ben as he drove the cruiser towards the apartment where Willy Parnell used to live.

"Grew up, like I said in Tylertown, went to a community college, and then applied to the police academy."

"Pretty young to get your detective shield. What are you, nineteen?" It had taken Ben over five years to get his gold shields up in Providence. Rumor around the station was that Burnside was well connected.

Burnside responded with a chuckle. "Nice guess Sherlock. I'm twenty-six."

"Got a girl?"

"Nothing serious at the moment. Lots of prospects. What about you O'Shea, people say you're married to the job?"

"I was married to a gal up in Providence, but it didn't work out.

"How did you end up down in Biloxi?"

"In Providence, you have to pay your dues," answered Ben giving Burnside a subtle jab. "After about five years as a beat cop, I made it to detective and joined the Narcotics Squad. Around that time I met a girl, and we ended up living together in a one-bedroom apartment over a Chinese restaurant. At first, things were pretty good. We both wanted the same things. You know, a career, home, making a difference, Moo Goo Guy Pan. Things started to change after we had been living together for a year. She wanted to get married, she wanted a family, she didn't like me working nights, she didn't like eating Chinese food anymore…We worked on it, I didn't give up. Meanwhile, at work, I was part of a team that made a big drug bust. Got a lot of play in the National Press. Lots of wise guys were charged. That's when the problems started. First, there was a fire in the Chinese restaurant, then some assholes hassled my gal at the market. Nothing heavy, but it was clear that the wrong people were watching. What I didn't realize was that the agenda had changed in the department. The DA dropped some solid cases, and the department shifted manpower away from Narcotics. A lot of it was bullshit, and I was tired of the politics. I wasn't happy at work and coming home to a scared girlfriend was no treat. One day she just packed up and headed home to Vermont. I have a cop friend who had moved down to Biloxi in the late sixties. I spoke to him, and before I knew it, I was offered a detective position on the force."

"So how do you find it down here, compared to up north?"

"I would say that folks here are friendlier. Little things like saying hello out on the street, talking to you in the elevator. Up north, people are a more reserved. I guess it might have something to do with the slower pace of things down here. The food is different, you know the grits, okra, and all the fried foods. "

"Give it time, and you will learn to love it. You asked about her religion back there, that was a good idea. Are you a Roman Catholic?"

"Not a very good one. That's another difference down here. Folks are much more public when it comes to their religion."

Burnside let that comment slide. "What about crime? Is it much different down here?"

"Crime is just about the same everywhere. Same dirtbags trying to take advantage of other people. You guys call it Dixie Mafia, in Providence, it's just the mob." Ben pulled the cruiser into the visitor parking lot adjacent to an eight-story brown apartment building. The apartment was on Belvedere Circle, which was next to Hiller Park. On the night in question, Willy Parnell would have set out around 9:30 p.m. to cross through the park from his daughter's place on Hillier Drive. At a normal walking speed, it might have taken fifteen minutes to travel the distance.

Burnside interrupted Ben's concentration, "So how do you want to handle this?"

"Let's start with Willy's apartment and then knock on some doors on his floor. See if anyone might have known him and whether they've seen anything suspicious."

As they approached the front door, an older black gentleman wearing an immaculate uniform held the door open for them.

Ben flashed his badge, "We're here to look at Willy Parnell's apartment."

"Of course sir. You be looking for room 803. The staircase is just to the right." The lobby was dark, finished in oak burnished to a glimmering shine. Ben noticed a bank of mailboxes off to the left and gestured to Burnside to wait. Taking out his notebook, Ben recorded the names of the other tenants on the eighth floor.

"Sure was a tragedy what happened to Mr. Parnell," said the older gentleman who was watching Ben.

Ben gave the man a nod and introduced himself and his partner.

"The name's Bruce...Bruce Smith, but folks just call me Smitty.

"Did you know Willy very well?" asked Ben recording the doorman's name in his notebook.

"He was a mighty fine man. Always saying hello and having something nice to say to everyone. I just can't believe what happened to him. I sure hope you catch the person responsible."

"Did Willy get many visitors?" asked Burnside, who had previously appeared to not even be listening to the conversation.

Bruce peered at Burnside over his glasses, "His two granddaughters came by most days. All full of spunk those two.

Really made my day when they'd come by." The old man suddenly looked sad, shaken by the recollection.

"Other than the girls, anyone else? asked Ben.

"No sir, poor man. He lost his wife a couple of years back and ever since then...." Bruce looked down hiding his emotion. "I see the girls, and every couple of weeks his daughter. That's it."

"Thanks, Smitty, we plan on catching whoever did this. Where's the elevator?" asked Ben.

"I'm sorry sir, the Belvedere dates back to the Civil War, weren't many elevators back then."

"Thank again," said Ben as the two detectives made their way to a very long staircase. After a couple of stairs, Ben turned back to the doorman.

"Anyone ever strike you as a bit off, maybe having a problem with you or Willy because of your....."

"Color? I saw the article in this morning's *Herald.* Wouldn't surprise me much. I've seen a lot in my time but nothing recently. No, wait, I had to put the run to a couple of punks a couple of weeks back who wanted in the building. I asked them who they were visiting, and they told me to mind my own business and then used the N word."

"Could you recognize them again?"

"Most likely, they were white with big, muscular, arms. They were maybe late twenties, t-shirts, jeans. Oh, they needed a shave. They both had brush cuts. Might have been brothers."

Ben caught Burnside' eye and made a note to have the doorman and Justyne sit with a forensic artist.

Ben looked around the lobby. It was a thing of beauty. "Quite the building," Ben said quietly to Burnside as he started the climb. "Pretty pricey I'm thinking ...doorman, heritage building, everything perfectly maintained. I bet Willy was paying through the nose."

"That's whacked man. This place is gloomy as shit. Reminds me of a fucking cave," responded Burnside.

*****

When Ben finally neared the 8th floor, he was out of breath. "How does an old guy like Willy make it up these stairs every day? Burnside was already standing on the landing above looking down at him like he was Rocky Balboa having just scaled the stairs at the Museum of Art.

"Relax Burnside, we have all day."

"I guess a few too many cheeseburgers huh?"

"Fuck off," said Ben, bent over trying to catch his breath. The hallway was dark with six doors leading to apartments. Willy's place was easy to spot. It was the one with the bright yellow sticker on the door warning that the site was off limits pending a Biloxi PD crime investigation. Recovering, Ben approached the door. "This is odd, someone's been in here." He pointed out to Burnside that the seal had been broken. Ben pulled out his service revolver and put his fingers to his lips.

"Maybe another detective team came by," Burnside said, ignoring Ben's command.

Ben shook his head and mouthed the words, "Shut up," as he tried the handle of the door. He found the door unlocked and opened it slowly. The lights were on, illuminating a small well-furnished living room. He could hear the sound of someone moving about, somewhere off to the left. Holding his revolver up, he directed Burnside to check out the rooms to the right of the entranceway. Ben quietly made his way down a corridor which he guessed contained bedrooms. As he neared the room he heard the noise again, this time sounding like someone rummaging through a box. He risked a quick peek and saw a woman bent over with her back to him.

"Biloxi PD" He yelled. The old lady straightened up briefly before resuming her search.

"Biloxi PD!" Ben repeated, this time, louder. The old lady straightened up again and turned around. This time giving out a gasp of surprise when she saw Ben with his gun pointed at her. The frightened old lady sheepishly held up her hands. She had to be mid-seventies with thinning curly white hair. She was wearing a blue flannel nighty with black socks.

"Well, are you going to shoot me?" she said, her expression going from surprise to boredom.

"Who are you and what are you doing in Mr. Parnell's apartment?"

"Are you going to handcuff me, young man? Maybe beat me with your big nightstick?"

"No, answer the question." Just then Burnside came into the room, gun at the ready.

"Ah isn't that cute, a younger, slimmer, much more attractive version. You make my heart flutter young man." She seemed to adjust something in her ear.

"Who are you and what are you doing in Mr. Parnell's apartment?" Ben repeated, this time much louder.

"You don't have to shout at me. I can hear just fine. My name is Maven, Maven the Raven was my professional name. You probably recognize it. I was a dancer, and well my hair used to be dark so the name kind of stuck. A few other things might have sagged a little." She reached down and cupped her sagging breasts and held them up. "Are you going to describe these in your little notebook? Do you want my numbers?"

"Ma'am, what are you doing in Willy's apartment? Didn't you read that it's an offense to break the seal on the police sticker on the door." Ben asked putting his gun away.

"I didn't break any seal, the door was open, and I just walked right in. I need to get my recipe cards back before someone takes all this stuff away."

"Wait, you say the door was already open?" asked Burnside.

"Aren't you a cute little Sherlock," she said, approaching Burnside. "Let me see your credentials young man. You are way too cute to be a cop."

Burnside' face went red as she reached out and stroked his chin.

"Knock it off lady," said Ben, although he was kind of enjoying the young man's predicament. Maven turned her gaze to Ben, "Yes, Mr. Detective do you want to frisk me, or can I frisk you?"

"We're investigating a very serious matter here."

Just then another old lady entered the room from behind them. "Mabel, Mabel get off the table the two bits is for the beer," said Maven. "I saw them first...they're mine." The newcomer was the spitting image of Maven, but instead of curly white hair, she had dark hair tied up in a beehive hairdo. She wore the same type of flannel nightie along with black executive length socks. While Maven had used an excessive amount of blue eye shadow, Mabel preferred green. "The older one has a big gun," Maven cooed.

"My name is Mabel Foster and my sister, the slut and I live in apartment 805 down the hall. Can I see some identification please?"

Ben and Burnside fished out their Biloxi PD identification and the two women took their time looking back and forth from the detectives and their ID. When they were done, Mabel said, "Why don't you men have a seat, and we can talk this through." Maven chose to sit beside Burnside on the couch while Ben sat in an old armchair. "Now what can we do for you gents?'

Burnside was a little tongue tied from trying to keep Maven's hand off his thigh, so Ben took the lead. "We're investigating a very serious matter, the murder of Willy Parnell. I'm sure you must have read about it in the Herald."

"Yes, Detective I did, and it was horrible. I really liked Willy. I can't believe that someone would hurt him like that."

"So you women knew him well?" asked Burnside. His question seemed to have awakened Maven, who had been silent for a few moments.

"This one's mine. He's so cute, asking his cute little questions. Don't let Mabel fool you guys, she was an exotic dancer just like me. She's just prissy because her fun bags haven't dropped as much as mine."

"You'll have to excuse my sister, detectives. Turn it off Maven." Mabel said before turning back to the detectives. "We knew Willy pretty well, had him over for a casserole once. He was totally devoted to those two granddaughters. Once his wife passed, he got depressed. Maven tried to ... show him a good time, but he wasn't interested. Right Maven?"

"He couldn't get it up. Had a bad ticker he told me. I told him that if you were going to have a heart attack, you might as well have a good time."

Ben wanted to change the subject. "This is a nice apartment and a pretty exclusive building. Would you say that Willy was well off?"

Mabel looked around the apartment appraisingly. I think he had money. Yeah, he had money. After we had him over for dinner, I guess we goaded him into reciprocating, so he took the two of us to Mary Mahoney's in downtown Biloxi. I got the impression that it wasn't his first time there, and he wasn't concerned about Maven here drinking her way into a good time."

"I had a few Martinis, at least I wasn't the one pushing my juggies in his face every chance I got." Mabel's mouth fell open at the accusation.

"I did not detectives. My sister has things a little confused. Now shut up Maven."

"As far as the other tenants in the building, do you know if Willy was having any problems with anyone?"

The two women looked at each other and replied in unison. "No."

"No, you don't know, or no he wasn't," asked Burnside.

"I mean we would know if he was having a problem because we know pretty well everyone, and Maven here has had sex with half of them."

"And you the other half," replied Maven.

Ben gave Burnside a look of exasperation. "Have you noticed a couple of big guys hanging around the building, late twenties, brush cuts?"

"Sound dreamy...what do you mean by big?" answered Maven.

"Shoulders, physique..." replied Burnside.

"No," replied Mabel with a look of admonishment at her sister.

"Listen, ladies, this is a very important question. Was the seal on the apartment door really broken before you came in here? We need to know," Ben gave them a serious look.

"As I told you before, the door was open about a foot. I didn't break any seal. I swear on my sister's bazongas," replied Maven.

Turning to Maven, Ben asked, "And what were you looking for when I interrupted you?"

"Why he loved my tuna casserole so much, he wanted the recipe. I wanted to get it back."

Chapter 9

The congressman kept Gabriel waiting another 10 minutes. During that time Charlie made another appearance, giving Gabriel a sympathetic look. "I gave your car a good oiling then played around with the carburetor for a spell. It should run a might smoother now, not perfect; that diesel is getting old like me."

"Thank you, Charlie. You didn't need to do that."

"It's kind of a nice break for me. Took me a time before I realized that the engine was in the trunk," Charlie laughed.

"You're pretty handy," Gabriel said, handing the man a $10 bill.

"No suh, all part of the service. I'm kind of a jack of all trades. The congressman he don't let no one but me, work on his cars. No suh," he said proudly.

"Was there anything wrong with Mrs. Rogers' car that might explain the accident?"

"No suh, that car was in perfect condition. The Sheriff he says she lost control of the car on account of her driving too fast and slipping on the wet pavement," Charlie explained in a way that made Gabriel think he was recounting the party line. Just then they were interrupted by the two double doors to his left being opened by a tall, handsome gray-haired man. He gave Gabriel a full, pearly white smile and approached with his hand outstretched.

"Why, Y'all must be Gabriel Ross. I declare Mr. O'Brien told me you were short, but I had no idea," he chuckled. Even after standing, Gabriel was almost a foot shorter than the Congressman. "Are all in your family this short?"

"My Mom and Dad are both a little less than average. I must have smoked too many cigarettes as a baby." Gabriel quipped. The congressman had a good laugh, clapping Gabriel a little too forcefully on the back and ushering him into the study. The room was large and lined with books and more paintings of serious looking men looking uncomfortable in their uniforms. At the far end of the room was a large oak desk, likely a hand me down from one of the serious men in the paintings. On the wall behind the desk, there was an autographed print of Richard Nixon. It was the one where Tricky Dicky had his hands raised in a victory salute. Looking at the picture, Gabriel wondered whether Rogers secretly recorded his meetings.

"Y'all already know Ashley," Rogers said, pointing to his aide who was standing obediently to the right of the desk like a faithful watchdog. "Grab a seat," he said to Gabriel, pointing again, this time to a green leather club chair.

"You have a beautiful home Congressman." Gabriel took in the immaculate room with its long windows. The congressman's desk was tidy without a stray paper or file folder hanging around. Gabriel put his iced tea glass on the desk, causing a circle of dampness to form.

The Congressman allowed a frown to cross his face and picked up a leather coaster and tossed it to him. "Care for another drink Mr. Ross? Maybe something a little stronger?"

"It's Gabriel....,"

Before he could finish, Rogers signaled Ashley, "Fix us all a drink, it's not too early for a little relaxation, right Gabe?"

Actually, it's Gabriel.

"I understand you come from up north Gabe."

"Yes. I came down last fall and started up the detective agency shortly after."

"Is that what you did up in Deeeeetroittt?" *I wonder if Deeeeetroittt was the same as Detroit. Interesting I didn't mention my hometown. He must have checked me out.* "No, I worked for Ford Motor Company...an accountant."

"A number cruncher. Quite a change in career. What all brought you down to the Magnolia state?"

"Just thought I needed a change." *I had no desire to get into the real reason. Not sure if Mr. Family Values would approve of my divorce.*

"That business with Sheriff Cooper must have been quite the ordeal." said the Congressman.

"It was. I was happy that I was able to resolve the issue."

"Right!" The Congressman gave Gabriel a wink. "What I told my lawyer, Mr. O'Brien, I liked best about that business, was your discretion in not piling on in the press. You had every right to crow, but you remained calm and composed." Gabriel decided to leave him with his impressions. "Well I have plenty to do, and I 'm sure you do too Gabe. Thank y'all for coming up here to see me. I understand from Mr. O'Brien that you understand the terms of our arrangement?"

"Yes I do," Gabriel replied stone-faced. *Although to be fair I barely have two nickels, let alone a million dollars. And I have already yapped to the Biloxi PD.*

The congressman nodded his head. "Ashley, why don't you fill Gabe in on what needs to be done?"

Before Ashley could respond, Gabriel spoke up, "I wanted to express my most sincere condolences on the loss of your wife, Congressman Rogers."

"Well thank you, Gabe, this is why this matter is so unsettling... it coming at such a bad time for my family and all. That's one of the reasons I want this handled discreetly. I don't want Esther's memory to be sullied."

Yeah, it wasn't your wife who was caught in a compromising position. Ashley, who had been fixing drinks, came back to the desk balancing three bourbons in crystal glasses. He gave Gabriel a disappointed look as he handed out the drinks.

"A week ago, a boy hand delivered this to Charles, our manservant." He handed over a white envelope, Gabriel wondered if his reference to boy meant a youth or just another black. The term manservant was also a strange choice of titles. Gabriel handled the envelope by the tips.

"How many people have handled this?"

"It's not even the original envelope. It was ripped open and discarded before we realized what it was."

Gabriel opened the envelope extracting a single piece of paper. The paper contained the standard blackmail threat with block letters cut out of a magazine.

PEOPLE DESERVE TO KNOW THE TRUTH. IF YOU WANT TO KEEP YOUR SIN QUIET, IT WILL COST YOU A MILLION

ENJOY THE PICTURE. WE WILL BE IN TOUCH."

"There's been no further contact," said Ashley.

Gabriel read the note over a couple of times and then looked over at the Congressman and said, "I presume there was a photo with this."

"Only one," replied pretty boy. "The congressman burned it in the fireplace."

Gabriel paused for a moment to register the lie, then looking at the Congressman, who was looking down at the ground, "Okay Congressman, why don't you describe the picture?"

Once again the answer came from Powder Puff, "It showed the Congressman in an embarrassing situation with another person."

"When did this happen?" Gabriel pulled out a spiral notebook from his pocket.

"It took place in May...of this year," replied Rogers.

"When exactly?"

"It was May 19th or 20th. Maybe 21st," replied Rogers, looking through his leather daytimer.

"Can't remember the exact day?"

"No, it happened over a 3 day period," said the man with family values.

"Where?"

"There was a function for the local Republican Party that took place on a steamboat," said Puff the Magic Dragon. "Listen Mr. Ross are the notes necessary?"

Gabriel ignored the question and turned away from Ashley looking again at Rogers. "So you had an affair May 19th, 20th and 21st on a steamboat, on, I expect the Mississippi, in front of a bunch of Republicans?" Gabriel tried hard to keep the disbelief out of my voice.

"I believe the boat was called the *Mississippi Queen*. It was all very discreet. No one knows about this other than, well you and Ashley here."

"That's not exactly correct is it?" Gabriel replied. "I think the person you were with would know, and so might the person who took the picture."

"I realize that what I did was wrong, and I have asked My Lord to forgive me. It happened once, and I want to do what I can to put this behind me."

"So are you saying you had sex once over the three day period or that you had sex multiple times on one of the days?"

"Once and now that I think about it I guess it was on the first night that would be May 19th."

"You sure?"

"I remember looking for the other person the next day, so yes I'm pretty sure."

"Ok, what's her name?"

"Her name?" Ashley asked.

"Yeah the boinkee, if you want me to make this go away, I need to know who was involved."

"I didn't get their name," replied the Congressman.

I hate bullshit, and these guys were swimming in it. "You mean to tell me that you never once said her name in passion? 'Oh God, Oh God Juicy Lucy!" Gabriel said with a touch of enthusiasm. "You get my drift?"

"If you don't believe the Congressman then our business is concluded. I will expect the return of the retainer," said Ashley acting as if his delicate sensibilities had been bruised.

I felt like punching pretty boy in the mouth. "Okay, let me summarize what you're asking me to do. You want me to make a couple of blackmailers go away, but you have no clue who they are. Further, you decided to burn the only piece of evidence. Congressman, you aren't the first elected official to be caught in this type of scheme, and you won't be the last. Most likely the boinkee set you up. That's why I would like that other person's name. How did you happen to meet this person?"

"It was at the social, I was at the bar. I guess I might have had more than I should, but everyone was drinking. I got talking to this person. We slipped back to my cabin and well ...you know."

"What exactly did the picture show?"

"The Congressman performing a certain sex act that is illegal in Mississippi," replied Ashley.

In Mississippi almost every sex act was illegal. It was even illegal for a man to be aroused in public. "Can you clearly see the Congressman's face?"

"Yes, as a matter of fact, it was a pretty good picture," Ashley said with a touch of admiration.

Gabriel tried to get the image of the Congressman with a farm animal out of his mind. "Can you be more specific about the sex act?"

"The picture showed the Congressman on his knees performing oral sex." replied Ashley, his tone clinical.

Gabriel looked at the congressman who was turning a different shade of pink. "So if he was kneeling, she was standing. Was the picture taken from the side, or from behind?"

The congressman was now looking down at his shoes as if he had discovered a bug. Ash clarified, "The picture was from the side."

"Okay, that plays, pretty hard to secretly take a picture of some guy going down on you, don't you think? Works better with an accomplice hiding behind the curtains," Gabriel left that hanging, waiting for the Congressman to chip in. When he didn't, Gabriel continued. "Of course, maybe the dame had a camera on delay or a remote control. Think that might be possible, Congressman?"

"I don't know. Like I said I had a bit too much to drink. I guess my head was elsewhere."

I think we already established that.

"Do you think there was an accomplice?" asked Pretty Boy.

"The ransom note refers to "we" so I would presume so. Okay, so here's my advice, just come clean, schedule a press conference and say that your wife's passing has caused you to have a "Come to Jesus" moment and admit your past indiscretions. The headlines will be brutal, but it won't take long for people to forget. Some might even like you more."

The congressman's expression hardened, and his voice went up a few octaves. "Who are you to give me advice as to what I should or should not do? I'm paying you to make this problem go away. No press conferences, no admissions. What's more, I don't want this to leak out to party officials."

It was pretty clear that Gabriel had hit a nerve. "Okay, what's the connection between this blackmail letter and your wife's accident?" *I know I'm breaking Pretty Boy's rules, but the two of them are starting to piss me off. Self-righteous, sanctimonious ...*

"There is no connection. You are quite rude Mr. Ross. I have a half a mind to give you a solid thrashing and throw you out on your ear," boasted Cream Puff.

The Congressman sensed the escalation of hostilities. "My wife, bless her soul, died in a terrible car crash in June, well before this letter was received."

Gabriel tried to picture Powder Puff trying to throw him out. He was pretty sure that if anyone was going to receive a solid thrashing, it would be the Fruit Cup. "So the indiscretion happened in May, and it is now mid-July. Why would the blackmailer wait two months?"

"I don't know," replied Rogers.

"Had you confessed your indiscretion to your wife?"

The Congressman gave Gabriel a look suggesting he had just urinated on the precious Confederate flag.

"Of course not, we had a loving relationship, and I wouldn't have wanted to hurt her by talking about this."

"So this babe, who for now is nameless, had an invite to this little shindig. Give me a description, and I'll find her. It might take me a while, but it won't be that hard."

"Average height and weight, dark hair, dark eyes, maybe late twenties, early thirties."

Yeah like 50% of the women in Mississippi. "Did she have a Mississippi accent?"

"She spoke normally like me."

"Right...so probably a native Mississippian. What about distinguishing features?"

"Like what?"

"I don't know, a confederate flag tattooed on her left breast? Pegleg? Hairy? No teeth?"

"Nothing like that."

"Did she have big wobbly tits?" Gabriel made a wavy hand gesture to illustrate.

"Mr. Ross, do you find this amusing?" asked the Congressman in a threatening tone.

"Not at all, but I'm sure you understand that I am just trying to do my job."

"Well, then I guess she did." The Congressman looked over at Ashley as if somehow he would know.

"Wait a minute. Ashburn were you on the same boat ride?"

"It's Ashley, and yes, I was there, but disembarked to attend to an important matter in Natchez."

"So do you remember wobbly tits?"

He shook his head, and Gabriel thought, *And you call yourself a senior aide?"*

"I saw the Congressman obviously, but he was with a bunch of people. I don't remember anyone in particular."

Turning back to the Congressman, Gabriel asked "What about jewelry, anything unique? Like a school ring either on her finger or her….?"

"Not that I remember."

"Did the drapes match the curtains?"

"I don't follow," replied Rogers.

Gabriel looked over at Pretty Boy who replied, "He wants to know if her pubic hair was dark like her hair."

"Yes," replied Congressman Family Fucking Values.

"Would anyone else have seen you chatting with this lady at the bar?"

"Maybe, I don't know. Clearly, I wasn't thinking."

"let's say I find this dame and convince her to give me the negatives, then what?"

"I don't care what happens to her, just as long as I get the pictures and never hear from her again."

"Okay, tell you what I'll do. I will make some discreet inquiries, try to put a name to this gal. Can you get the GOP to fax over the invite list?"

"I don't want to have them involved," said Rogers.

Gabriel shook his head in frustration. "Let me know as soon as you hear from the blackmailer. In situations like this, it helps if you can play this out, give me some time to get ahead of this. Tell them you need time to get the cash together. I will do the drop for you and take it from there." Gabriel was talking like he had done this before. The closest he had ever gotten to a blackmailer was Mary Louise Ponder, who said she would tell his parents he smoked dope if he didn't take her to the prom.

They chatted for a little longer before the Congressman looked at his watch, and said he was late for a meeting. This left Gabriel with Pretty Boy, who Gabriel was sure had been feeding him bullshit all afternoon. He just didn't know why.

Chapter 10

Gabriel was still smelling the bullshit an hour after he left the Congressman. This might have been because of all their lies, or simply because some farmer had been spreading manure on his fields. He felt Rogers and his pretty boy were playing him for a sucker. *For a man in his position having an affair was bad enough, but for a Congressman to do this at a GOP meeting and not even remember the floozy's name, was as large a stretch as selling rocks as pets. My name's Tucker, not Sucker.*

For the blackmail to take place right after the Congressman lost his wife in a horrible accident was either a terrible turn of events or maybe an interesting coincidence. Tomorrow he would call the cruise people and get them to send him a passenger list. He would then brace the lady and get the pictures back and collect his other $5,000. Easy Peasy, Lemon Squeezy!

By the time Gabriel got back to Gulfport, it was late. He wasn't anxious to go back to his sweltering apartment only to heat up a Swanson's TV dinner and watch the latest *Barnaby Jones*. Instead, he decided to drive through Gulfport looking at the type of homes that were for sale. He had suggested to Arnie over coffee that buying a small cottage near the beach might be a good investment. After about a half an hour he found himself in the neighborhood where Jacqueline used to live with her husband,

William Cooper. Gabriel parked out front of the house and let his mind drift back to earlier that year. The house had a beautiful pool in the back and while on surveillance for his client – who happened to Jacqueline - he'd tested out his new camera by taking pictures of the house from a little knoll across the street. Well, that's not quite right. He had taken pictures of Jacqueline in a skimpy bikini lying by the pool. Everything would have been fine except he mixed up envelopes and mistakenly gave Jacqueline the pictures he had taken of her by the pool. He shook his head remembering how angry she had become when she opened the envelope only to find that he been spying on her.

Now, the house lay empty. Victim of a marital dispute. Before leaving for Chicago, Jacqueline had started legal proceedings to sue for divorce. The fact that there was still no "For Sale," sign was confirmation that suing someone in the witness protection program wasn't straightforward.

As Gabriel sat watching the house, a smile flashed across his face as he remembered Travis Franklin, the young kid who lived on the next street over and had caught Gabriel spying on the Sheriff. Travis had a vivid imagination and had claimed imperiously that the knoll was part of his kingdom and that Gabriel was trespassing. The two of them had become friends and Travis proved instrumental in helping to gather evidence against the Sheriff.

Gabriel put the car in gear and drove around the block. When he got to the house where Travis lived with his younger sister and parents, he noticed that the house had a for sale sign on the lawn. When Gabriel had been spying on the Sheriff, he'd discovered that Travis' father, a deputy in the Sheriff's office, was deeply involved in a case he was working on involving missing teenagers. He'd never forget arriving at Travis' house to see a couple of wise guys go into the home, and hearing gunshots minutes later. Gabriel was able to get away with Travis, but Travis' father was found later shot to death. Travis' mother wisely chose to gather her family and escape to Hattiesburg to live with relatives.

For the past few months, Travis and Gabriel had stayed in touch. The last time he spoke to Travis, he'd said that his mother had decided to put the house up for sale. Looking at the banner "Reduced- New Low Price" on the For Sale sign, Gabriel concluded that potential buyers might be put off by the previous owner having been brutally shot to death in the living room.

Chapter 11

Ben finally shooed Mabel and Maven out of the apartment with promises to look for Maven's recipe card. They hadn't learned anything of any significance from the two old ladies.

"So what do you think about the door being open?" asked Burnside once they'd left.

In answer, Ben got up and went to the hall and came back with a log sheet that was used to record all visitors. The only names were the initial detective team that first checked out the apartment. He picked up Willy's phone in the kitchen and dialed the precinct, asking for Detective Robinson.

After a few minutes, "Hey Bert, it's O'Shea. ....Yes, Chuckles. We're at Parnell's apartment, and we found the door open. Any thoughts?" Ben listened for a few minutes before saying, "Yeah he's here. I think he has a new lady friend. I'll let him tell you about her later."

Ben put the phone down and said, "Robinson's sure the door was locked with the seal in place when they left. My guess is either Maven's lying, or someone else was here before us looking for something. Maybe the old guy had jewelry or money."

"Do you believe Maven's story?"

"She was a little over the top. Maybe an act to try to distract us? Not sure if I believe that she came into the guy's apartment to get her recipe for tuna casserole." Ben went back out into the hall and returned a couple of minutes later. "There are little scratches on the door lock which might suggest that whoever came in here picked the lock. I don't see the old ladies as the type. Let's do our own search of things and see what we come up with. If we don't find recipe cards, then that might tell us something."

"Don't you think the person who broke in might have already taken what he wanted?"

"Maybe so, but there is no harm looking. Besides, maybe the clue is really about what's not here and should be."

Burnside shook his head and started to pull open the drawers in the bureau under the TV. Mumbling under his breath, "We're looking for something that's not here but should be. That's whacked man! What the fuck does that even mean?"

"I'm going to check out the kitchen. Look for something that looks suspicious," instructed Ben.

Ben checked out all of the drawers, cupboards, and closets. He looked in the freezer and found nothing other than a year's supply of frozen peas. From the kitchen, he moved to the bathroom and found more heart medicine in the cabinet. Other than that, there was just a normal assortment of men's toiletries.

"Hey, I found some jewelry," Burnside yelled as Ben returned to the bedroom. Burnside was holding a couple of women's rings and necklaces. Ben looked at the stuff before saying that the whole bundle might get a grand at a pawnshop.

"Find anything else?"

"There's a suitcase under the old man's bed. It's full of kid's books."

Ben nodded and said to look under the drawers of the dresser and to look for loose boards in the closet. Meanwhile, he would tackle the smaller bedroom. He imagined that Willy used it as an office except when the kids stayed over. As he was going through a file folder, he found a bunch of papers containing the lease for the apartment, a will leaving everything to his daughter. There was also a Power of Attorney appointing Willy's son-in-law to act on his behalf. Ben thought about that. The document was dated last year and was notarized. In his experience, it was unusual to appoint in-laws over your own daughter.

Ben found some old bank passbooks showing only a few transactions each month. Willy kept a low four-figure balance and received a couple of regular deposits which he guessed were social security payments and a pension. There were a few checks each month. A grand came out on the first of the month, most likely for rent. Lastly, Ben found an insurance policy for $250,000 on the lives of Willy and his wife. He also found a bank receipt for a deposit where Willy had invested a similar amount into a T-Bill.

Ben walked into the other bedroom and asked Burnside if he had found anything suspicious.

"Yeah, something really off."

"Yeah? What did you find?"

"The guy's underwear. I swear it's older than me."

Ben shook his head, and after putting everything back the way it was, they concluded that if there had been something of value in the apartment, then it was no longer here. "I didn't find anything that should have been here...and wasn't or whatever you said," proclaimed Burnside.

"Neither did I. I wonder what the old guy did with Maven's recipe cards?"

Before leaving, they knocked on the other four doors on the floor to see if anyone had anything to add. They were in luck, getting responses from three of the apartments. All of the answers, however, sounded the same. Willy was a very nice man, always smiling and enjoying the kids, no they didn't know if he had enemies, and no, they have not seen anyone suspicious hanging around.

Chapter 12

Later that afternoon, Ben was sitting in front of Chief Willis, who was having a very one-sided telephone conversation with the Mayor. It was clear by the way that Willis was holding the receiver away from his ear that the Mayor was demanding action. Ben listened as Willis' *yes buts* soon became *yes Sirs* and then finally *absolutely Sir, right away Sir*. Ben was working hard to keep the smile off his face and prepared himself for the verbal onslaught that was most assuredly about to come his way.

As soon as Willis hung up the phone, he looked at Ben, "Where the fuck is Burnside?"

"He was with me all day, but said he had a dentist appointment."

"A dentist appointment? What the fuck is going on around here?" Willis was close to shouting. It didn't really matter whether the office door was closed or open. Everyone in the squad room could hear everything anyway.

"I'm not sure, but I think he had it booked for some time." Ben lied, not wanting to tell Willis that his junior partner cut out early to meet someone.

"Yeah?" Willis asked in a tone that suggested that he knew Ben was covering for him.

Ben nodded his head and decided to try to change the topic. "I don't know if this Parnell thing is what it appears to be."

"Well, the Mayor thinks it's one big clusterfuck. There's a rally scheduled for tonight down at city hall by some Black Action Movement. You know who they are?" Without waiting for a reply, he continued, now standing up behind his desk glowering at Ben. "They're a bunch of fucking radicals. Not the peaceful ones with the cute little signs. They're the fuckers that smash windows and turn cars upside down. It's going to be Watts all over again," a reference to the race riots in California. Willis stopped to catch his breath before picking up his stapler and flinging it against the wall in frustration. Ben thought it would have been a good education for Burnside to be sitting with him, listening to their boss freak out. "Ever since that story in the paper this morning, more graffiti is turning up all over the place. Probably fucking copy cats. This is getting out of hand."

Willis eventually sat back behind his desk and stared at Ben. "Okay Detective, why do you think this is anything but a couple of crackers beating on an old black man?"

"It's just a feeling."

Willis drew a breath in and slowly exhaled. "The Mayor wants more than your feelings O'Shea. He wants us to find the people responsible and string them up before this gets any worse." Willis paused for a moment considering what to say next. "O'Shea, I'm sorry if I sometimes call you a clown. I shouldn't do that. It's insensitive of me. I promise you, when there's no one else around, I say to myself that you're my best detective. If you have a feeling, then, I, as your boss, the man in charge, who reports to that cock-sucking Mayor, should just accept that. You have a feeling." He made a gesture with his hands suggesting that the feelings might be magical. "If it ever comes to trial, the DA can just tell the judge that you had a fucking feeling." The compliment about being the best detective had only hung in the air a brief moment before Willis resumed angrily, "BUT WHAT THE FUCK ARE THESE FEELINGS BASED ON?"

"Okay, this might still be a random, racially motivated attack. But maybe someone wants us to believe that, so we don't go looking for the real motive. You know what I mean?"

Willis opened his desk drawer and pulled out a package of cigarettes. He had been trying to quit, but most of the squad were openly hoping he would just continue to smoke. To Ben, the guy was just as irritable with or without cigarettes. Willis lit a cigarette taking a deep breath before putting the cigarettes back in the drawer which he angrily slammed shut. "Detective you could say the same thing about every fucking thing that happens around here. Was that arson or was it just meant to look like arson? A mugging? Or maybe someone beat themselves up and just said they were mugged. Was that person robbed or could a fucking Irish leprechaun named O'Shea be yanking our chain?"

"When we interviewed Willy's daughter today, she told us there were a couple of thug-like guys, brush cuts, jeans, t-shirts, just hanging around outside her building. When we interviewed the doorman over where Willy lived, he told us that he had to put the run to two people with the exact same description. One called him a nigger. Same guys, two different buildings."

Willis looked unconvinced but took a moment to take a couple of drags from his cigarette before responding. "Can either of those witnesses pick them out of a lineup?"

"I think so. I'm going to have the forensic artist sit down with both independently, and then we can compare."

"Okay, but even if it's the same thugs, that doesn't mean it wasn't a racially motivated killing. The two buildings aren't that far apart. Maybe, they're just punks hanging around looking for an old black man to beat up."

"I think that the people who did this didn't know Willy had a bad ticker. After the medical examiner does their work, they'll see that Willy didn't die from the beating."

"Who else knew he had heart problems?"

"No one according to the daughter."

"So you think someone who didn't know Willy had a bad heart wanted him to teach him a lesson, and beat the shit out of him causing the old guy to have a heart attack?"

"Yes," Ben replied, not feeling totally convinced himself.

"Kind of a circular argument. It doesn't matter what the Coroner finds. The person that beat the old guy still caused his death. If they didn't know about the heart, it's still murder. So none of this matters." Willis glared at him, silently communicating that Ben was wasting his time. "So I'm all ears O'Shea, what's the real motive for killing a 64-year-old man ...and don't tell me it's because he's a nigger."

Ben wisely decided to keep Maven and Mabel and their missing tuna casserole recipe to himself.

Chapter 13

The following morning, Gabriel woke up early drenched in sweat. There was no end in sight from the Biloxi heat wave. He found a toll free number for the Delta Queen Steamboat Company in the yellow pages and figured he had nothing much to lose by giving them a try.

A pleasant sounding woman answered his call right away, "Morning, thanks for callin' the Delta Queen Steamboat Company, How may we assist you?"

"My name is Gabriel Ross, and I would like to speak to someone about the Mississippi Queen."

Gabriel was connected to a fast talking man named Cash, who identified himself as a booking agent for the greatest cruise experience on the Mississippi. "Thank you for taking my call Cash, my name is Gabriel Ross."

"Hello, Gabriel Ross when were you thinking of cruising? July is a pretty popular time on the Mississippi, and we are getting booked up quickly. Yes siree Gabe, best you move fast partner."

'Thanks, Cash. I was actually looking for some information about a cruise that took place back in May. I'm calling on behalf of the Republican Party."

"Sure, sure that was a lot of fun...You don't have a complaint do you?"

"No, not at all; and I think folks would be predisposed to book again. This time maybe for a longer campaign rally."

"Well, that's wonderful Mr. Ross. We get all kinds of compliments on the Mississippi Queen. When would the group like to sail again?"

"Well we're not quite ready to book, but I'm trying to locate one of the passengers that was on the cruise back in May. You see she was a delegate and promised to make a rather large contribution to a Congressman's campaign, and well this is embarrassing, but we have somehow lost her information."

There was a bit of hesitation in Cash's voice before he responded, "I'm not sure I can help you, Mr. Ross."

"Would you have a list of everyone that was onboard?"

"I'm sure we have something like that. But now that I think about it, not everyone got on board right from the beginning. If I remember correctly that was a 3-day cruise starting from

Vicksburg, then stopped in Natchez before docking in New Orleans. There were people getting on and off at each stop."

"Would you have something showing those passengers that were on the boat from Vicksburg?"

"This is about a passenger making a donation? Seems to me you guys should already have that information considering each passenger was an invited guest."

Gabriel decided to play the waiting game. After about twenty seconds Cash continued "Since you're considering another event I think we can provide you with something. I still have your fax number up in Jackson where I sent the original contract."

"Rather than fax it to the Republican Headquarters, how about if I pick it up?"

"Suit yourself Mr. Ross, but we're a piece from Jackson. We're based out of Missouri."

"Where would the Mississippi Queen be now?"

Cash excused himself for a moment before replying, "She'll be docking in New Orleans tomorrow morning."

"Any chance you can fax it to the Queen and I can meet the ship in port? I have to be there tomorrow to meet some of the Louisiana people."

"Well okay, this will be a list of the hundred and fifty or so who came aboard in Vicksburg. It would take a might longer if you wanted to know the names of passengers who boarded mid cruise."

"That's okay Cash, what we have discussed would be fine."

"When you get to the ship ask for Captain Kelly, I'll be faxing the list to our office to his attention."

"Thanks, Cash, and I'll get back to you on dates for the next event."

After hanging up from Cash, Gabriel thought about how to handle the list. His thoughts were interrupted by another call coming in. Gabriel answered using his standard office greeting, "Good morning and thank you for calling the *Eye on You Detective Agency* for *When You Really Need to Know*. How can we help you?

"Hi Gabriel, that's quite the mouthful," Rachel replied.

"Oh Hi Rachel, I was just thinking about you."

"Yeah? Why is that?"

"I have to go to New Orleans tomorrow to check out a riverboat. Did you want to come with me? Maybe we can make a mini vacation of it. Check into one of those cheap, sleazy motels... have a nice dinner in the quarter...."

Rachel laughed, "Why are you interested in a riverboat? Planning a cruise?"

"No, it's a case...I might get you to help spin a little story for me."

"Alright, but I bet you forgot that tomorrow is Wednesday night."

"Wednesday night, yes I know that," Gabriel said, madly reaching for his day timer.

"You forgot that you promised to come with me to dinner at my boss' house."

When Gabriel didn't immediately respond Rachel prompted, "You remember I wanted you to say how bright and caring, decisive, fair and effective, I am."

"Oh, that's right. Let me make a list, so I don't forget, that's beautiful, funny, sexy, what else did you say?"

"How about bright and well liked?"

"Oh yeah, busty and well proportioned."

Rachel laughed again, "You're silly. As it turns out, I have tomorrow off so if you want company I can go with you. We will have to be back by 6 so that you can help me suck up to the boss."

"Great, I'll pick you up at 9." Before hanging up, he added, "Let's save the dinner in the French Quarter and the sleazy motel for next weekend."

Chapter 14

The next morning Ben and Burnside met in the parking lot after Police Chief Willis' daily briefing, taking a few minutes to enjoy the warmth of the sun before getting in their cruiser. Ben filled Burnside in on the ass-chewing that he had missed the day before. For his part, Burnside said his date with a young model had gone very well. He went out of his way to describe the sex as being out of this world and that she was most likely too much for him to handle. Only when he described her as a double-jointed gymnast did Ben catch on that his young partner was yanking his chain.

"What about you Ben, are you involved with someone?"

"Nah never seems to be the right time," he lied.

"I could ask Foxy if she has a friend....an older friend ...like a grandmother."

"That's her name ...Foxy? Does she spell that with one "x" or three?"

"I don't care."

"Thanks anyway. There's a girl I met a few months back through a busi...." Ben had caught himself before he mentioned his business partner Gabriel. That would be a mistake, as Ben still wasn't sure that his new partner could keep a secret. "She's younger than me and lives in New Orleans, but we seemed to have hit it off pretty well." Ben thought for a moment then added, "I guess the next step is mine, I need to call her or go see her. She plays the sax and works at a café in the French Quarter."

"You should man...do you have any other pastimes or are you the kind that goes home and watches the ballgame on TV every night?"

"There's a bar not far from me, O'Toole's. I know some lads there, and there's usually a college game on the tube. I shoot a little pool....the usual stuff."

"I should check it out sometime, maybe you can introduce me to your gal...What's her name?"

"Chevon, and she's not exactly my girl."

"Kind of a different name, not exactly on par with Foxy but ...." Burnside paused for a moment before adding, "She black?"

"Not that it matters, but yes."

His partner opened the driver's door and said, "We had better get rolling." When they were both in the car, he added, "So where to?"

Ben thought the conversation with Burnside had taken an abrupt turn when he'd said Chevon was black, and he didn't know what that meant. "We have a 10 o'clock with the son-in-law at his office. I thought we could ask him to give us his perspective on what happened."

The younger cop drove into downtown Biloxi parking the cruiser in the lot adjacent to a building housing some professional businesses. Morgan Armstrong worked on the eighth floor of an investment firm called *Laity and Associates*. The temperature was already mid-eighties, so when they opened the office front door, the air conditioning fogged their sunglasses. Ben approached the front desk where a young man sat typing on an IBM Selectric. "We're here to see Morgan Armstrong." Ben flashed his badge.

The man took a glance at the badge and gave Ben and Burnside a quick smile. Picking up his phone he buzzed someone to say they had visitors. The office was well appointed and had been finished in a preppy style using a lot of pastels and chintz. The floor was a bold black and a white checkered pattern. Over a background of Muzak, Ben could hear a man's voice responding from one of the inner offices. A few moments later a smiling man, Ben assumed was Morgan Armstrong, bounded out of an office, his hand outstretched in greeting. Ben introduced himself and his partner. Willy had described the son-in-law as extra white which wasn't far off the mark. The black and white photo at the daughter's apartment did not do the guy justice. The man had curly red hair, floppy ears and a complexion dotted with more freckles than you could possibly count.

"Why don't we make ourselves comfortable in our boardroom. Can we offer you coffee, Detectives?"

Ben declined, but Burnside enthusiastically asked if they had espresso. Morgan asked the receptionist, "Jules can you fix the Detective here an espresso?" Once again Ben made a mental note to speak to his young partner.

The boardroom had a long glass table and lush leather chairs. Once they were all seated Morgan broke the ice, "Sorry I wasn't able to be home when you came by yesterday. It's been a zoo in here lately."

Ben tried to reconcile the comment with the absence of any traffic in the waiting room. "We're very sorry for your loss, Mr. Armstrong."

A look of grief flashed across Morgan's face wiping away the smile that had up to that point been painted on. "It's been tough...we told the girls last night, they were very upset as you can imagine. They loved their grandpa very much," then he added, "we all did."

"Any thoughts on the crime, Mr. Armstrong?" asked Ben pulling out his notepad.

"You can call me Morgan if you like. What do you mean by thoughts?"

"Any idea why someone would want to hurt him?" asked Ben.

"No, none at all. I read in the paper that it was a racially motivated crime. This sounds like the wrong person in the wrong place at the wrong time."

"That might be, we're just trying to cross all the T's on this," responded Ben.

"I would think that with the demonstration last night, people would be pushing for a quick resolution to this. Any ideas as to who did this?"

Morgan was referring to a violent protest down on the main drag in Biloxi that had taken place the previous evening. On the way to their meeting, Ben had seen some shops boarded up, their windows smashed by vandals. "We were going to ask you the same question?" responded Ben.

Morgan looked back and forth at the two detectives before shrugging his shoulders. "Probably the same redneck that's spray painting all of the horrible graffiti down near the boardwalk."

Ben noticed that his partner had not said anything since they arrived and had looked over his shoulder at the boardroom door a couple of times. Morgan picked up on this and said, "Let me go check on that espresso for you Detective."

When he stuck his head out the door, Ben gave his partner a look of consternation and said, "Do you want to add anything to the conversation?"

Moments later Morgan returned and put a miniature cup and saucer in front of Burnside. "I hope you like it. Enjoy." Burnside thanked Morgan and when he was seated again, Ben continued, "We were trying to get a handle on your father-in-law's financial situation and Justyne told us you would be the best person to ask."

Morgan seemed to take a few moments to collect his thoughts. The silence was broken by the sound of Burnside sipping his drink.

"He has investments, I would categorize him as comfortable, but not wealthy. I think he had what he needed."

"What do you do here?" asked Burnside, who seemed to all of a sudden wake-up.

"I'm an Investment Counsellor."

"What does that entail?" Burnside followed up.

"I work with clients, many of them corporate, and help them grow their financial positions by taking advantage of various market opportunities."

"So you're a stock broker?" jumped in Ben.

"Not exactly. Brokers are usually no more than commission sales people. They've got a bad rap for churning accounts to earn a commission. We manage investments and earn a fee for that management." Morgan's answer displayed a holier-than-thou attitude.

"So I understand that your father-in-law received $250,000 in insurance when his wife passed. "

Morgan again took a moment to consider the question and then shrugged his shoulders, "Yes, I might have heard something about that."

"We found a few things searching his apartment. For example, we found a bank T-Bill certificate in that amount taken out a couple of months after his wife died."

"Then I guess that confirms things," replied Morgan. "How was that espresso, Detective?"

Burnside nodded his head, and Ben continued, "The other thing we found was a Power of Attorney naming you and not his daughter as his representative for his finances." Ben let the statement hang there but didn't have to wait long.

"Justyne doesn't have the expertise in financial affairs and would have just deferred to me anyway."

"It must have been a comfort to him to have a son-in-law who could help look after things," replied Burnside, finishing his espresso. This caused the smile to return to Morgan's face.

"We just have a few more questions," said Ben. "We understand that your father-in-law had some medical problems."

"Hmm...I think he said something about his back once."

"Heard he had a bad heart?" asked Ben matter-of-factly.

"News to me. Justyne would know more about that. Want me to get her on the phone for you?"

"No, it's okay. Anything you can add that we haven't discussed?"

"I don't feel like I've been very helpful."

"That's okay Mr. Armstrong, thanks for taking the time to see us." Ben handed him his business card, "If anything else comes to mind we'd appreciate a call."

Chapter 15

Burnside was barely in the car when Ben turned to him, "Don't feel you need to accept everything that's offered to you."

"I don't know what you mean."

"Like today with the espresso and yesterday eating practically a plate of cookies."

"I was just trying to be friendly. Down here when folks offer you stuff, it's rude to say no."

"I would buy that if it had been one cookie - and he offered coffee, you asked for an espresso. I want you to have a professional detachment."

"You think I might go light on someone because they gave me a cookie?"

Ben was about to respond when the cruiser's radio started squawking their call numbers. Ben picked up and responded to the call. "Chief Willis requires your presence at the station house right away. A suspect has been apprehended in the Parnell case."

Burnside immediately put the car in gear, thankful to not have to continue the conversation.

After they had gone a few miles in silence, Burnside said, "The son-in-law seems like a pretty nice guy."

"That because you liked the espresso."

"I should have asked him for a little biscotti on the side."

Ben ignored the comment, "We didn't learn anything new, although, he seemed pretty convinced that this was a hate crime."

"Isn't pretty well everyone, other than you, convinced that this was a hate crime?" replied Burnside.

The comment irritated Ben. " I think that's what we're supposed to believe."

"Well, maybe you'd believe it if we got to the station and found the suspect wearing a fucking hood."

Ben just looked out the window and wondered how he could get Willis to assign him a new partner.

*****

When they got to the station, they went right towards Willis' office. As they crossed the bullpen, they found Lawson and Munroe giving each other a high five.

"So what's up...we have a suspect?" asked Ben of the two detectives.

Willis had heard Ben's voice and came out of his office. "Yeah, these fine detectives caught the suspect spray painting hate messages on the wall. The suspect is in interview room B."

"Did he say he did it?"

"Not exactly, I'll let you form your own conclusion."

*****

Ben and Burnside stood in front of the two-way glass looking in at the kid who had been arrested in the act of tagging a wall along the boardwalk. The kid was small, not at all like the man described by the doorman or by Justyne. He had dark brown hair hanging down almost to his shoulders. He was sitting alone at a table staring at the floor, his hands cuffed in front of him.

"Kid looks to be pretty young." Ben turned to Willis, who had followed them to the interview room. When Willis didn't reply, Ben pointed at the file in Willis' hand. "How old does it say he is?"

"It doesn't. He had no identification on him, and he's been less than cooperative," replied Willis, handing the file to Ben. "Maybe you can get him to open up."

"It's a long stretch to go from vandalism to murder," said Ben.

"Check out the photo."

Ben took a look at the photo and knew right away why the kid was a suspect.

"He spelled the word 'die' the same way, as "dye." There hasn't been anything about that in the *Herald*. I know he's young, but he was probably hopped up on weed or something." said Willis.

"Pot doesn't make you violent unless of course, you're a bag of potato chips," said Burnside, speaking up for the first time.

Willis just gave Burnside a sad look, "Get in there and do your magic Detectives. I want a confession from the little shit."

Ben turned to his junior partner and said, "Follow my lead."

"He's pretty young, he might relate better to me. Why don't you let me question him first? I have some experience with this."

Ben thought about that for a minute then nodded saying, "You've got a short rope, Burnside. I'll take over if it looks like you are striking out."

"Don't worry he'll be singing like a canary in minutes." bragged Burnside.

The pair went into the small interview room, which was maybe 10' by 12'. The only furniture was an old wooden table, and a couple of cheap wooden chairs likely sold at Kresge's fifty years ago. A solitary light hung from the ceiling, positioned over the table and casting a bright glow. The room was like most interview rooms, gray brick with a window that looked like it hadn't been cleaned in years. The only thing remarkable about the room was the large mirror which reflected the face of the kid looking up as they came into the room.

"Hello, we're Detectives Burnside and O'Shea of the Biloxi Police Department." Once the detectives sat down, "Can we talk about this situation for a spell?" asked Burnside.

The suspect remained unresponsive, slumped in his chair like a kid in grade ten English class.

"Let's get those cuffs off you," said Burnside gesturing for the kid to extend his arms. "There, isn't that better?" Burnside asked once he'd unlocked the cuffs. The kid was rubbing his wrists trying to reestablish some feeling.

"So, I've introduced myself, can I ask your name?" said Burnside, opening the police file in front of him.

After a moment or two, the kid proved his skill at reading upside down by saying his name was "John. John Doe."

Burnside looked over at Ben, who gestured that he should continue.

"Where do you live John?" asked Burnside.

"With my parents."

"Okay, that's good," replied Burnside, appearing more confident. "Where do your parents live John?"

"With me."

"I understand that. Where do you all live?"

"Together," came the reply. The kid's scornful look was replaced with a smug grin.

"I want to know where your house is."

"Next to my neighbor's house."

Burnside looked over at Ben again, showing frustration. "Where's your neighbor's house?" asked Burnside, his tone showing his mounting annoyance.

The kid shook his head and smiled. "If I tell you, you won't believe me."

"Where's your neighbor's house?" Burnside repeated through gritted teeth.

"Next to my house!" The kid laughed and pointed a finger at Burnside.

Burnside looked up at the ceiling and finally pushed the file folder over to Ben. Ben stared at the kid until they made eye contact. The kid gave Ben an impudent smile.

"So I'll just call you Sonny Boy. How's that?"

"Ain't your son."

Ben ignored the answer, looking down at the kid's hands resting on the table. There were flecks of paint on his fingers. He also noticed something else. "So Sonny Boy, did the policemen read you your rights?" The kid shrugged his shoulders in response. "Okay, it doesn't matter Sonny Boy 'cause they told me they did. You had no ID when they picked you up."

"That a crime Dad?"

Ben mimicked the kid by shrugging his shoulders. "The cops say you were caught with a can of spray paint down on the boardwalk."

"What can I say? I'm an ar-tis-te. One day I'll be famous. The famous John Doe." The kid started laughing again, now leaning back and balancing the chair on its back two legs. Ben got up and stood for a minute looking at the mirror.

"Who's the a-hole behind the glass?" asked the kid.

Ben nodded his head and walked around the room until he was standing next to the kid. In a flash, Ben used a leg to knock the chair over backward throwing the kid to the floor. "Didn't your teachers ever warn you about sitting like that Sonny Boy? Detective Burnside, can you help Sonny Boy back onto his chair?"

"That was police brutality, I could have hit my head." the kid yelled. Burnside meanwhile righted the chair and helped the kid up. Just as the kid was about to sit down, Ben yanked the chair out from behind him causing the kid to once again fall to the floor.

"Now that was funny," said Ben, laughing. Before long Burnside was laughing as well. The kid got up, glaring at Ben, "My dad will sue you over that!"

"That so? Your daddy's a lawyer is that right Sonny Boy?"

"Don't call me that anymore, my name is Alex."

"Alex, now we're getting somewhere. What's your last name?"

"Bell... Alexander Graham Bell," said the kid. "And my Dad's not a lawyer, he's an inventor."

"Would you like to use his invention to call him and tell him you're in big trouble, Sonny Boy?" Ben resumed his seat across from the kid.

"Big trouble? Okay, lock me up Sherlock, arrest me for ...decorating."

Ben pulled out a Polaroid from the file, the one the cops had taken of the graffiti they found on a cement wall by the beach.

"That what you call art?" The picture showed "Dye Nigger" in a flowery curved script.

The kid sat back and said, "Different strokes for different folks."

"Detective Burnside, you heard the suspect confirm that he spray painted this mural, correct?" asked Ben.

Burnside nodded, and then Ben said, "Well take a look at this picture." This time, he extracted a police glossy black and white of the body of Willy Parnell. The kid looked at the picture. For the first time in the interview, the kid's expression showed a trace of confusion. "What the fuck?"

Ben then showed him a close-up of the note that was found beside the body. The kid was still looking at the police photo when Ben added, "Not very funny what you did to that old man, Sonny."

The kid went from zero to ten on the interest scale. "WHAT ARE YOU TALKING ABOUT? YOU CAN'T THINK THAT I HAD ANYTHING TO DO WITH THAT?"

Burnside broke in at this point and spoke in a conspiratorial tone, "Listen, son, it's not a crime to not care for niggers. Lots of people don't, but they just keep it to themselves. They go through life bottling up their feelings, never having your courage to act."

"What? I didn't ...."

"It's okay kid." Burnside continued.

"I spray painted a mural, that's it. Lots of kids do it."

"You notice the way the word die is spelled in both pictures? I'm pretty sure a police expert will be able to testify at your trial that both pieces of "art" were done by the same person," said Ben.

"You guys are on drugs...I just copied what's on a lot of murals downtown. Spelling was never my best subject."

"The penalty in Mississippi for a racially motivated, cold-blooded murder is life up in Parchment Penitentiary. Now it's a shame because most of the prison population up there is black and they're going to know about your artwork. Want me to describe what they're likely to do to a pretty little white boy like you?"

"When did this happen? Last Saturday right? I was at home playing Atari with a bunch of friends. I was home all evening. You can check with my dad."

"Okay, what's his name and it better not be Benjamin, Fucking Franklin," said Ben.

"His name is Frank Mitford, and we live at 4320 Belair Avenue, you can call him at work at 654-3498. He'll vouch for me being at home all night.

"Detective put the cuffs back on little junior here, and I'll run this down." Ben turned to the kid, "You better not be messing with me kid."

When Ben left the interview room, Willis was waiting with a big smirk on his face. "When he said his name was Alexander Graham Bell, you should have seen your face!"

"Lucky for him by that point I was pretty sure he didn't do it."

"How do you figure that?"

"With Willy Parnell's injuries, if that kid were responsible there wouldn't just be paint on his hands. His knuckles would be swollen and torn to shreds."

*****

Luckily, Ben was able to reach Frank Mitford at work. The firm was called Mitford and Sons Trucking. Ben hoped Frank had more than the smartass in the interview room to leave his business to. Once Mitford came on the line, Ben spoke. "Mr. Mitford, it's Detective Ben O'Shea from the Biloxi Police Department. Do you have a few minutes?"

"What's this regarding, we're in the middle of a staff meeting, and I need to get back to them."

"It's about your son Frank Junior. He's okay, but he was picked up earlier today." This was a moment of truth when talking to a parent. What they said next often dictated how things were going to progress.

"What did the little prick do now?"

Ben smiled and said, "He was caught spray painting walls down by the boardwalk. Normally it would be a minor thing but what he wrote was racially motivated, and with the tensions in the city being pretty high, we had to make sure he wasn't involved in anything else."

There was a pause before Mr. Mitford spoke, "Do you mind me asking what exactly he wrote?"

"No, but he claims this was all an instance of copying someone else's thoughts so we would prefer it not be made public. He wrote Dye, Nigger."

"Jesus H. Christ! What a little shit! Did he tell you to call me?"

"Once he realized we were following up on a murder investigation he offered you up as an alibi. Can you confirm what your son was up to last Saturday evening around 9 o'clock?"

"I feel like saying I can't remember and have you keep him a little bit longer, Detective. He's not my son by the way. I married his Mom, who just happened to have a son named Frank from her first marriage. This little prick is an embarrassment to my name. Okay, I don't know what he told you, but he was playing video games in our living room with his little punk friends. They made a complete mess which of course his mother had to clean up. Detective, I hate to say it because I hate the little shit, but his tough guy act is all smoke and mirrors. You know what he plays on his Atari? Pong!"

"Thanks for clearing this up Mr. Mitford. When you come to pick up your step-son, you'll need to sign a statement to that effect. I will get everything set up. The Department may decide to press charges for vandalism so you might need to bring him back. Will you be able to come right down?"

"Is he in a cell?"

"No, I think he's drinking a coke and sitting in one of our interview rooms."

"Tell you what, I could come down there if you insist, but why not throw him in jail and let him learn a lesson."

"I'm sure that can be arranged but don't leave him here overnight. Some pretty nasty characters get thrown in there." Ben was about to hang up when a thought came to him. "Listen, Frank, I think I can talk the chief into not pressing charges if your son was to agree to repair the damage."

"Is there a city crew with a real mean son of a bitch supervisor? If you can line it up, then I will personally see that the little creep shows up first thing in the morning."

"Sounds good Frank, let me talk to the boss. If everything is cool, then I will leave something for you to sign as well as to where Frank Junior needs to show up tomorrow."

Ben had just hung up from Mitford when he noticed that Burnside was coming down the corridor towards him drinking a coke.

"Ben," Burnside called out. "That kid was some piece of work wasn't he?"

"Yeah, it's pretty hard to get through to kids like that." Ben brought him up to date on what he had arranged with the father.

Burnside nodded. "Say, how about going for a beer? I don't know about you, but it's been one of those days. First, the son-in-law wasn't very helpful, then we have our only suspect turn out to be just a kid with a spray can."

Ben looked at his watch, "It's half-past 4, and I want to talk to Willis about the deal with Mitford senior. Also, we got a call from the Coroner. I guess he's ready to tell us about the cause of death."

Burnside said fine but then asked Ben if he was cool with getting caught up tomorrow after the daily briefing. Ben said okay but thought the whole conversation sounded odd. One minute the guy wants to go for a beer than all of a sudden he has to be somewhere. Ben watched as Burnside walked away. In the next few weeks, Ben was due to write a progress report on his young partner, and he didn't look forward to the exercise. Burnside lacked in a couple of areas. Ben wondered if the younger generation of cops would prove to be less willing to put in the extra time. He couldn't put his finger on it, but he couldn't help think there was something off about Burnside.

Ben went in to talk to Willis and found the chief was not in a receptive mood. "Listen, O'Shea, I told the Mayor we had a suspect. So what does he do? He organizes a fucking press conference for tomorrow at 11 a.m. I know you don't think the kid's the murderer, but maybe we shouldn't be too quick to release him."

"Ah boss, the kid's just a punk. I already made a deal with his dad and believe me the kid needs a good lesson, but he didn't beat Willy Parnell to death."

"Fine," Willis pointed at Ben, "then you need to be there at the press conference, and when they ask me for a fucking update on the case, I am going to call on you. You better have something Chuckles."

"Shit fuck, I hate those things."

Chapter 16

As he drove over to the Harrison County Medical Examiner's office in Gulfport, Ben's thoughts slid back and forth between Burnside and the case. There had been more rioting last night, and he was sure pressure to close the case was being put on Captain Willis. If it hadn't of been for Bruce Smith and Justyne Armstrong describing the same people, he would probably let it go.

When he got to the Coroner's building, Ben was directed to the lab where he would find Brian Tifton. Opening the door to the lab, he found the Coroner standing over a cadaver with a saw in his hand. In Mississippi, a county coroner was a political position, and many of those elected had little or no medical training. Up until 1974 a coroner's jury would have been convened to investigate and order an autopsy whenever a violent death occurred. Since that time, the law had changed, leaving it up to the local Coroner to determine if there were enough grounds to warrant a full investigation, and whether such an investigation would be in the public interest.

"Ahem," Ben tried to get the old man's attention. Tifton looked like he could have just as easily been on a gurney himself.

The doddering old man had Albert Einstein-like hair and was well past his prime, a veteran of municipal bureaucracy.

"Oh, Detective you didn't have to come over. I could have sent the report in the interoffice mail."

"I was in the area, Brian. I don't mean to interrupt your work." Ben gestured to the saw which Tifton continued to hold over the body.

"That's fine Detective, I'll get back to this later," Tifton said as if he had been about to carve a roast. He walked over to another metal table and handed Ben a file. Pulling back the sheet to expose Willy, Ben was once again taken by the sight of all the bruises and scratches on the body. *What kind of bastard would do this?*

"So Detective, I have decided that Willy Parnell died of misadventure which in turn led him to have a heart attack."

"Misadventure? I don't understand."

"Well, Detective there is no doubt that the man had a bad heart, and that will be the official cause of death."

"What about all the bruises, someone beat the crap out of him?"

"Perhaps, but I don't think it's conclusive."

"You're full of shit, Tifton."

"You're entitled to your opinion Detective, but Mr. Parnell was found in the forest. These scratches on his face could have been caused by tree branches, the bruises perhaps from bumping into trees."

"I don't believe this. I suppose he just wrote Dye Nigger on a piece of paper before the heart attack?"

Tifton remained quiet for a moment before saying, "I cannot, by that fact alone, conclude that Mr. Parnell was murdered. I have no idea when that was written or whether it is even related. It would not be in the public interest to speculate."

Ben suddenly realized what was happening. If there was no murder, then there was no murderer. Therefore, everyone could just go back about their business and forget about Willy Parnell. "I can't believe this. I suggest you not sign off on this quite yet. Let me make a couple of calls first."

"Don't let me inhibit your investigation Detective, but I will be advising Police Chief Willis that the old man died of a heart attack."

Ben was beside himself. The only saving grace was that based on their last conversation about the press conference, Willis could not have seen the report yet.

*****

Ben decided to drive back to police headquarters rather than risk an awkward telephone conversation with Chief Willis. He was dumbfounded by the Coroner's decision. You didn't need medical training to see that Willy had been beaten. At heart Chief Willis was a good cop, they may have disagreed more than once, but Ben was cautiously optimistic that he could get Willis to stop the investigation from being swept under the rug.

Ben parked the cruiser and raced into the building, avoiding a couple of people who wanted him to stop and chat. When he got to the nearly deserted squad room, he was relieved to see Willis still in his office talking on the phone. As Ben sat at his desk in the bullpen, he could see his boss was becoming more animated. His hands were gesturing, and even through a closed door, Ben could hear his raised voice. *Go get 'em chief!*

Ben looked down at his desk and amidst all of the inter-department memos, he saw a manila envelope addressed to Detective O'Shea. He was tempted to leave the mail until the next morning, but he had requested the forensic artist pay a quick visit to both Justyne Armstrong and Bruce Smith. As he watched Willis give the middle finger to whomever he was speaking to, Ben opened up the envelope. What he found was a set of drawings. The first sketch had the name Bruce Smith scrawled on the bottom and depicted two men. The two men looked to be mid-thirties, short brush cuts, stubby beard, with one clearly sporting a nose that had been broken at least once. The first thing that came to mind was a longshoreman. At first, he thought the two might have been twins, but upon closer examination, the one without the broken beak had a slimmer face and narrower lips. *No not twins, but brothers, isn't that what Bruce Smith had said?*

Ben's heart jumped when he looked at the second set of sketches, this one with Justyne's flowery signature on the bottom. While they weren't identical to the first set, there was a remarkable resemblance. There was a note with the sketches from the artist, saying that neither witness had seen the other set of sketches or been made aware of the similarities.

He was still ruminating about the drawings when Willis' door opened, "O'Shea, my office."

Grabbing the drawings, Ben moved into the captain's office and took his normal seat. As he sat down, he saw something fly across the desk and break into pieces against the far wall.

"How many staplers do you go through each week?"

"Never mind the fuckin stapler." Willis opened his side drawer and extracted a large bottle of Excedrin, shaking more than a couple in his hand. He popped what sounded like a half dozen in his mouth crunching on them before washing them down with coffee. Judging by the face he made, Ben figured that the coffee must have been sitting on his desk all day.

"Just got off the phone with the Mayor. Jesus what an asshole. He's somehow got that fuckin' Tifton to rule that this was a fuckin' accident."

"Yeah, I just got back from meeting with him. What a load of bullshit! We can't let them whitewash this." Ben's tone mirrored that of his boss.

Willis opened up his right-hand drawer and extracted a half-empty bottle of Wild Turkey. Ben felt like asking if the cocktail was a good chaser for the pills but knew enough to just go with it. Willis poured a healthy two fingers into two glasses and pushed Ben's glass towards him. "O'Shea, I've learned something about being the police chief here. Something that doesn't sit well with me, but it's something you need to learn. You ready?"

Ben nodded and wondered how full the bottle had been before Willis started drinking. "Here it is. You can't fight city hall."

Ben remained quiet for a moment thinking there might be more. He took a sip of the bourbon and grimaced. Wild Turkey was not his drink of choice. The bartender at O'Toole's used to say that Wild Turkey could make a man walk sideways. "Listen boss can I show you something?"

"What the fuck you got?" Willis asked with a grin. Clearly, Willis had been drinking; the liquor was having an effect on his speech. Ben spread the sketches out on the desk in front of Willis. As Willis looked at the drawings, Ben continued, "Remember I said that two witnesses had reported seeing a couple of tough looking guys hanging around their apartment buildings and one of them used the term Nigger. So I had the police artist sit with both witnesses independently, and this is what they came up with." Willis poured himself another few fingers and picked up the drawing of the suspects done with the doorman. "You already have a name for this guy...Bruce Smith?"

"No that's the witness, the doorman. The artist just gets the witness to sign the drawing to tag it as coming from his description."

"Oh okay," Willis swallowed half of his drink. He put the drawing down and looked at the four sketches again. "Fuck, it's four fuckin brothers. Ugly bastards to boot. They look like cab drivers." Willis held Ben's gaze for a moment, neither saying anything. "So what?" Willis said finishing his drink and pouring another. Ben reached over for the bottle and poured a small amount into his glass, putting the bottle on the floor away from Willis.

"So these guys targeted Willy Parnell either because he was black or for some other reason. This was murder, Chief."

"Tomorrow at that cocksucking press conference, the Mayor is going to say the bruises were the result of bumping into fucking trees. The scratches came from branches, and that old Willy got disoriented in the forest and suffered a heart attack."

"Fuckshit!" Ben responded.

"Listen Chuckles, you have a good theory, I'd be able to see it better if you gave me the bottle back."

Ben reluctantly poured a half a finger into his boss' glass. "I'll drive you home, okay?"

"I'll take a cab. Maybe I'll meet one of these four brothers. Maybe this one...his name's Justyne. So what do you want to do Chuckles? We've got cases stacked up the wazoo, our detectives wasting their time with punks doing graffiti, and chasing down the cab drivers."

"Boss, all I want is your okay to run with this... maybe get these sketches in the paper tomorrow. We can set up a dedicated tip line, maybe someone will know who they are." Ben wasn't sure if Willis grasped the meaning of what he had said as Willis nodded and changed the subject.

"What the fuck is happening with Burnside? You're supposed to be showing that kid the ropes.... Where is he today?"

"Ophthalmologist."

Willis spat out his mouthful and started laughing. That's good O'Shea! Of-ta-mogisssst! Last week it was the podiatrist then yesterday it was the dentist. I just wish I had a partner like you when I was starting out."

Then he forced himself into a fleeting moment of sobriety and gave Ben a serious look, "You need to make a call on that kid." I hate fucking politics, but his uncle is some big fuckin' politician. So if he isn't cutting it, you'll have to be careful."

"I still have a couple of weeks before I have to write the assessment."

Ben collected the sketches and got up to leave. Willis was still mumbling about four fucking brothers. As he was about to open the door, Willis called out, "See you at 11 for the press conference and Chuckles please, please, I beg of you, wear something fucking normal."

Chapter 17

"So a riverboat? I'm excited," said Rachel as she slid into the passenger seat of the VW. She was wearing a long slim-fitting skirt with a cream blouse and a pearl necklace. "You said to dress professionally. Is this acceptable sir?"

"You look absolutely stunning." He noticed that she had put her shoulder length brown hair in a bun.

"So tell me about the mission," Rachel said as Gabriel pulled the car out of the parking lot.

"The case involves someone who apparently was on the riverboat back in May. I need to get a name and find the person. The head office up in Missouri faxed a list of passengers to the captain for pick up. Once we get the list from him, I would like to get a tour of the boat and check on a few things. Maybe talk to some of the staff."

"That doesn't sound very difficult. You said something about having to spin a story."

"Well the reason I'm getting the list is because they think I'm with the Republican Party, which is the group that chartered the riverboat last May. They think that the person I'm looking for pledged a large donation and that somehow we neglected to get her name."

"But that's not true, is it? Is the Republican Party your customer?"

"Not directly, it's pretty complicated, and I can't really disclose too many details." Gabriel pulled onto the interstate towards New Orleans. He slipped on his shades; it was going to be another scorcher.

"Can't you just ask the Republican Party who this lady is? Surely they must have a list of the people they invited to their little party."

"They probably do, and if I have to, I might have to come up with a story and do that." For a few minutes, Gabriel drove in silence thinking about how best to present themselves to the captain of the Mississippi Queen.

Rachel broke the silence, "So how many names will be on this list and what else do you know about the person you're looking for?"

"I understand there were approximately a hundred and fifty passengers on board. As for what I know about the person, all I know is that she is late twenties or early thirties, dark haired, average height and weight."

"You've just described me. I guess the good news is that most Republicans are rich, old white guys, so there might only be thirty or forty women. If you could figure out how to get their ages, I bet you could narrow this down to a dozen."

"That's good Rachel, I hadn't thought about it that way."

"So this mystery lady was on the cruise as an invited guest of the GOP?" Rachel slipped off her high heels. "These shoes kill me, but they're all I have that goes with this outfit."

"In answer to your question, someone in the GOP must know who she is but remember I'm not working directly for them. The client doesn't want the party to know that I'm looking for her."

"Very mysterious. I'll quit asking questions now."

They drove in silence for two minutes before Rachel asked, "Have you considered that maybe this mystery woman might be a member of the crew?"

Gabriel thought about that and conceded that Rachel had a good point. Rogers had said he met the lady at the bar, could she have been a waitress? You'd think the Congressman would know if his boinkee was the one serving him drinks. "No, I haven't considered that, remind me to ask the ship captain about the number of women that he has on staff."

For the rest of the drive, they fell into a conversation about Rachel's courses, which she thought were boring. She also said that her job at the hospital was equally dull.

"So why the charade with your boss tonight?"

"Because I don't know what I want my future to be. To tell you the truth, the most exciting time I've had at the hospital was that time you came in to see Mr. Dermody, and we had to try to figure out what he wrote on that piece of paper. Do you remember?"

"Yes, that was fun. It was the key to solving the case. I'm going to tell your boss how smart you are."

"Tonight's about getting to know my boss and her husband on a more social level so that if I wanted to progress within the hospital, then I would have the right person backing me. Plus it was her idea. If I had said no it would have been awkward." Rachel pulled out a *Kleenex* from her purse and blew her nose loudly.

"You catching something?"

"I've had the sniffles for a few days, kind of goes with working in the hospital."

They hit traffic when they got to New Orleans and arrived at the dock on Toulouse Street later than planned. It wasn't hard to find the riverboat. It stood majestically moored to the dock, the largest boat in the harbor. Looking up at the tall white structure it looked like a large white apartment building. Emblazoned across the front in gold was "Mississippi Queen." The aft of the ship had a huge bright red paddlewheel that had to measure 35 feet in width.

"Wow, it's bigger than I thought," said Gabriel in awe.

"My Daddy took me to see the boats once, but I don't remember ever seeing anything this big." replied Rachel.

The dock was a bustle of activity with a procession of ant-like workers carrying boxes along a gangplank. "I guess we should ask someone where we can find Captain Kelly," said Gabriel parking the VW in a nearby lot. As they got out of the bug, Gabriel asked, "Are you good with the plan?"

"You sure we should use our real names?"

"Well, let's see, I can be Mr. P Ennis, and you can be the lovely Patricia Squatpump. We can give it a try, but what do we do if the captain wants to see our identification? No, let's stick to our real names. Besides, I told the guy in Missouri that my name was Gabriel Ross."

As they made their way towards the riverboat, Rachel was walking awkwardly in her heels. "I'm a little nervous, I don't want to mess this up for you."

"Don't worry Rachel, let me handle it. I'm a professional."

Gabriel asked a couple of workmen where they might find Captain Kelly and was directed to an older gentleman standing off to one side. The large, overweight man was peering over the tops of his glasses making a notation on a clipboard. He was dressed in a white shirt with suspenders holding up navy trousers below his generous belly and a white captain's hat with gold trim. The most remarkable thing about him was the Santa Claus beard that dominated his face.

Sharing a look with Rachel, Gabriel walked over to the man and tried to get his attention. "Ahem."

The Captain yelled at a workman man who had stumbled on one of the boat's bow lines, causing him to drop a bunch of boxes he was carrying. "Listen, man, if you can't carry the load without dropping it, you'd best be finding a job more suitable for those dainty little hands."

"Ahem," Gabriel repeated. This time, Kelly gave him a dismissive look before returning his gaze to the loading activity.

The man towered over Gabriel standing at over 6 foot and most assuredly over 300 pounds.

Gabriel was about to say something else when he heard a voice behind him. "Excuse me, Sir, my name is Rachel Henderson, are you the famous Captain Kelly?"

"Not sure I'm famous young...lady. Probably infamous." The captain smiled as his eyes took in Rachel. "Captain Patrick Kelly at your service Miss. You can call me Patty."

"Nice to meet you, Patty," said Rachel, giving Kelly her best smile. "I'm a special aide with the Republican Party of the great State of Mississippi. This man is Gabriel Ross, you might have heard of him, he's a rising star in the Party."

Looking over his glasses at Gabriel, "He'd have to rise a might more before he'd get my vote."

Rachel laughed at the comment, which Gabriel thought was unnecessary. Captain Kelly then asked, "Well, what can I do for you, pretty lady?"

"Ah! Thank you, Patty! Gabriel here was talking to a man named Cash in your head office in Missouri. You see Cash was to fax you something that we were hoping to collect."

"Yeah what might that be?" Kelly let his eyes travel over Rachel's figure.

Gabriel spoke up and said, "It was a passenger list for the cruise which the GOP took on the Mississippi Queen back in May." He added, "You would be helping out the GOP."

"Don't give a rat's ass about politics kid. What do you want with that list?"

Rachel broke the momentary pause giving the Captain her best smile as she put a seductive hand on his sleeve. "Well, it was my fault, Patty. I misplaced the information about one of the passengers who made a rather large pledge to the party. I'm going to get in a lot of trouble if I can't find this person." When Kelly didn't immediately reply, Rachel added, "If I see the list then I'll probably remember the name right away. You would be helping me out big time if you could look for that fax. Pweassse."

"Well young lady, I don't mind helping out a beautiful woman. The fax is in my cabin aboard ship. Maybe Mr. Up and Comer can stay here while you and I go aboard for the fax."

"Actually Gabriel here is in charge of booking the next campaign cruise, and he was hoping he could get a quick tour."

Kelly gave Gabriel another look and then barked out an order to the worker who had dropped the box. "Hey, twinkle toes. Got a job for you." When the man came over, Gabriel placed him as early thirties with a slight build. "This little man is supposed to be a big man in politics. He needs you to give him a tour of the Queen."

Ben's guide introduced himself as Curtis and wore his long dark hair tied in a ponytail. The four of them climbed aboard the boat, with Rachel giving Gabriel an apprehensive look before heading off with Captain Kelly to his cabin. Gabriel mouthed the words "thirty minutes" to her. Curtis led Gabriel through some double doors to a beautiful foyer with a giant staircase. A mixture of polished brass and glass gave the lobby a lavish look.

"We might as well start at the top and work our way back down again. Anything special you would like to see?"

"I guess just give me the standard tour, but I am particularly interested in the layout of the cabins."

Curtis directed Gabriel to a pair of gold brass doors leading to an elevator. On the ride up Curtis started rambling, a spiel he had no doubt delivered hundreds of times, "The Queen was built in 1976 up in Indiana. She's the second biggest riverboat on the Mississippi. We're going up to the 7th level, that's called the Promenade Deck. The boat has 199 cabins and assuming double occupancy, that would give us a capacity of 398. Most cruises are pretty well booked." The doors opened up to an enclosed area overlooking the deck, offering a fantastic view of the New Orleans Harbor. "Lots of folks come out here to check out the view and walk off the booze they've consumed at one of the bars on board." Curtis lead the way to an area with about fifty tables set up in the aft part of the ship. A bunch of workmen were cleaning a 16 foot Jacuzzi. "This is called the Calliope Bar, and it's usually the most popular party place on the ship."

"Impressive," said Gabriel, taking in the view and trying to picture Rogers up at the bar or frolicking with Wobbly-Tits in the Jacuzzi.

"The ship also has 6 other decks, there's a movie theater, a gym, a sauna, a library, and all kinds of shops including a hair salon and barber. After touring the Promenade deck, they walked to the stern of the ship and then Curtis lead the way down a short flight of stairs. "This is the observation deck. It's where most of the entertainment happens. Over there is our Grand Saloon," he pointed to a large ballroom. "They have a Dixie band playing every night. The place is a veritable Who's Who in the entertainment business. Frank Sinatra and Dean Martin are regulars on board."

"How fast does the riverboat go? Gabriel asked.

"Average speed is 8 miles an hour, but if Captain Kelly wants to, he's been known to get her up to 14 miles per hour." When they looked in at the Grand Saloon, it was clear that nothing was done on the cheap. Huge chandeliers hung from the ceiling, and the chairs were all done in gold leather.

"Tell me Curtis how many crewmembers are on board?"

"Counting the officers, chambermaids, cooks, dishwashers, porters... I think the number is a little over 150."

"Any idea how many of those are women?"

Curtis gave Gabriel an appraising look, "I reckon you have a reason for asking that. I figure more than half would be women."

"Would most of those be women under forty?"

Curtis nodded enthusiastically. "I was seeing a girl who works as a waitress up here. We broke up recently because she would get jealous of all of the sleazes that work onboard." Gabriel wasn't surprised that Curtis, who had fine features and brown eyes, was popular with the ladies.

The two made their way back to the elevator and went down to what Curtis called the Texas deck. "Of the 199 rooms, there are 26 suites. They contain a separate sitting area, a private veranda, and a king size bed. All rooms have FM radios and a separate bath and shower." Pulling a master key out of his pocket, he opened the door to one of the suites. Gabriel walked into the stateroom and was immediately impressed. The room was finished in dark wood and gave the spacious room the appearance of wealth. "This is a Triple-A suite, one of the nicest," said Curtis.

As he looked around, Gabriel noticed a large armoir off to one side. He opened one of the doors, half expecting someone to jump out. Curtis led him out to the veranda which offered a fantastic view of the harbor. Gabriel was more interested in whether someone could hide out here and take pictures of the show happening inside. A vision of Rogers on his knees in front of the mystery woman flashed across his mind.

Curtis brought him back to the present, "Did you want to see the regular cabins?"

"Absolutely, this is very nice."

"The smaller cabins on the next deck are much smaller. No veranda, no armoire."

But still, someone could be hiding behind the shower curtain. Surely, they would put a sitting Congressman in a suite.

As they moved about the cabin deck, Gabriel paid particular attention to what Curtis called the Public Rooms. Gabriel had counted 4 bars in addition to the Grand Dining room and the Grand Saloon where the Congressman could have met the mystery woman. Curtis finally led the way down the main deck where they looked around for Rachel and the Captain. The tour had taken almost thirty minutes, and there was no sign of them.

"Thank you for the tour Curtis," said Gabriel, handing him a $1 tip. "Mind if I ask you a few more questions?"

"Wow! A whole dollar....awesome." Sarcasm dripped from Curtis' voice.

Gabriel reached for his wallet and pulled out a Franklin, holding it up in his fingers.

"Sure, want to see the engine rooms? There are the crew's quarters too, but most folks want to see the passenger areas."

"Maybe you can show me where the Captain's cabin is in a few minutes. How long have you worked on the Queen?"

Curtis snatched the finsky and thought for a moment, "It's going on two years now."

"What duties do you have when the boat sets sail?"

"I used to work in the kitchen, but about six months ago, I was moved up to busboy. Of course, after dropping those boxes today, I'll probably be in the kitchen washing dishes again."

"So you were a busboy when the Republican Party cruised this past May?"

"Yeah I remember that cruise. Lots of rich white guys."

"Would you know Congressman Rogers if you saw him?"

"Sure, I cleared his table in the Grand Dining Hall. He's not a big lover of Cajun cooking."

"Cajun cooking?"

"Yeah, it's a 5-star restaurant and has a full menu with some down home Cajun cooking. I remember the Congressman asking for American food."

"Do you remember who he was sitting with?"

Curtis looked off into the sky as if some plane might have written the answer across the blue sky. After a moment, he just shook his head..."Don't reckon I do."

"Do you know if there were women at the table?"

"I'm sure there was. The group that organized things wanted each table to have a couple of women."

"Do you remember seeing Congressman Rogers on more than one occasion, maybe in one of the bars?"

"I only ever saw him in the dining hall on account of that being my job. I heard he was up at the Calliope Bar though, because my ex told me. I guess she spilled something, and he didn't appreciate it. She said he called her a name under his breath. She said he was drunk."

"I'd like to meet your ex. What's her name?"

Curtis gave Gabriel a quizzical look. He pulled out his wallet proudly displaying an attractive dark haired woman. "Her name's Jessie. The picture is the best I can do, though. She dumped me and quit right after that cruise."

They were interrupted by the sight of Rachel running, carrying her high heels in one hand and the fax in another.

Gabriel thanked Curtis and got the last phone number he had for Jessie. When Rachel and Gabriel were safely in the car, Ben asked, "My God, Rachel...what happened? Do you have any paw marks on you?"

"No, but only because I'm faster than him. Captain Kelly is one horny old dog. Once he had the cabin door closed, he was like an octopus. I couldn't keep his hands away from me. I kept asking for the fax, and he kept on trying to get me to drink this 'genuine Irish whiskey.' I finally humored him and had a sip, it was awful. Anyway, he got the fax for me, and I told him I needed to visit the washroom. That's when I split. I took my heels off because I was afraid he would run after me."

"Wow, thank you, Rachel. I feel like going in there and teaching him a lesson. You went beyond the call of duty." Gabriel took the fax sheets.

"How was the tour?'

"Interesting it's a beautiful ship, we should come back and go on a cruise, and I'll chase you around the cabin. I'm starting to believe that your thought about the woman being part of the crew is a possibility." Gabriel told her about Curtis' girlfriend and that he had her number and wanted to check her out.

"Gabriel you don't realize something."

"What's that?" he asked, putting the VW in gear and backing out of the parking space.

"For the GOP cruise, the organizers brought a bunch of local girls on board to help provide entertainment."

"Entertainment?"

"Yes, entertainment....that kind of entertainment."

"Like boinkee, boinkee?"

"Like boinkee."

Chapter 18

The following morning there were over one hundred people standing in the foyer of City Hall. The Mayor stood on the second step of the long circular staircase with Chief Willis and Ben O'Shea. The latter was wearing a black blazer with a teal green shirt and a pumpkin tie. Willis took one look at what O'Shea was wearing and groaned, complaining about the impact it was having on his hangover. A collection of microphones from the various media outlets in the area were poised to capture everything.

"Okay let's get this going," said Mayor Baxter. As soon as the crowd quieted down, Baxter approached the microphones. "Last Saturday night a terrible tragedy befell one of our valued citizens. Mr. Willy Parnell, 64 years old, died a tragic death in the woods around Hillier Park. Mr. Parnell was born and bred in Biloxi and was a longtime longshoreman. He was predeceased by his loving wife and survived by his daughter Justyne Armstrong, his son-in-law and his two granddaughters." He looked over at the family for a brief moment, "My most sincere condolences on your loss. My heart and, I'm sure the heart of everyone in our city, goes out to you."

Ben made eye contact with Justyne and nodded. The two girls were holding their mother's hand in what looked like a vice grip. The Mayor stopped briefly and took a drink of water before continuing. "Willy served his country valiantly during the Second World War. There will be a ceremony on Saturday at the South Baptist Church where he worshiped. Much has been written about Willy's death and this press conference is to help people who are inflamed by this event to better understand the circumstances of his death. Sadly some people in our community are taking advantage of Willy Parnell's death to promote anarchy. Once again last night, there were people in the streets carrying signs. While most of the protesters were peaceful, there was a group of thugs who took advantage of the situation to loot stores and vandalize property. I would like to caution everyone that people who break the law will be held accountable. I urge everyone to remain calm. I would like to turn it over now to Police Chief Willis to give us an update on what the Coroner had to say about the event. Chief?"

Chief Willis held the Coroner's report in a trembling hand and spoke slowly as if he was having a tough time focusing. "Harrison County Coroner Tifton has fully examined the body of Mr. Parnell and has concluded that the deceased suffered a myocardial infarction. In layman's terms, that means a blood clot blocked a major artery causing Willy's heart to fail. Mr. Tifton's conclusion was supported by our investigation indicating that the deceased had suffered from heart problems and was under doctor's care. Much has been written and speculated about Willy's death in the *Herald*. Some of the speculation was that he had been beaten to death because of his race. While the case has not been closed by any means, the Coroner is labeling Mr. Parnell's death a misadventure. An older, disoriented man under doctor's care ventured into the trees in the dark on his way home. The scratches on his face probably caused by branches and the bruises from running into trees in a panicked attempt to find his way home." There was a rumble of voices amongst the crowd, a cry of "Bullshit!" and another of "Cover-up."

Willis raised his voice over the increasingly loud crowd. "I, like you, feel terrible about this and would like to remind everyone that the case is not closed, we have our best people chasing down all leads so that we can be sure about what happened. So I would like to turn it over to the lead Detective, in this case, to update you on the investigation. Detective...O'Shea."

Ben thought Willis had been about to call him Chuckles. "Thank you, Chief Willis. I have a couple of brief comments and then would like to give everyone a chance to ask questions. We are pursuing a couple of people who have been identified as persons of interest in this case. We have witness statements identifying them as individuals who may have information. Later today you will see an article by Dana Lorimer in the *Herald* with a sketch artist rendition of the two men. I want you all to take a good hard look at the sketch. These two men live in our community, someone knows them, and we will be setting up a tip line to handle your calls.

While I understand Mr. Tifton's findings, I am convinced that there is more to Willy Parnell's death, and I can pledge to each and every one of you, that I will find those responsible."

A murmur of approval came from the crowd and Ben could see from the nodding of heads that he had won them over. He heard a man cry out, "Go get'em O'Shea!" from the back of the room. A smattering of applause was interrupted by Mayor Baxter who spoke into the microphones. "My office is in direct daily contact with Chief Willis and his team, and we will ensure that any information about this tragic accident is shared. I would like to speak directly to all of our wonderful community residents and urge you, whether you are black or white, to remain calm and have patience as our police force does its job."

Baxter's remarks were once again labeled as bullshit from the crowd. Ben spoke up, "I understand your anger, does anyone have a question they would like to ask?"

A reporter for a New Orleans paper spoke up. "Detective O'Shea, how do you reconcile the Coroner's report on the hunt for the two people of interest?"

Ben took a deep breath, "The Coroner was unable to conclusively point to a homicide, as I mentioned the investigation into Willy's death continues."

The same reporter remained unconvinced, "Can you confirm the presence of a note found near Mr. Parnell's body that would prove this was a racially motivated crime?"

Ben looked over at Willis, who like the others was looking at their feet. "The answer is yes and no. There was a note found near the scene with a racial slur. As to whether it proves that the murder of Willy Parnell was racially motivated is another issue. It might be what the killers want us to believe. Until we have completed our investigation we are not prepared to comment on what led to this crime."

There was another murmur in the crowd, and a different reporter from the Memphis paper asked, "Detective O'Shea, have similarly worded statements to the one found near the body been found around downtown Biloxi? And was a suspect not arrested?"

"That's a good question. A young man was apprehended for spray painting a mural with the same message. He has been released to his father and will be properly dealt with. He is not a suspect in the murder. As to the graffiti messages that are showing up, the sheer number of instances would suggest the work of copycats who are most likely teenagers. This is an open avenue of our investigation."

Chapter 19

Gabriel drove through the streets of New Orleans. He wished he could talk to Rachel about the case. He was used to having Ben as his confidante. With being sworn to secrecy, that option was gone. He was sure that Rogers was not being straight with him. Given the new revelation about the pros being invited on the cruise, he had to conclude that the blackmailer was most likely one of them or one of the staff. "Take a look at the list Rachel, how many are women?"

Rachel looked at the list which was six pages long. She counted silently as he drove. She gave up part way, blowing her nose once again. "I'm not sure because there are some first names that are just initials. There are others that could be male or female, like Pat Gains....is it Patricia or Patrick. Here's an Ashley is that a man or a woman."

I've met him, and the jury is still out, thought Gabriel.

"If we count just the names that are clearly women and then say half of those that are unisex, then I would say at most 40 names. They're a lot of Phyllis' and Gladys, ' so I would wager that you will find most of these are old ladies. Wait, the list isn't in alphabetical order, but there must be some husband and wives because they have the same room number. Like Gladys Philpott is in cabin 26 and so is Rudy Philpott. Does that help?"

"Sure it does. Likely I'm looking for a woman who is not sharing a room with her husband."

"I would have to take the list home and cross reference everything. But if you subtract all of the ones that are clearly with their husbands as well as those whose name would suggest that they are as old as the hills, I bet you won't have many left."

"Is there no other information other than the name?"

"Just a room assignment."

"Is there any indication which people got triple A rooms."

Rachel looked through the sheets stopping to blow her nose again. "There are three. Michael Retzner, Thad Cochran and an Emmett Rogers."

"Retzner is the chairman of the Republican Party in Mississippi, Cochran I believe is a senator, and Rogers is a Congressman. Can you see if a woman is sharing one of those AAA rooms?"

Rachel shuffled through the pages one more time. "You owe me lunch for this, I am starved." After a couple of minutes, she said that Mildred Cochran shared a room with Thad. But it looks like both Retzner and Rogers were singles."

"Okay, thanks, Rachel that is really helpful. What would you like for lunch?"

"I would rather you told me the truth about your case and what we're doing here. You already said the business about finding the big donor was bull, so it has to be something else tied to the Republican Party. Did some spouse hire you to prove their husband, this Retzner guy, was having an affair with someone?"

"Rachel, I really appreciate all your help. I wouldn't have made it past Captain Horny Dog without you, and you have really helped me get a handle on this case. Believe me, when I say this, nothing would make me happier than to share this case with you. But I cannot. I can't even discuss this with Ben."

"I wouldn't tell anyone. Pinky swear."

"Please don't ask me again."

"Okay, then I want to go somewhere expensive and before we leave New Orleans."

*****

Gabriel and Rachel stopped at a place called the *Three Muses* in the French quarter. As you would expect, the restaurant had two specialties - one was to serve fresh fish caught that morning and the other, taking advantage of the fresh suckers who agreed to pay their prices.

The restaurant itself was small and crowded with a party atmosphere thanks to the jazz band playing in the front corner. They decided to go with their waiter's recommendation, a fresh smoked salmon omelet together with a carafe of Pinot Noire.

"Do you like Jazz Music? asked Rachel.

"Sometimes, when I'm in the mood." Gabriel looked at the stage where an old black man played a washboard, accompanied by a bass player, drummer and a familiar looking black girl playing the saxophone. "I know the girl up there," said Gabriel gesturing to the girl on stage.

"How do you know her?"

"She's Jacqueline's friend." Gabriel had to speak loudly to be heard over the music. "There were three of them that drove down to Mardi Gras, Jacqueline, a girl named Catharine and this girl Chevon. That was the trip where Jacqueline met her future husband, Sheriff Cooper." As far as Gabriel knew, Jacqueline and Chevon had stayed close. "When Jacqueline's husband went nuts and tried to kill his wife, Chevon came to the rescue. She went ballistic and attacked him. She ended up in the hospital, but she probably helped save Jacqueline's life."

"Wow! She sounds like a pretty good friend, not a bad sax player either."

The band was playing a song called the *New Orleans Wiggle* which featured Chevon doing a solo. Gabriel and Rachel listened while waiting for their food. As if on cue, the waiter brought over their dinner as the band announced that they would be taking a short break. They had just started eating when Chevon walked over to Gabriel's table, "I thought that was you when you came in!" Gabriel stood up to greet her. She gave him a big hug. "It is so great to see you again Gabriel."

"You sound fantastic up there Chevon, the music classes must have paid off."

"I'm not sure it was the BA in music, it was probably more likely all those years of playing at college pubs to drunken students that helped the most." The mention of Jacqueline must have triggered something as Chevon looked at Rachel for the first time and gave her a smile. "Am I interrupting something...a business meeting?"

"This is Rachel Henderson, a colleague helping me out on a case." Rachel gave Gabriel a quick look, then returned Chevon's smile. "Why don't you join us...Chevon?"

"Okay, nice to meet you, Rachel." Chevon pulled out a chair and sat down. "I hope your case doesn't involve a crazy husband looking to have his wife dig her own grave."

"No, it's nothing like that...I hope. I'm just getting started. We were down here to check out the Mississippi Queen. It's part of the case."

"Oh! My band and I played in their Grand Saloon once. It was fun."

"Recently?"

"No, it was after I got out of the hospital." Turning to Rachel, "Some asshole tried to kill my best friend and me."

"Gabriel was telling me, that must have been awful," replied Rachel.

"Are you living here full time now Chevon?" Gabriel interjected.

"Yes....my uncle owns this place ...how's the food? I'm supposed to mingle during the breaks and find out."

"The food is wonderful," said Rachel, who had almost finished her omelet."Do you want to have a glass of wine with us?"

"I would, but wine makes me sleepy. Believe me, it wouldn't go over well if the sax player suddenly started snoring."

There was an awkward silence for a moment before Gabriel decided to address the elephant in the room. "Have you heard from Jacqueline lately?"

Chevon gave him a sympathetic look and flashed a look at Rachel. "I spoke to her last week. She's still trying to work out a few things. Her Dad was recently diagnosed with Hodgkins, so I think she has her hands full helping out. You know taking him for chemo."

"That's too bad, I didn't know that," replied Gabriel. *Was that the reason she hasn't been returning my calls?*

"How's that partner of yours, Mr. O'Shea?" Chevon had a playful smile on her face.

Gabriel laughed, remembering the sparks of attraction between Ben and Chevon. "He's good. I'll tell him you asked about him."

"Why don't you drag him down here and the four of ....," Chevon caught herself "We could all go out, and I can show you the sites they don't tell tourists about."

Gabriel felt awkward for not having introduced Rachel as his girlfriend. What's more, he knew that Rachel had picked up on it.

Eventually, Chevon had to resume her spot on stage. She asked Rachel if she had a request, but Rachel admitted that jazz was not something that she normally listened to. When Chevon got back on stage, she had a short word with her bandmates before speaking into the microphone. "We would like to dedicate this next song to everyone who is here today, but missing someone they love, the song is an old favorite written by Billy Rose, it's called "*I Miss You Every Evening.*"

Chapter 20

Everyone scattered after the press conference, which was fine with Ben. He figured Mayor Baxter would be incensed over how his attempt to cover up the case had blown up in his face. Similarly, he wanted to avoid Willis, who he was sure was too tipsy to remember authorizing the sketches being put in the paper.

Before the press conference had begun Ben had dropped off the sketches to Dana Lorimer with an update of where the case stood. He had also dispatched Burnside to set up the snitch line and to ensure that a couple of volunteers were enlisted to help. When he met with Lorimer, she assured him that she would have the story in the afternoon's edition. She had asked him about motives, and he had been honest with her. "Dana, it looks to me like Willy Parnell was targeted. He wasn't just an old black man stumbling into the forest. This could very well be a racially motivated crime, but because these two guys were seen in front of both the old man's apartment and the daughter's, I sense something more happening here."

"What have you been able to uncover about the old man?"

"That's just it...nothing. A loving grandfather. A man who led a simple life which revolved around his family and the church. When his wife died, there was a little bit of money, but I have confirmed that the money has been sitting in a T-Bill account. The daughter and the son-in-law confirm that the old man had no enemies." Once again Ben decided to not bring up Maven, Mabel, and the missing recipe card, only because he didn't want to end up being a laughing stock. "I really hope that we catch a break with these sketches. Someone has to recognize these two."

"Oh don't worry, at least two people will."

Chapter 21

He recognized the voice on the phone. "Have you seen the paper?"

"We don't get paper."

"The job was to push the old guy around a little. Get him to mind his own business. Now the cops are looking for you guys on a murder rap. That was pretty stupid."

The man didn't like being called stupid. He took his time before answering. "Accident, just like the police on TV said. Mis-adv-en-ture," said the man with a thick Eastern European accent.

"It was supposed to be a lesson, a fucking lesson you idiot! The customer is not happy."

The man didn't like being called an idiot either. The only idiot was his stupid brother, who was sitting on the couch watching reruns of the *Six Million Dollar Man*.

The man on the other end of the phone took a deep breath, "You and your brother are on the front page. Everyone is talking about you. It's just a matter of time before someone fingers you."

"You not say man was sick. Your fault."

"Fuck you. You didn't need to beat him so badly." There was a silent standoff on the phone as tempers dissipated. "What's with all the nigger stuff?"

"Pretty smart I think. People hate Niggers, so all is good."

"You'd better get lost somewhere. Get on your bike and get out of town."

Chapter 22

The drive back to Gulfport was quiet. Too quiet. Rachel spent most of the time staring out the window. Meanwhile, Gabriel was stewing over not having introduced Rachel properly. As they approached Gulfport, Rachel finally said, "She seems like a really nice girl. You should do as she suggested and get Ben to go with you to New Orleans. Everyone should have someone special in their life."

Passive aggressive? Gabriel nodded, "I'll definitely suggest it, maybe the four us can go out."

Rachel responded to the offer by honking into another Kleenex. "Yeah, that would be a lot of fun." They drove on for a few more honks before Rachel said while looking out the window, "I'd like to stop at my apartment so I can get freshened up. Don't worry, you can stay in the car." Gabriel thought her voice was starting to sound phlegmy. "I'm sure your boss will understand if you told her you were too sick."

"It's past 5 p.m., only someone rude would cancel at this point. She would have already started to prepare the meal."

I think she just suggested I was rude. "Speaking of the meal, while you freshen up, I'll go to the bakery and pick something up to contribute."

"That would be big of you."

Chapter 23

The day after the tip line went up, the crackpots and lunatics started calling. At the daily briefing, Willis told everyone about the Coroner's findings and the press conference that morning. He avoided any comment on the *Herald* story and the sketch of the two suspects.

When Ben had a chance to speak, he updated the squad on the Mitford kid that was released and handed out sketches of the two suspects. "Burnside set up a tip line yesterday afternoon once the sketches came out in the late edition. I don't imagine that you would have received many calls yet?" He looked over at Burnside.

Burnside stood up and said the tip line would be staffed all day by volunteers. Referring to his log sheet, "We have seven reported sightings of the suspects." Then raising his voice, "Seven crackpots and weirdoes." This got everyone laughing with shouts that the two guys looked like pizza delivery men. In the middle of all of the laughter, Ben looked over at Willis, who had an, "Are you happy now?" look on his face.

"Okay, let me say something," yelled Willis, quieting the room. "Shut the fuck up. I want Chuckles' drawings to be stapled to every telephone pole and every bulletin board in town. Wherever you fuckers go today, I want you to circulate them. Chuckles, you and Burnside need to chase down all of these leads. Every fuckin' one of them." With that he grabbed the blackboard eraser from the front of the squad room and threw it at the back of the room, barely missing Detective Munro, who had continued to talk.

Once everyone had cleared the room Ben told Burnside to grab his log sheet and meet him at the cruiser. He was angry at his junior partner for making a joke about the tip line. Ben tried to get a grip on his emotions, but he was still grumbling as he slid into the driver's seat of the cruiser. When Burnside finally arrived sipping a coffee he said, "Don't want me to drive, Boss?"

"Nah I feel the need to take charge today. Just get in and tell me where we need to go."

Once Burnside got in and closed the door, Ben put the car in gear and pulled out of the parking lot a little recklessly, causing his partner's coffee to spill on his lap. "Fuck, slow down man," screamed Burnside.

Ben continued the recklessness out on the road and asked, "What's the first name on the tip sheet?"

"Wait you don't have poopie pants about what I said in the squad room do you?"

"The address?" repeated Ben, his voice showing his anger.

"Mildred McCallum, she said she definitely knows who these guys are. She lives over on Playfair Drive in Gulfport."

After about five minutes, when the cruiser stopped at a traffic light Ben turned to his partner. "You need to learn how to be more supportive Burnside. When your partner has a lead, you're supposed to go along and help, not make fun of him in public. Everyone in that squad room knows you think the sketches are a stupid idea. What's more, I guarantee you that every one of them thinks you're a punk ass, lousy partner."

"I'm sorry I guess I'm just trying to fit in. I didn't mean to be disrespectful."

"Okay, apology accepted but let this be a lesson. Partners are to work as one. You have each other's back. Always."

Burnside didn't say anything for a moment. "Does it piss you off when Willis calls you Chuckles?"

Ben looked down, he was wearing a gray jacket with a red shirt and yellow striped tie. He started to laugh. Burnside tentatively joined in as Ben continued through to the next intersection.

Mildred McCallum was working in her garden when Ben drove up and parked at the curb in front of her small bungalow. As they approached her, Ben figured she was in her mid to late sixties. The age didn't fit with the get up as she was wearing - a loose halter top and a pair of cutoff jeans.

"You guys cops?" she asked as they approached.

"Yes Ma'am," said Ben flashing his ID and introducing himself and his partner. "You called the tip line saying you recognize the two men in the paper...."

"Yes, Detective, I did, and you can just drive down this street take a left at the stop sign and you'll find them at Gulfport High School. One is the arithmetic teacher and the second is the physics teacher. But they're not teachers, not really. I know more about arithmetic and physics than either of them."

"Why do you feel that way?" Ben was starting to get a bad feeling about things.

"One, they failed my grandson. In both their classes," Mildred fixed the detective with a determined gaze as if that fact alone would satisfy. Ben waited a moment, and the old lady continued, "I went to the parent-teacher night with my daughter, and I'm no fool. I figured things out pretty quickly."

"That's so?" asked Burnside.

"Do you Detectives ever watch the news with David Brinkley?"

"Sometimes Ma'am," replied Burnside.

"Then you might remember the reporting a few months back about how these horrible people who took over "Eeeran" and got rid of the Shah. These two were front and center, yelling death to America and burning our flag. Now that "Aya-lola" has sent them over here to spy on us and flunk our children."

Ben gave Burnside a quick glance and scribbled something in his notebook. "Thanks for calling us Mrs. McConnell, we'll follow this up."

The second and third tips didn't turn out much better. Alice Hooper, who lived in D'Iberville, told them that the two men were the same ones that had been peeking through her bedroom window hoping to catch a glimpse of her cooter while she prepared for bed. Mrs. Hooper, who Ben figured to be in her early fifties, was a widow who lived alone. She told Burnside that if he wanted to catch them in the act, he should come over himself around 10 p.m. the next night. As they thanked Mrs. Hooper for the call, they were called over by an older man who was out cutting his lawn. "Don't believe a word the old gal tells you. She's a kook but pretty harmless. She's often heard yelling out her bedroom window and calling the police reporting a prowler watching her."

"Okay," Ben said as they got back in the car. "This town's got its share of lonely women."

"I'm going to get the volunteers to screen the tips a little bit better. We're going to waste a lot of time out here Ben."

"Are you going to visit Mrs. Hooper tomorrow night?"

"Fuck off Ben, she's more your age. The next one is a guy who lives in Pass Christian, maybe he might be a bit more normal. We can squeeze one more in before lunch."

Mr. Ezekiel Carson turned out to be just as squirrelly as Mildred and Alice. He told the Detectives that he would need to see the color of their eyes to be sure. "Why's that?" asked Burnside.

"Unless I am mistaken they will both have brilliant blue eyes."

"So you've seen them before?"

"Oh absolutely. I saw them yesterday at the German market downtown. They also hang out at the beer gardens down in the park, mean looking bastards."

"Do you know their names, or where they live?" asked Ben, looking over at Burnside smugly, finally thinking he had a solid lead.

"No they all have normal names. You know, to fit in."

"Not sure I follow you, Mr. Carson?" Ben was puzzled.

"At the end of WW II, a Nazi scientist experimented with cloning. I happen to know that," he whispered conspiratorially. "These clones all look alike and resemble the two in the paper. They were dispatched at a certain age all around the globe to carry out Hitler's final solution. Ridding the world of all the niggers and kikes."

*****

Over chili dogs down by the waterfront Burnside resisted the temptation to say "I told you so."

"We definitely need to get the volunteers to get more detail on the phone to screen out people like Mr. Carson." Burnside started laughing, "There's a movie called the *Boys from Brazil*. I bet he watched that movie, and it seemed real to him."

Ben laughed and shook his head, taking a huge bite of his dog and then washing it down with a gulp of Coke. "Out of a hundred calls all you need is one to pan out. Look," he pointed to the sketch which a cop had already posted on a bus shelter. Someone had drawn a mustache and goatee on one face while the other sketch had a pointy-eared representation of Spock, a popular figure on the TV show *Star Trek*.

"Okay but this has been a wasted morning Ben. We aren't accomplishing anything."

"I wouldn't say that. You have an invitation to check out Mildred's cooter."

"Fuck off."

"I hear you Burnside, but Willis gave us an order. If you think he isn't going to follow up, you don't know him." Burnside rolled his eyes, a look that once again threatened to send Ben on the warpath. "Tell you what, there's four more to run down. Why don't I drop you off at the station to work with the volunteers? I'll run down the last four. If I don't come up with anything, we'll talk to Willis about changing it up somehow."

Chapter 24

Rachel's boss lived in an upscale part of Gulfport near the Golf Course. Gabriel had selected a freshly made Mississippi Mud Pie at the bakery and handed it to Rachel as they parked the VW in front of her boss' home. Rachel seemed to be a little bit more upbeat after freshening up.

"Remember you're supposed to sing my virtues. I'm going to hold you to it."

"I got it. Not to worry. What's your boss' name anyway?"

"Mitford. Hazel Mitford. I think his name's Frank."

They walked up the walkway and Gabriel rang the doorbell. He was feeling a little nervous about the performance he was expected to deliver. He knew nothing about the Mitfords and Rachel was already upset over the way he'd introduced her to Chevon. The doorbell chime rang through the house and then he heard the "Woof, woof, woof," of a dog.

"Sounds big," said Gabriel. He had never had a problem with dogs but considered himself to be an avowed cat person.

Rachel nodded her agreement, "I think I hear someone coming." Sure enough, the door opened, and a middle-aged lady wearing a summer dress under an apron opened the door. Behind a wooden gate, a large bloodhound continued to woof.

"Rachel, I'm so glad you could make it." She gave Rachel a hug and a fake kiss before setting her eyes on Gabriel, "This must be the boyfriend you've told me so much about. Come on in both of you. My goodness, it is so hot out. Gabriel, it is nice to finally meet Rachel's beau."

Gabriel looked over at Rachel's reddening face and did his best to hide his feeling of being a heel. The awkward moment seemed to last minutes, but the silence was broken by Rachel, who handed her boss the pie.

"I hope you like Mississippi Mud Pies," said Gabriel. "Rachel baked it herself. A real good little cook there."

"That's so? I never heard of baking a mud pie Rachel. I can't wait to taste it."

Rachel glowered at Gabriel, shaking her head as her boss put the cake on the side table and escorted them to the living room. "You have a beautiful home, Mrs. Mitford," said Gabriel.

"You can call me Hazel, and thank you, Gabriel but you haven't really seen it yet have you?"

"Well, from what ...." Rachel jumped in and said, "What's your dog's name, Hazel?"

"Oh that's BJ he's harmless. Y'all like dogs? 'Cause if you do, I can leave him out to visit?"

"Oh sure Hazel, we love dogs, hope to have one someday, but we both live in apartments," replied Rachel.

Hazel let BJ lose, and he made a beeline straight to Gabriel, standing up on his hind legs and slobbering all over his face. "Whoa, nice boy, down," Gabriel said, trying to push the massive dog down. BJ was very strong and determined to show his affection.

"My, look at that, BJ he's just about as tall as you Gabriel," Hazel said laughing. "For some reason, he has a real hankering for men. Don't much bother with women."

Gabriel had managed to push BJ down, but now he discovered another problem ...the dog was a very persistent crotch sniffer. Try as he might, Gabriel couldn't seem to rid himself of the big dog. Hazel and Rachel started chatting about the weather totally impervious to what was happening to Gabriel. Gabriel tried to move further into the house, only to have BJ continue to stick his nose where it didn't belong. "Excuse me, Hazel, is there a command to get BJ to leave me alone?"

Rachel and Hazel started to laugh at Gabriel's predicament. Rachel turned to Hazel, "Tell me, why do you call him BJ?" Gabriel was sitting on the couch covering his private parts.

"I'll show you." Hazel walked over to the stereo where she had a bunch of vinyl records stacked in a milk crate. She selected one and put it on the turntable. "Now listen to this, he only does this when we play this song. The next sound they heard was the warbling voice of B. J. Thomas singing *I'm so Lonesome I Could Cry.* All of a sudden BJ started howling along with the music. "Oh my God that's hilarious," Rachel laughed.

They were still listening to BJ's howling when the front door opened, and a mountain of a man walked in. "BJ you showing off again? Not sure if B. J. Thomas would find it funny but the dog don't do that to any other record."

"This is my husband, Frank. This is Rachel Henderson, who works for me at the hospital, and her sweetheart Gabriel Ross."

Frank shook hands with Rachel and then looked down at Gabriel with a smile. "Might short aren't ya?"

"Yes, but perfect height for BJ I think."

"BJ have you been sniffing Mr. Ross's dangly bits? Just means he likes you...I think."

Hazel had everyone sit down in the living room then went and dragged BJ out of the room, while Frank fixed them all a cocktail. Passing out the drinks, Frank asked Gabriel what line of work he was in and was quite interested when he found out that he owned a private investigation business.

Gabriel told them about starting up the business from scratch and then his first big case involving Sheriff Cooper.

"That was you?" asked Frank, clearly impressed. "I read about that in the *Herald*. Didn't you hook up with the Sheriff's wife too? That Chinese girl?"

Gabriel caught Rachel's eye and said, "After the trial, she moved up north to live with her parents."

"That's a shame, I saw a picture of her, she was quite a hottie."

Gabriel nodded and then changed the topic, asking "What kind of business are you in Frank?"

"I own Frank Mitford and Sons Trucking. We own the big rigs you see on the highways. We handle most of the Southern States."

"Interesting, do you do much driving yourself?"

"I do my share. Hazel here has to hold down the fort sometimes when I'm on the road." Hazel, hearing her name came out of the kitchen and sat down beside her husband.

"How did you two meet if you don't mind me asking?" Rachel asked, hoping to continue the focus on the Mitford's.

"It's the second marriage for Hazel. Her first husband ran off with his secretary. Hazel and I met up at a Sadie Hawkins dance."

"That's right, Frank swept me off my feet dancing to B. J. Thomas. How about you two?"

Gabriel saw an opportunity to impress Rachel's boss. "Well, I was on a case, the case of the missing teenage girls, you might have read about it. There was a potential witness who was totally paralyzed and a resident at Gulf Oaks. I went out to see for myself, and I met Rachel. Rachel is so smart and quick-thinking she was able to communicate with the man when no one else could get through. It's like she has a sixth sense. Anyway, it was her charm, humor, and creativity that finally reached the man. He was able to scratch out a clue that in turn allowed me to break open that case."

"Wow! That's quite the accomplishment young lady," said Frank. Hazel, who had already heard the story continued, "We are all very proud of Rachel. She has a special gift."

Gabriel looked over at Rachel, who was beaming. The beam, however, faded quickly when Gabriel noticed that Rachel had a booger bubble coming out of her left nostril.

"Ah, Rachel?" Gabriel said gesturing nonchalantly at his nose. Rachel looked down and tried a reverse sniffle but to her horror saw the bubble just grow larger.

"Wow that's sure is one big snot bubble," said Frank.

Rachel was horrified and ran out of the room in search of the bathroom. While she was gone, Hazel went to check on dinner, and Frank freshened up everyone's drinks. After five minutes had gone by, Gabriel went to the washroom door. "Rachel are you ok?"

"It just wasn't going away. Why didn't you give me a handkerchief?"

"I'm sorry I didn't think of it, and I don't carry one anyway."

"What kind of a man doesn't carry a handkerchief?" Gabriel heard her say quietly through the door. "I'm so embarrassed."

"Rachel listen to me. You will be even more embarrassed if you stay in there much longer The Mitford's are going to start wondering."

He had no sooner said this when all of a sudden he heard screaming coming from the kitchen. Gabriel abandoned Rachel and joined Frank in running to the kitchen. They found Hazel lying on her backside on the floor, her summer dress all covered in brown poo looking stuff. More shit was on her face and hands.

"Eeww," Frank and Gabriel said in unison, their faces contorted in disgust. To make matters just a little bit worse, BJ sauntered into the kitchen and started licking things up.

Gabriel thought he was going to gag, "Oh my God."

"It's the pie, it's the pie," screamed Hazel. "BJ got loose. When my back was turned. He climbed up on the table, got the pie," she gasped, trying to catch her breath. "I turned around and screamed at him. But when I reached for him, I slipped and fell in all this pie filling."

Gabriel noticed that Rachel had finally joined them in the kitchen. Taking a look at Hazel, she said "Eeww."

"It's the pie!" Frank and Gabriel said quickly in unison.

"Your freshly baked Mississippi Mud Pie!" cried Hazel, starting to laugh hysterically.

Everyone pitched in to help clean up the mess. This was not going to be an evening easily forgotten. After it had been cleaned up, Hazel told them to take their seats in the dining room. "We'd better eat this pot roast before something else happens."

The meal was exquisite. The pot roast was perfect, and the sweet potato pie and cornbread were wonderful. Gabriel held his glass up, "I'd like to make a toast to BJ, Mississippi Mud Pies and snot bubbles." Everyone laughed again.

After a few minutes, Hazel asked, "Have you read the stories in the paper about that poor man that died in the woods?"

"Yes, I read about it the other day. Terrible," replied Gabriel.

"Well, I don't know if you've seen today's paper but the Coroner's saying that it was all just an accident."

"What?" said Gabriel, not having seen the paper all day.

"They had the press conference, and the County Coroner said that the old man got disoriented and bumped into a tree."

"That sounds a little out there...." Gabriel shook his head. He wondered how his partner Ben was taking the news.

"Anyway, I hope this quells all of the niggers protesting downtown."

"Don't use that word in front of company," said Frank.

"Why? It's a perfectly acceptable word. I heard Richard Pryor on TV last week using it. Nigger, there I said it again. Would you rather I said, spook or jigaboos?"

Frank shook his head. He then turned to face Gabriel, "I was speaking with a Biloxi police detective today. Little Frankie, that's my stepson who's over at his cousin's place, was caught red-handed by the police spray painting that nigger hate stuff all around town. Little creep is going to end up in juvie if you ask me. I had to go down to the station to rescue his ass."

Hazel's expression made it clear that her husband hadn't shared that news previously. "I didn't know that. Were you going to tell me?"

"Well, I wasn't even going to bring it up in front of our company until you started with all this nigger stuff. Where do you think he gets it from?"

"I'm not prejudiced. I'm not. But you tell me, one old man bumps into a tree and suffers a heart attack, does that justify all the spooks vandalizing and looting businesses downtown?"

Thankfully Rachel and Gabriel had finished the meal, and since dessert was taken care of by BJ, they decided to leave the Mitford's to work this out for themselves. The older couple were still going at it as Rachel and Gabriel walked out the door.

Chapter 25

Ben dropped Burnside at the stationhouse and headed towards downtown Biloxi where the next two tipsters were located. Once again nothing much came from these interviews, and he was starting to wonder whether Burnside had been right. By mid-afternoon it had gotten uncomfortably hot, and Ben stopped at a variety store for a Coke. As he sat on a bench beside his cruiser, he thought about his young partner and the upcoming review he'd need to complete on him. Ben tried to think back to his own early days as a detective and whether he had been the same kind of pain in the ass as Burnside. Ben had had over a dozen partners; some had gone on to have excellent careers while others had ended up flaming out under the pressure of the job and the impact it had on their personal lives. He even knew one who, after Ben had left Providence, ended up on the wrong end of a gun after making the fatal mistake of not having a partner who had his back.

He wished that he could have someone like Gabriel as a partner. Here was a man who would never embarrass him. Ben wondered how Gabriel was making out with his hush-hush blackmail case and made a mental note to call him.

The next name on the list was a man named Zachary Harper. Getting back in the cruiser, Ben drove to Harper's address which turned out to be a business. He pulled into the parking lot next to a motorcycle shop called *Wheels in Motion.*

When Ben opened the front door to the shop, a little bell rang throughout the store. Other than a man reading a magazine at the cash the place was deserted. Ben nodded to him and checked out the Yamahas and Hondas that were on display. Lots of chrome and bright colors.

"In the market for a bike?" asked a man as he approached Ben. The guy was as skinny as a rake and had a straggly, ZZ Top-like beard. He was wearing jeans along with a leather vest over a Wheels in Motion T-Shirt.

Ben flashed his shield at the man. "Looking for Zachary, that you?"

"Nope, Zach's in the back working on a bike. What did he do?"

"Nothing." Ben shook his head. "Just wanted to ask him a few questions."

"Like what?" Asked the man. "Sorry, I'm not nosy. I'm the boss here, and Zachary's my employee."

"I got it. It's personal, but if you want, I can come back when he goes on break."

"Nah, it's fine, go on back there through those curtains. But if he's in trouble, I want to know about it. He's my sister's kid."

Ben nodded and followed directions to the back of the store and a hallway that led to a garage where he found a teenager bent over a Kawasaki. "I'm looking for Zachary Harper," announced Ben, getting the kid's attention.

"You here about the phone call?" said the teen, who Ben figured was barely old enough to shave.

Ben nodded and flashed his badge once again. He looked at the parts spread out over the shop floor. "This a summer job for you?"

"Sort of. My mother got me the job. I work out back here fixing bikes except when the owner Terry goes for lunch, then I watch the store."

The kid had long blonde hair and gray eyes. Ben revised his estimate of his age. "How old are you Zach?"

"I'll be 18 next month. I hope to be able to afford my first bike then."

"That right? Listen, about your phone call...."

"Would it be alright if we sat outside? There's a picnic table out back."

"Sure whatever you say, Zach," replied Ben looking back at the storeroom. He followed the kid to an old picnic table set up under a Magnolia tree. The tree was no longer blooming, but it still provided some shade from the afternoon sun. "So about that call Zach?"

"Well, I don't want my name to be linked to any of this. I don't think my uncle, the guy inside, would approve. But I think I saw those two guys a couple of weeks ago."

"Sure Zach, we don't have to tell anybody anything. So where did you see them?"

"In the store, I was covering for Terry. These two guys rode up on Harleys. I think they had FXS low-riders. The store was empty, so when they came in, I was all over them. If I make a sale, then Terry said he'd give me a bonus. Anyway, I thought they were brothers, and so I told them about our family discount. I'm pretty sure that they're the guys in the paper. The one with the nose," He made a gesture twisting his nose with a finger making it look broken, "did all the talking. He said he was looking for a rebel. That's a special edition Harley Davidson. They call it the Confederate Edition on account it has gray paint and the rebel flag on the gas tank and a bunch of other stuff. Well, we don't sell

Harleys at all on account of the owner wanting to focus on regular folk."

"So what happened?"

"I just told him we didn't sell them. They didn't look the types that would go for a Kawasaki, so I suggested they try *Thunder Twins* in Gulfport. I think they already knew about it. Then they left. I didn't give it a second thought until I saw their pictures in the paper."

"Why do you think they already knew about *Thunder Twins?*"

"The one with the broken nose just kind of waved me off."

"Did you get the impression the guy was from around here?"

"I don't know. They had an accent, but it was different. Oh, and broken nose said something to the other guy. It was in some other language."

"Any idea?"

"There's a kid at school his name is Luka and his family is Croatian. I went to a party at his place once, and his dad was yelling at him in Croatian. It might have been that."

"Okay, this is good Zachary. You think they could be Croatian, and you think they were familiar with *Thunder Twins* in Gulfport?" Zach nodded and asked if there was a reward. "No, there's no reward as of now, the family didn't have much, but if they decide to have one, and this information leads to anything I will let you know." An idea came to Ben, and he scribbled a note to himself in his notebook. "Did you only ever see them the one time?"

"Just the one time. I kind of remembered them on account of the jacket."

"Jacket? Were they wearing jackets?"

"Only the guy with the nose. I noticed it when he left, it had a big A with an eagle stitched into the back."

"An A? With an Eagle?"

"Yeah, it was kind of cool."

Chapter 26

Gabriel couldn't believe just how messed up the dinner party had been the night before. Things couldn't have turned out worse if he tried. When he and Rachel left, she once again resisted any attempt at conversation on the road home. As they arrived at her apartment, she said, "I'm not feeling well, and I have a terrible headache." Not waiting for an answer she got out and slammed the passenger door.

As Gabriel had driven off to his apartment, he'd known Rachel was upset because of that Judas moment when he'd introduced her as a colleague and not as his true love. *Was that because Chevon was talking to Jacqueline and he didn't want Jacqueline to think he'd moved on?*

Rachel, on the other hand, must have told Hazel that he was more than that. The rest of the evening had been what Gabriel liked to call a clusterfuck. The booger bubble, the dog, the pie was bad enough, but for Rachel to witness her boss showing a dark side and getting into an argument with her husband would just make things awkward for their work relationship.

The only good news Gabriel could think of this morning was that on the drive to work he heard the local radio weatherman announce that the current heat wave would end on Saturday after a run of thunderstorms passed through the Gulf Coast.

Once he got to the office, Gabriel put on a pot of coffee and opened the window, expecting Bourbon to come sauntering in looking for his tuna breakfast. It was still too early to call anyone, so he read the story in the *Herald* about a press conference held by the Mayor. While the black community's reaction to Willy Parnell's death and the graffiti that was showing up around town was understandable, Gabriel agreed that the violence and looting were not helpful. As for the Coroner's report, he wasn't surprised. He wondered what would have been different had a white man been beaten in the park and died.

Gabriel wanted to call Curtis' ex-girlfriend Jessie but figured it might be a little early to call. He grabbed the Mississippi Queen passenger list and spread it out on his desk. Selecting a fresh notepad, he set about analyzing the list. After thirty minutes he had written down the following,

Total # of cabins=199

Total number of names on the list =301

Crew (from Curtis) approximately = 150 (mostly women)

Number of party girls brought on board =?

Number of passengers sharing a cabin=102

Number of passengers not sharing = 97

Number of male passengers not sharing= 88

Estimate of females not sharing =9

Gabriel still thought that the likelihood was that Rogers' bedmate was one of the pros that had been brought on board, or a member of the crew. It was likely that Rogers would know all of the women who were delegates or GOP staffers. To kill time, Gabriel wrote the contact information for the 9 women not sharing a cabin. He knew Ashley Loewen wasn't a candidate, so he stroked his name off the list. Similarly, he thought Stacey, Courtney and maybe even Robin could very well be unisex names.

1. Stacey Manderville
2. Courtney Vickerson
3. Leila Cartwright
4. ~~Ashley Loewen~~
5. Gwynneth Coors
6. Sue-Ellen Mitchell
7. Daisy Hagan
8. Robin Michaelson
9. Gladys Harding

Next Gabriel grabbed the business directory and searched for the names. The only ones he was able to find were Daisy Hagan, who lived in Pass Christian and Leila Cartwright, who lived in Biloxi. The others he figured were either unlisted, listed under another name or were not residents of the area. Over coffee, he considered how he should approach the calls. He dialed the number for Daisy, imagining in his mind an old spinster.

"Hello," a woman's voice answered.

"I'm looking for Daisy Hagan."

"You're speaking to her." Gabriel was surprised, as the voice sounded younger than expected.

"Is this the Daisy Hagan who participated in the GOP cruise in May on the Mississippi Queen?"

"Yes, what's this about?" Suspicion now creeping into the woman's voice.

Gabriel had not considered whether he should use his real name. "Not to be alarmed, my name is Peter Ennis, and I'm calling from the head office of the Mississippi Queen. We are calling to determine whether our passengers enjoyed the cruise. "

"Oh...yes, it was very nice."

"Do you work for the Republican Party?"

"Not directly. I run the local constituency office."

"What did you think of the food on the cruise?"

"First class all the way. I've always liked Cajun cuisine. Are you calling all the passengers, Mr....what did you say your name was?"

"Peter Ennis. I notice that your accommodations were on the cabin deck. Were you in a room by yourself?"

"Yes. By myself. The cabin was very nice if that was going to be your next question."

Gabriel wondered how to ascertain the lady's hair color. "Mrs. Hargan, just one more thing."

"It's Miss Hagan. What is that?"

"Miss Hagan there was some jewelry found after the cruise. We think it probably belonged to one of the passengers. One of the waiters seems to remember a dark-haired woman in the Grand Saloon wearing it. I don't suppose you have dark hair?"

"I'm not missing any jewelry."

"Ok, but do you have dark hair?"

"Why in heavens name do you need to know my hair color?"

The lady sounded very suspicious now. Gabriel blurted out, "My boss just gave me these questions to ask. Thank you for answering my questions Miss Hagan."

Before Gabriel could hang up the lady said "Redhead."

Gabriel was happy to get off the phone. Being a serial liar was a necessary part of the job, a part he didn't particularly enjoy.

He crossed Daisy Hagan off the list and wondered what kind of parents would saddle their kid with that name.

Before he had a chance to make a second call, Bourbon came through the window meowing about wearing a fur coat during a heatwave, and why wouldn't Gabriel have sprung for an air conditioner? "Well, I would buy one of those windows units Bourbon, but how would you get in here?" Bourbon's response was to lie down on Gabriel's passenger list.

Gabriel picked up the phone again and dialed the number he had written down for Leila Cartwright. The lady was clearly middle-aged and said that she had been an aide for Senator Thad Cochran for over twenty years. He didn't even bother asking her about the color of her hair. Crossing her name off the list, he decided to call Jessie who had a New Orleans number. Looking at his Cassio, he figured surely she would be up by 10 a.m.

"What IS it?" answered a sleepy voice after a half dozen rings.

"I'm looking for Jessie, the girl who used to work on the Mississippi Queen."

"What?"

Gabriel began to realize the girl wasn't fully awake and repeated himself. Rather than answering the question, "Whatever you're calling about I didn't do it."

"Curtis gave me your number," Gabriel said quickly, fearing she was about to hang up and go back to bed.

"Curtis? Why...did he do that?"

"My name is Peter, Peter Ennis and I'm calling from the head office of the cruise line."

There was a pause on the line before she said, "Wait your name is ...what Penis?"

"That's very funny Miss. I've gotten that all my life."

"Well, what are you calling about Mr. P-Ennis?" she started to giggle.

Gabriel wished he had worked out a better script. "We're following up on a complaint from one of the passengers."

"I told you Penis. Whatever they said I did is pure bullshit."

"Jessie, do you mind me asking why you quit right after the cruise?"

"You can ask if you want Penis." After a moment of silence, "I was tired of being paid crap and then having to let old rich guys put their hands all over me just so I could get a decent tip. So what was the complaint?"

"Something about spilling drinks all over Congressman Rogers and then calling him a name."

"WHAT A FUCKER! LISTEN PENIS. THAT OLD COOT WAS DRUNK, AND HE SPILLED HIS DRINK, AND THEN WHEN HE TRIED TO PICK UP HIS GLASS, HE KNOCKED OVER A WINE BOTTLE. IT WENT ALL OVER EVERYTHING. I TRIED TO HELP HIM CLEAN UP. WHAT A FUCKER! HE COMPLAINED ABOUT ME? I WON'T BE

VOTING FOR THAT OLD TURD. THAT GUY CALLED ME A WHORE? WELL FUCK HIM!!!"

"Was he one of these rich old white guys that you ....you know, flirted with?"

"Did I smile at him? Did I laugh at all his jokes? Yeah. But as far as playing touchy feely with him I didn't get the right vibe from him."

*****

After dinner, Gabriel called Gulf Oaks Hospital wanting to apologize to Rachel again for last night's fiasco. He was told that Rachel had called in sick that morning. Gabriel then tried her at the apartment, but the call went straight to her answering machine. He was contemplating ordering flowers to be delivered with another sucky message when the phone rang.

The caller interrupted the standard *Eye on You* greeting. "It's Ashley Loewen, I'm calling for a progress report."

"Progress report?"

"Yeah, what precisely have you been doing about the case?"

"You mean since Tuesday afternoon?"

There was a pause on the line, "You've had the case for almost 3 days."

"I guess that's true. It's not my only case you realize Ashton."

"It's Ashley, our case takes precedence over everything else. You're to drop everything and work this case. Now, what have you accomplished?"

"Well, I had a lovely dinner yesterday with a young lady and then last night....oh last night was something else. Now that I have you on the phone, you probably could have expected results by now if you weren't feeding me a line of bullshit."

"What do you mean bullshit?"

"That brown stuff that comes out of a bull's ass."

"The Congressman and I have been as honest and straightforward as we can be on this matter."

"You didn't tell me about the girls Ashlynn."

"What girls?"

"The hookers that were invited aboard to do the... you know, boinkee-boinkee with the horny male passengers. Since I am being charged with finding the little tart that's blackmailing Rogers, wouldn't that have that been a nice detail to have?"

"I don't know anything about hookers. I told you I got off the boat early."

"That's just more brown stuff Ash. Your crap is so thick it's coming through the phone line." Gabriel proceeded to bang the phone on his desk. Picking up the receiver again, "Listen, Ash, I'll let you know when I have something solid, which won't be for a while. I have to go and meet a bunch of hookers."

When Ashley didn't respond, Gabriel continued. "Maybe you guys aren't playing me, and really don't know who this dame is. I doubt it, though. I just can't figure out your angle. But here's a tip Loewen, you call me again, and you'll be solving this on your own."

Gabriel hung up and picked up the receiver, dialing Ben's number. He was still muttering about lying politicians when a Detective Burnside answered. When Gabriel asked for Ben, he was told that he was currently out of the office.

Gabriel asked Burnside to get a message to Ben to call him when he got a moment. Standing up, he stretched his legs to try to relieve his frustrations. He began pacing back and forth in front of his desk, wondering what his next step might be. He could interview every female employee on board, he could somehow find the pimp that arranged for the girls, get their names and call them up. Or he could just bang his head against the wall calling all the old ladies on the passenger list. Bourbon was sitting on his desk, his feline eyes following Gabriel as he paced back and forth.

Chapter 27

It was almost 5 p.m. when Ben finally left Zach at Wheels in Motion. It was likely too late to do much else. There was still another name on the tip list, but Ben decided that following up on the information provided by Zach was a better use of his time. He called Burnside at the station and was told that he was gone for the day. Resolution of this case was supposed to be a priority, and his partner had bailed on him just about every day that week. Not wanting to stew on that, he called a detective he knew in the Gang Squad.

Mike McShays was also unavailable, but Ben knew Mike well enough to call him at home. When the call went through Mike answered right away. "Hey Ben, how are you keeping?"

Ben heard the sound of people laughing in the background. "Did I catch you in the middle of something Mike?"

"Naw...just relaxing by the pool watching the kids playing. You'd think if a parent were going to let their 9-year-old come over for a swim, they would make sure the little fucker could swim. I had to jump in and rescue this kid who swore to me that he was the world's greatest swimmer. Yeah well, Mark Spitz he's not, I got my new shorts all wet."

They chitchatted about a few things before Ben got to the point of the call. "It's about a case I'm working on."

"Oh...heard you caught the Willy Parnell case. Getting anywhere?"

"Yeah, I have a couple of leads I'm chasing. I think you can *probably shed some light on a couple of things.*"

"Why don't you come by and play lifeguard with me. The beer's cold and I am going to barbecue some tube steaks for the little bastards."

Ben agreed to head over right away. He remembered Mike as a good cop, who'd spent a lot of time undercover and was caught in the middle of a bank heist when bullets started to fly. Mike had taken a bullet in his leg and was now in charge of directing the department's activities involving gangs. The gangs were starting to become a menace with The Bandidos and the Hells Angels having local Mississippi chapters.

Ben got to Mike's and found his way through a walkway to a gated area where he heard kids yelling and splashing. He saw Mike lecturing a kid about running around the pool. When Mike spotted Ben, he pointed to a cooler. Ben reached in and popped the caps off a couple of cold Budweiser's. Taking off his jacket and loosening his tie, he grabbed a lawn chair under a patio umbrella.

Mike joined him a couple of minutes later, shaking his head when the kid resumed his racing around the pool.

"So I heard a rumor the other day," said Mike once he was seated.

"What's that?" asked Ben.

"I hear you're playing nursemaid to some politician's nephew."

"I guess that's true, not sure who the politician is. The guy's name is Burnside, and well I kind of have mixed feelings about whether he'll make it. Willis is warning me that if I give the kid a bad report card than all kinds of shit will hit the fan."

"I hear Congressman Rogers is his uncle."

"That so?" That was the same guy involved in Gabriel's blackmail case. "Well I'm not big on politics, I've got some time before I have to complete a fitness report on him. If I can't trust him, then I'm going to blow him away, and I don't give a rat's ass what any politician has to say."

"That's my Ben...nice performance at the press conference by the way. I thought the Mayor was going to blow a valve when people started cheering you on. Catch any shit for that?"

"Probably would have, but I think Willis has my back. But if these leads I'm working on don't pan out, then I may be back directing traffic."

Mike and Ben clinked beer bottles and toasted, "Here's to traffic cops."

"So these leads you're referring to...you talking about the mugs on the front page of the *Herald*?"

"Yeah, recognize them?"

"No. I assume you think they're gang bangers?"

"Someone told me they were in a local shop looking to buy a Confederate Edition Harley."

"Hmm, not exactly the kind of bike for the average citizen. There was a time before I pulled the desk job, I knew all of the Outlaws, and Bandidos plus what kind of hog they rode. It's been almost five years riding a desk instead of a bike."

"Miss it?"

"Sure do. 99% of the people in these clubs are fine. Accountants, business owners....but the other 1% are definitely trouble. They call themselves 1%'ers."

"I heard there might be a connection with a place in Gulfport called Thunder Twins."

Mike nodded his head. "The guy that owns that place used to be a 1%' er with the Angels. I think his name is Horvat, but everyone knows him by Spider. He'll probably have to order the confederate model. The company didn't make that many."

"Apparently one of the guys was wearing a black leather jacket with a patch on the back with an A and an Eagle. Ideas?"

"Just a minute." Mike got up and went into the house and came back with a binder. Ben noticed that his friend walked with a noticeable limp. "Take a look in here. You might find what you're looking for." The binder had page after page of gang patches. There was a number which featured Eagles, but there was only one that had an eagle superimposed over a huge letter A. Ben tapped that one and handed the book back to Mike.

"Sons of Silence," he said nodding his head. "They call themselves a motorcycle club. They are definitely all 1% ers. If memory serves me correct, they were founded out west. Colorado? Now they're springing up in a lot of states including here in Mississippi."

"The logo kind of looks like the logo of this bottle of Budweiser."

"That's probably how they came up with it. These guys are not rocket scientists."

"What can you tell me about them?"

"Stay away from them. They're probably the most ruthless and violent of the gangs out here. They recently had a change at the top with a guy by the name of Richardson stepping down, and now it's a real bad-ass named J. R. Reid. They have a loose connection with the Hells Angels. So they're probably not too pleasant if you happen to be a member of the Outlaws. I'm not surprised they're down in Biloxi, I guess it was inevitable. They're involved in illegal gambling. That, of course, is in addition to other rackets like blackmail, fraud, gun running, money laundering and murder for hire."

"What's this saying at the bottom of their emblem?" Ben finished his beer.

"The words *donec mors non separat* is Latin for *Until Death Separates Us*. The context is that once a member always a member."

"These two guys apparently spoke another language, maybe Croatian. Does that fit?"

"It could. There are a lot of them down here. The Sons might be looking to become more of a force down here. I can ask my team to see if anyone knows more. But if your guy is wearing that patch, then he is a member of the most vicious motorcycle gang in America."

Chapter 28

Gabriel dialed the number for Travis Franklin up in Hattiesburg. He was disappointed when once again he got the family's voicemail. At the beep, he blurted out, "Hey Travis, it's Gabriel. I'm just checking in. I was thinking about you the other day. I happened to be driving through the old neighborhood and noticed that the For Sale sign was still up. I hope you guys are being inundated with offers. Anyway, I miss you, buddy, give me a call."

He had no sooner hung up the phone when he heard a knock on the office door. When Gabriel opened the door, he saw Arnie's smiling face.

"Is it too late in the day for my afternoon coffee?"

"H, Arnie, what brings you to my humble office?" Gabriel ushered his friend in.

The black man's eyes took in the small office, "I knocked on your door yesterday. When you didn't answer, I figured you were up to your ass in alligators. And left early."

"I had to leave early, long drive to New Orleans."

"On a case I presume."

"Yes, one I can't discuss I'm afraid. As much as I could use the extra brain power."

"So make me an employee and swear me to secrecy."

Gabriel knew he shouldn't, but he was at a loss about what to do next. "But what I'm going to tell you is strictly confidential Arnie."

"I promise on my Mamie's grave never to breathe a word."

Gabriel told him about the blackmail, Congressman Rogers, and Ashley, as well as his lack of progress so far in trying to figure out the identity of the blackmailer.

"Hum...interesting. I think trying to find the right pimp and then getting them to tell you anything is asking for a whole heap of trouble. They'd be just as likely to skin you alive."

"I know, but what else can I do?"

"I would probably go back to the crew. They might not be involved, but chances are they know something. I'd talk to the cabin maid. They have the awful job of cleaning up the next morning. With the client being a dignitary of sorts the gal will likely remember something."

"That's great," said Gabriel, "maybe I should hire you."

"Well, I am getting kind of bored being a superintendent." Arnie paused for a moment and then continued, "I could source my own cases too. Seems to me half the people I know claim their spouse is cheating on them...Now that I think about it, the other half are the cheaters."

For the next hour, the two talked about detective work, and they agreed to think about trying it out part time. When Arnie left, Gabriel called the head office for the Mississippi Queen and found out that the steamship was still in New Orleans until Sunday.

Chapter 29

After the call, Gabriel decided to pack it in for the day. When he got back to his apartment, he decided to go for a run on the beach and changed into a pair of gym shorts and a t-shirt. One of the biggest advantages of living at the Trade Winds was that it was right on the beach. Before going out the door, he decided to give Rachel one more call. This time, she answered right away. Her voice showed signs that she was feeling better. Rachel asked about the riverboat case, and he told her that he was going to go back to try to interview a cabin maid. "If you want to come along, I can use the company."

"I'm sorry Gabriel, but I need to get back to work otherwise she might hire a private detective to come and check up on me."

"It's great that you're feeling better Rachel." He was going to ask her out, but there was something in her tone that was different. She didn't make him wait long.

"I've had a lot of time to think about things, and I've made some decisions about my life. Now that I've made them, it's like a huge weight has been lifted."

"Tell me about them."

"One, I am not going to pursue opportunities at the hospital. The patients are great, but it's not for me. I'll stay there until I can find something else that I want to do."

"Is this because Hazel is a bit of a bigot?"

"Not at all, she just speaks her mind, there are all kinds of others that are thinking the same thing, but just don't say it. At least she's honest."

"So you think most people down here are ....racists?"

"No, and I would be careful with that label. People from her generation just think the way their parents thought. The way they were brought up. Back then, things were separate, and the colored people had their place. I'm not saying I agree with the way she thinks, but I guess I understand that they like the way it used to be."

Gabriel didn't want to get into an argument with her, so he quickly changed subjects, "What else have you decided?"

"I've decided that I like what you do, being a private detective. Working cases, helping people, catching bad guys."

"It can get kind of boring, and the money is only as good as your next retainer. But hey, I don't want to discourage you. I just hired an associate. Otherwise, I would offer you a job. You're a natural."

"Well keep me in mind, I have also decided that taking law classes is too boring. So I'll finish the semester but come the fall I'll be taking something more interesting."

"Sounds like you have really thought things through. Anything else?"

There was a pause on the line, and Gabriel's mind flashed back to when his wife had dumped him. "Gabriel you would be a fantastic guy to work for, and you will always be my friend. But this romance thing just isn't going to happen."

"You want someone taller?"

"No silly, I guess I don't feel that we're right for each other. I know there's an attraction, and a few weeks ago I would have gladly jumped into bed with you. But to be honest, it would have been for the wrong reasons. I thought it would help you get past Jacqueline. But now I think you need to do just the opposite."

"What do you mean?"

"Seeing you talk to Chevon last week made me think that you don't need a girlfriend, you need to get Jacqueline back. At least satisfy yourself that the door is really closed."

"So we can still be friends right?"

"Of course Gabriel, just don't say any more sucky, flirty things to me."

Chapter 30

Ben didn't work every Saturday, just those that followed a Friday. His apartment was a mess, his laundry was piling up, and his fridge was empty, but he couldn't summon the will to do anything about it. Some of his pants had felt a little tight lately with the waistband starting to curl under his belly. He knew he should get some exercise. Maybe go for a walk. One look out the window at the impending storm squashed that thought.

He was surprised he hadn't heard from Gabriel all week and wondered how his protégé was progressing with Congressman Rogers. It was an interesting turn of events that Burnside was the Congressman's nephew. Mike had said the Sons of Silence were involved in blackmail and wondered if there might be a connection to Gabriel's case. Dialing Gabriel's number at the Trade Winds Apartment, he was disappointed that the call went straight to voicemail.

Ben poured himself a cup of coffee and looked out the apartment window at the graying clouds. The wind was really kicking up. He could see the trees bending as if in silent prayer to the angry wind. Not a very nice day for a funeral. Now that the Coroner was finished with his findings, Willy's body had been released to his daughter. Ben wanted to attend the funeral just in case the suspects showed up. He thought of the sketch of the two men in the paper; he had a stack of the sketches on the counter. He tried to imagine them wearing gang leathers and riding Confederate Edition Harleys. An idea started to form, and he threw on a pair of jeans and a t-shirt and headed out.

He got to Thunder Twins for 10. a.m. and sat in his car watching people come and go into the store. The store was a renovated warehouse with a bunch of motorcycles parked in the front parking lot. The first few splashes of rain hitting his windshield gave him the impetus to get out of the car and go into the store. It was much bigger than *Wheels in Motion,* and their inventory of chrome was primarily Harley Davidsons. There were plenty of customers in the store, a few wearing leather jackets with different patches. Ben waited patiently at the counter for a large tattooed man wearing a leather vest and sporting a black ponytail to finish chatting with a customer. Ben noticed the Confederate flag prominently displayed behind the counter.

The man eyed Ben suspiciously as he sold a pair of leather chaps to a guy. When the customer left, the large man looked at Ben sourly and said, "Cop?"

Ben nodded and flashed his badge. He'd been hoping to ask his questions under cover. The large man took a quick look at Ben's identification before lighting up a cigarette and exhaling a cloud of smoke at Ben. "So?'

Ben decided to put the flyer with the sketch of the two suspects on the counter. "You the owner?"

"Yeah, folks call me Spider." He blew a second cloud of nicotine Ben's way and gave him a "So what?" look.

"I was hoping you would agree to have this sketch on your counter. It's the two men wanted for questioning in the death of the old man last weekend."

"Haven't seen 'em," said Spider without looking at the picture.

"Maybe if you actually looked at the picture."

Ben noticed that Spider had a Hells Angels Tattoo on his meaty forearm. The man looked down at the picture for a half second and shook his head again.

"Are you willing to keep this flyer up by the cash? We're trying hard to find these two."

"Naw...I don't like a bunch of crap around here. Fuckin bake sales will be next."

Ben nodded his head and fought to restrain himself from slamming the guy's head into the cash register. Spider seemed to sense the impending violence and reached down behind the cash and put a Louisville slugger on the counter. "What makes you think anyone here would recognize them?" Spider asked, crumpling up the flyer.

"We got a tip that they might ride with the Sons of Silence," said Ben. Turning and gesturing to the bikes, "Looks like you cater to that type of customer."

"Nah you got the wrong store. We see any of those punks in here we put the run to them."

"Really?" Ben said, looking around the store and counting at least a half dozen who could fit the mold. Then deciding on a different strategy, "So you were an Angel....a 1% er?"

"Don't know anything about that. I just run a respectable bike business. After work, I run a prayer group. I'll say a prayer for your soul, brother."

"The tattoo on your arm might give you away."

"That's just ink. Nothing illegal about a little artwork."

That was the second time in a week Ben had heard that comment. "I'll get out of here but don't be surprised if the Gang Squad comes in here looking for your records."

"Oh, I'm scared," said the big man doing a mock shiver.

Ben was pelted by rain as he ran back to his car. He pulled the car out of the parking lot and parked across the street with a clear view of the store. He hadn't expected cooperation, but he wanted to rattle Spider. If the big guy looked out the window and saw him so much the better. He would be willing to wager Spider knew who these two thugs were.

Ben watched the store for the next hour. The rain most likely discouraged riders from stopping by. He made a decision to continue the surveillance once the weather cleared. Putting the car in gear, he headed home to change for Willy's funeral.

Chapter 31

Since arriving in Biloxi, Branko and Juraj had concentrated on keeping a low profile except with the people who could help them get connected. Reid had sent them to the Gulf Coast to establish a chapter and to scout out business potential. When the only restriction on your business activities was to money, that opened many doors. So far Juraj had found a girl they could run, while Branko had made good drug connections. They had gotten the word out that they were open for business. The nigger thing had been a referral that netted over 5 large. Earlier last month they had scored big time on a job worth twice that amount. The brothers were ambitious, and Reid and the others were pleased. There was an old Croatian saying, *Velike ribe male proždiru* or loosely translated, *Men are like fish; the great ones devour the small.*

Branko was tinkering with his bike when he got a call. It was the man again.

"Hey, I want you to know I have a line on that Confederate Edition for you. It might take a few weeks."

"Yeah...good."

"Listen, there was a cop in here. A big guy, he was flashing that sketch of you and Juraj. He knows about the Sons."

"How?

"I don't know, but I think he was just fishing."

"What you say?"

"I told him to fuck off and get out of my store. I also noticed him parked on the street watching people come and go into the shop. Kind of bad for business."

"Okay, we take care of this man. His name?"

"Detective O'Shea. There's a picture of him in Wednesday's paper. He's the guy heading up the investigation into the nigger's death."

Chapter 32

Gabriel looked out the VW's window as he drove down Beach Blvd to the grocery store on Saturday morning. The sky was tar-black, and the large clouds were unsettled, moving quickly. He heard a tapping on the window and then it became a pitter-patter. He watched as people ran for cover outside. People walking along the boardwalk were opening umbrellas as the clouds spat out their beads of water. Puddles began plinking as the rainfall became heavier. The roofs of the cars danced with spray, and he could hear the pelting of the rain through the window.

His ego had been a little bruised after the call with Rachel. If he was going, to be honest with himself, he felt conflicted. Gabriel thought about Detroit and whether he should fess up and tell his parents that Jacqueline was no longer with him. His father still hadn't forgiven him for what happened at Ford and for the breakup of his marriage. He knew he had to close that loop, just like he had unfinished business with Jacqueline.

Last night after his run on the beach, he'd gone down to the basement to do laundry. When he'd gotten back to his apartment, he'd found the phone ringing. Racing to pick it up, he'd been pleased to hear a familiar voice.

"Is this the infamous trespasser?" said a youthful voice.

"Hi Travis, I'm sorry ...my liege. I did indeed hail your name."

"What does thou want, my faithful subject?"

"I was riding my noble beetle past your former castle and noticed that the sign indicating its offering for sale was still up."

Travis started to laugh. "Okay, Gabriel knock it off. Mom's real estate agent said that with interest rates on the rise it's a buyers' market. I guess people in Gulfport are reluctant to buy a home where someone was murdered. Mom still wants to sell it, but she said we can't afford to lose money."

"Hey, maybe you guys should move back."

"I've asked her before because I kind of miss stuff, but she's scared that somehow the Mob would come back for us." There a pause on the line before Travis asked, "How's Bourbon?"

"He's complaining a lot lately. I think the heat is getting to him."

"You would be too if you had to climb eight flights on the fire escape wearing a fur coat, only to find that you're not there. Have you got any exciting cases?"

Gabriel sketched out the broad details of the blackmail case. Of course, his young protégé had tons of questions, most of which Gabriel couldn't answer. With a familiar touch of bravado, Travis declared that were he able to come down and join him, cases would be solved in no time. There was a pause on the line before the inevitable, "How's Jacqueline?"

Gabriel felt a lie bubble up in his throat before he finally decided to tell Travis the truth. Travis listened to Gabriel explain why she'd left and how he was feeling. In his youthful simplicity, Travis said, "So, you're telling me your true love is in Chicago, and you're down there wondering why she hasn't returned your call? Has it occurred to you, that the reason she hasn't returned your call is that she wants to know whether you love her enough to go get her? Have you ever seen *Gone with the Wind?* You're like this really short version of Rhett Butler, and she's a Chinese Scarlett O'Hara."

As Gabriel pulled the VW in the parking lot of the local Piggly Wiggly, he wondered why complicated things always seemed to be so simple to young people.

Chapter 33

The downpour had not let up by the time Willy's funeral started. A sea of umbrellas gathered in a procession from the parking lot to the First Baptist Church like a sea of black mushrooms. Ben had parked a couple of blocks away from the church and joined the throng of attendees heading into the Church. His umbrella with its distinctive yellow with black stripes drew a few looks. He caught a glimpse of Chief Willis walking beside the Mayor and decided to stay clear.

The service was what he'd expected. The Pastor spoke about asking God for help in understanding what had happened to Willy Parnell. Speaking to a predominantly colored congregation, he spoke of tolerance and acceptance for all races and religions. Ben wondered how many of those assembled were involved in the protests that continued to happen in downtown Biloxi. After the service, Ben stood at the back of the church and watched as people left to go to the grave site. From what he could tell the two suspects had not made an appearance.

As the rain pelted down, people gathered around the grave site, and the pastor quoted a few more lines of scripture. Ben saw Justyne standing beside her husband, huddled under an umbrellas.

Two teary-eyed girls held onto Justyne's hands like she was a life preserver.

As they were lowering the casket, Ben looked over and caught Chief Willis glaring at him. There was still no sign of the suspects, and Ben started to move with the crowd filing out to their cars. He nodded to the doorman Bruce Smith and recognized a couple of other tenants they had interviewed. Ben saw Maven and Mabel holding court with a couple of the younger men, no doubt exchanging recipes. There was still the matter of the seal placed on Willy's apartment being broken. Was Maven lying about not having opened the door, or did someone else come by looking for something else? He made a mental note to have the apartment dusted for fingerprints.

Ben picked out a couple of plainclothes cops who were busy watching the crowd. There was no sign of Burnside, which was surprising. His junior partner had assured Ben the day before that he would be there. Ben was just leaving the church grounds when he heard a voice call out his name.

"Detective O'Shea!" Ben turned in the direction of the voice and was surprised to see Morgan Armstrong walking towards him. "Hello, Mr. Armstrong. Once again, I'm sorry about Willy."

"Thank you, Detective, I wanted to speak to you about something."

"What's that?"

"All of this has been very hard on my family. Like the Pastor said, we need to pray to God to help us deal with this tragedy. The community needs to heal. That's what I'm trying to do. But I guess I'm a little confused about your investigation."

"How so?"

"First, the story in the paper came out saying that this was a random, racially motivated crime. That Willy had been beaten to death because of the color of his skin. As distasteful as that is, I can accept that. Then I heard that the Coroner found that my father-in-law wasn't murdered. It was an accidental death, a heart attack suffered when he grew disoriented. Then I saw the sketches in the paper of two men. Persons of interest. It claimed that you think someone tried to make it look like a race thing. I am confused, so yesterday I called the police station looking for you. I got your partner Detective Burnside. He told me that the investigation was winding down and that the department was going to accept the Coroner's report."

Ben bristled at the mention of what Burnside had said. "Mr. Armstrong, I guess the Coroner felt the note found by the body wasn't conclusive enough. You should probably accept the Coroner's findings for what it is. No more than a political move aimed at quieting the unrest that's happening in the city. But mark my words your father-in-law was beaten so badly he suffered a heart attack. He was murdered. What's more, he was specifically targeted by those two men in the paper. I can't say any more than that, but we're making progress."

"You're making this difficult for Justyne and the kids."

Ben stepped forward to within inches of Morgan, "Funny, I don't feel the need to move on, and I won't until I catch these guys."

Armstrong was still glaring at him as Ben turned around and walked to his car.

Chapter 34

Gabriel figured that the day before sailing would bring most of the crew to the ship and that his chances were pretty good to speak to some of those who had worked the GOP cruise. Sure enough, he was waiting by the car watching the workman carry supplies to the ship when he spotted Curtis.

"Don't drop those boxes, Curtis. Kelly will have you working in the latrines."

Curtis turned to look at Gabriel, "Oh it's you. Say, do you have any more of those finskys?"

"Actually, how would you like to earn ten bucks?"

"Wow!" Curtis said sarcastically, "You must be desperate for information," he said, continuing towards the ship.

"I spoke to Jessie," Gabriel called out.

That made Curtis stop and turn back, putting a box he was carrying on the dock. "Did she say anything about me?"

"Nah, she didn't have much to say, but remembered Rogers as having a bit too much to drink."

Curtis picked up his box and said, "Keep your money pal, Kelly reamed me out after you and your girlfriend left last time."

"How about an Andrew Jackson? All I need is one name."

"Make it quick."

Gabriel handed Curtis the $20. "The Congressman stayed in one of the triple-A rooms you showed me on the tour. I want the name of the cabin maid who made up the room."

"That's easy, all of the AAA rooms are looked after by this one girl. Her name is Sofia Gonzales."

"How can I find her?'

"That's two questions."

Gabriel pulled out his wallet giving Curtis another $20. As Curtis went to grab the money, Gabriel pulled it back, "For an introduction."

"No problem, I'll send her over to you when she goes on break. Stay right here."

Gabriel waited for about twenty minutes before a tiny woman dressed in a white uniform and apron made her way to him. She looked in her early thirties with dark hair and brown eyes.

Very attractive. Kelly must have personally selected her for the assignment.

"You friend of Curtis?" she asked in broken English.

"Yes, Sofia?" she nodded and looked at Gabriel warily.

"Curtis say, you give me money."

Gabriel pulled his wallet out and wondered about her expectations. He bet that a girl like her would be used to getting tips from the AAA customers. Pulling out two twenties he said, "I need some information about one of the AAA guests.

She held the twenties in her outstretched hand as if to say "Is this all?" I am not supposed to talk about the guests. Captain Kelly would fire me."

"Well, I don't want you to be out of income." Gabriel placed another twenty on her palm.

"What cabin?

"The one that Congressman Rogers occupied during the Republican Party cruise last May. Do you remember that cruise, Sofia?"

"Ah! Politico! He tall, fancy gentleman? He get drunk."

"I want to know about the woman he was with who shared the cabin with him."

At first, Sofia looked confused and then, "I see a woman leave his cabin the first night."

"Can you describe her?"

"Taller than you."

Gabriel gave her a sarcastic look and said, "As tall as Curtis?"

"No." She held her hand up about 4 inches over Gabriel's head.

"What was she wearing?"

"Pants, long dark coat. Sunglasses. But dark outside?" she said with a questioning look.

"Hair color?"

"Black like mine. Bufanda," Sofia said, making a twirling motion with her hand.

"A scarf? Was she wearing a scarf? When Sofia nodded, "Was she a white woman?" Once again she nodded. "I don't suppose you know who she is?" Sofia shook her head. "Did she look like a prostitute? A puta?"

"No senor, she was not like that. She not dressed like that and ...too old. I can tell you something else, but it is not so nice."

"Go ahead Sofia, I won't tell anyone."

A smile broke out across her face as she said, "The next morning I must change sheets, they had big sex."

"You mean there was ...."

She nodded, "Really big party."

Chapter 35

Ben got into work early Monday morning hoping to have a word with Willis before he dealt with Burnside. He hadn't had a serious conversation with his boss since the press conference. Willis had steered the daily briefings away from the Parnell investigation, probably in the hope that the case would just disappear. As soon as Ben stuck his head in Willis' office, he knew he was in for a rough ride.

"Where the fuck was Burnside on Saturday, and don't tell me at the podiatrist?"

"I was going to say, orthodontist."

"He wants to have braces?" Willis asked incredulously. When Ben just shrugged Willis continued, "Seriously Ben. I don't want to get involved, because of the potential blowback on me from telling that little twerp what I think of him. That's why I'm counting on you to have a man to punk talk with him."

"So I'm the sacrificial lamb?"

"There are worse things."

"Well, I was planning on having a heart to heart with him after the briefing."

"Fuck the daily briefing. I have another question for you."

"Sure what's up?"

"What kind of a fuck brings a yellow striped umbrella to a fucking funeral? You looked like a bumble bee."

Ben, who was wearing khakis along with a pink polo shirt and green tie, "Just trying to show some character."

"Character? Right. Listen, Ben, I know you're counting on these phone tips amounting to something, but no one saw those guys at the funeral, and everyone was talking on Friday about how all the tips have been from crackpots."

Once again Ben felt his blood pressure rise. "It's true that most of these leads are crap, but Friday afternoon, I got a solid hit." Ben proceeded to tell Willis about Zack, his discussion with Mike from the Gang Squad, Sons of Silence and then his visit to Twin Thunder. To his credit, Willis listened without interrupting.

"These motorcycle gangs are often a bunch of Neo-Nazis, which brings us full circle to the original premise that the old guy was targeted because of his skin color."

"So you don't believe the Coroner's report?"

Willis took off his glasses and used a handkerchief to wipe his forehead. "Officially, the guy died of a heart attack because he got confused and wandered into the forest. If asked, that is what I am supposed to say. That is what you're going to say. But between you and me, some punks beat him to death until he had a heart attack. End of story."

"Now resources being what they are, I have been told to reassign people to other cases. So officially no murder, no investigation. Ben, I'm going to make a suggestion. I want you to listen carefully just in case someone ever questions it. After you have your chat with Burnside why don't you take some time? I think you probably have some coming to you. You've been working hard, and I know this case has you twisted in knots. I'll temporarily assign someone else to be Burnside's nursemaid. The break will do you guys good."

Ben understood what Willis was saying and got up to leave. "Okay, boss I have a few things to do."

"Be careful Ben. And get some new fucking clothes."

Chapter 36

When Burnside came in, he wanted to tell Ben about some of the new crank calls that come in after he got back to the office on Friday. Ushering the younger officer to a private interview room, Ben said, "Let's go in here and have a chat. Have you set the volunteers up to better screen the calls?"

"Yep, that's why I know they're cranks. One guy said he recognized them from the local Dominoes. According to him, they were shorting him on the pepperoni, so he went down there and had it out with them." Burnside started to laugh but stopped abruptly when he saw that Ben wasn't laughing.

"What is it, Ben?" Burnside took a seat in the interview room.

"Burnside, I'm going to take a few days off, and when I get back, things are going to be different. Maybe you need a new partner." Ben continued to stand, hovering over Burnside.

"Have you already spoken to the boss?"

"No, I wanted to tell you first. Burnside, you have everything going for you. You've got youth, and you look more like a cop on TV than I do. But here it is. Let's get real. I've been covering for you. You left early every day last week, and you blew off the funeral on Saturday."

"Something came up...."

Ben held up his hand cutting him off. "Don't even bother. As for the tips, they're bound to be crap, they always are. That's police work. But every once in a while one pans out, that's police work." Ben repeated what he had told Willis about Zachary, the Sons of Silence and his visit to Twin Thunder.

"Shit, motorcycle gangs? There are some really bad dudes in those gangs, a cousin of mine..."

Ben cut him off again. "You have a ton to learn about police work and how to support a partner, which includes not running your mouth off because you're too caught up with yourself to see things clearly." Burnside looked down, knowing that he had screwed up. "I'm not sure why you ever wanted to be a cop, but the way you're going, it'll be a pretty short career." Burnside looked like he wanted to interject but was biting his tongue. "So here's the plan...I'll be away for a few days, and then maybe we'll pick this up at that point. I still have to complete a fitness report on you. You've got between now and then to decide what you want to do. If you want to go in and talk to Willis about wanting a new partner, be my guest. But when I get back I'm going to wrap this case up, with you or without you."

"I can run down this motorcycle thing while you're gone."

"No, stay away from this. Willis will get you working on other cases."

Burnside looked dejected, which made Ben feel like a bully.

"I'm sorry I let you down Ben," said the young cop, but Ben had already left the interview room.

Chapter 37

Ben had made arrangements to meet Gabriel in the lobby. Since he was technically on leave, he left the keys to his unmarked cruiser with Burnside.

"How has your week been, Ben?" asked Gabriel as they stood outside the stationhouse and basked in the early sunshine. Yesterday's storm had cleared some of the humidity away.

"It's been bullshit. It's bad enough I have to find a murderer, but I have to do it fighting City Hall and the County Coroner." Ben brought his partner up to date on the press conference, the sketches of the suspects and the possible link to the Sons of Silence. "I also feel like I have one arm tied behind my back with this partner of mine."

"Burnside?"

"Yeah, turns out he's Congressman Rogers' nephew, and I've spent the week either arguing with him or covering up for him. I wish I could have a partner like you."

"Why don't you just tell him to smarten up?"

"I did this morning. I bet he's never had anyone speak to him like that. To be honest, I feel like a bully. I really unloaded on him."

"You did what you had to do, to get his attention. You probably saved that kid's life. You've said before, being a cop is dangerous, much more so if you can't count on your partner for backup. So he's either going to smarten up or find something easier. Either way, you did him and the Department a favor."

"I hope you're right. I kind of blame his uncle, Congressman Rogers. If Burnside had come through the ranks like everyone else, he would have been better prepared. His uncle probably thinks he was doing him a favor, but he was actually hurting him."

"Speaking of Rogers, let me tell you about the latest developments." Gabriel filled Ben in on the discussion yesterday with the cabin maid Sofia.

"So does the description bring you any closer to finding the woman?"

"Not really but it did confirm a couple of things. One, Rogers' description wasn't bullshit. I was starting to think that they were lying to me. Two, the cabin girl didn't recognize her as being a crew member, and she didn't think she was a pro. Which brings me back full circle to one of the invitees."

"You sound just as frustrated in your case as I feel about mine."

"As we discussed, I cleared my schedule. How can I help?"

"If you're up for it, I thought we could head over to the old man's apartment. There was one tenant who wasn't home when we did the initial canvas. Then I would like your thoughts on the son-in-law. He cornered me at the funeral trying to pressure me into dropping the case. We'll have to take your shit box, I'm technically on leave."

When Gabriel gave him a quizzical look, "I've basically been given free rein to either put up or shut up within the next few days. I'm not blaming Willis, he's trying to walk on both sides of the street."

They got in the VW, and while driving to the apartment, Gabriel filled his partner in on the discussion with Arnie Sims. "He's been a big help. I would like to bring him on as an associate."

"Can we afford that?"

"That's the good part. He thinks he can bring us enough new customers to keep himself busy."

Chapter 38

After introducing Gabriel to Bruce Smith, Ben took a moment to speak to him, "Thanks again for working with the forensic artist," said Ben. "We have a pretty good lead thanks to you."

"Thank you for giving me the opportunity. Everyone here loved Willy."

As the two detectives started to climb the stairs, the doorman called out, "Just so you're not caught by surprise, Willy's daughter Justyne is up in the apartment sorting through things."

When they got to the 8th floor, Ben took a moment to catch his breath before knocking on the door. After a couple of moments the door opened a crack and Justyne peeked out at Ben, "Oh it's you Detective, the knock kind of startled me." She let them into the apartment and Ben introduced Gabriel as his colleague.

Following Ben's gaze at the empty boxes, Justyne added. "Just putting some things away. The landlord is anxious to rent the apartment.

"How are you, Mrs. Armstrong? I'm sorry I didn't get a chance to speak to you at the funeral," Ben offered.

"I saw you, but there were so many people. The girls pointed you out because of the ...umbrella." Justyne said giving him a grin.

"Are the girls here?" Ben noticed dark rings under her eyes.

"No, they're at the sitter's. I thought seeing Dad's empty apartment would upset them. This has been so hard on them." Justyne's gaze went to Gabriel.

"How is that nice Detective Burnside? Is he off the case?"

"He's fine, and working another case. That why I called in a favor and brought Gabriel with me."

"I'm sorry for your loss Mrs. Armstrong," said Gabriel. "You must be a strong woman to hold yourself together."

"Thank you, Mr. Ross. I thought I could handle this, but everything I touch is something that Dad wore or treasured. The smell of the apartment reminds me....."

"I understand," said Gabriel, seeing that Justyne was close to tears. From the bags under her eyes, he wondered if she was taking anything to help her sleep.

"I spoke to Morgan at the funeral. Did he tell you?" Ben asked, sitting on the couch.

"He said that he spoke to you and told you that he wants everyone to just move on. He can be a little awkward sometimes. I think he meant the protests."

Ben was pretty sure Morgan was referring to the investigation and not the protests, but he decided not to say anything. "I'm sure there must be others who feel the same way. I gave him my promise that we are going to get to the bottom of what happened to Willy."

"Thank you, Detective, we appreciate it. Am I in your way? Were you looking for anything in particular?"

"Actually, we're here to interview a tenant who wasn't here during the initial canvas."

"Oh, okay, I would offer you a coffee, but I've already packed things away."

"That's fine I've already had my morning cup, but since you're here, there are a couple of questions that maybe you could help me with."

"Sure."

"I know your husband was the Power of Attorney for your dad..."

"Morgan told me you asked about that. I really don't know anything about financial things, and, well Morgan is very smart."

"That's great. What about the estate?"

"Well, I guess we'll have to go see a lawyer. Now that the funeral is done, I don't see the urgency. Morgan said he'll look after everything for me."

"Okay, that makes sense. Thank you again for working with the forensic artist. We're pursuing a pretty good lead on these two men."

"Glad to help. Detective, I saw the sketch in the paper." After a moment, "Can I ask you a question?"

When Ben nodded "Now that I identified these people, are we in any danger?"

"I don't believe so, but if anything happens to make you think otherwise call me."

Before leaving Gabriel handed her one of his business cards. "If you can't reach Ben, call me, and I'll come running.

Chapter 39

Ben led Gabriel down the hallway to Apartment 806, and the tenant who had yet to be interviewed. After a few knocks, he was tempted to leave a card under the door when he heard rustling in the apartment. Ben had the distinct feeling that he was being watched and not just from Apartment 806. Holding up his gold badge to the peephole in the door, he said, "Biloxi Police Department, just a few questions please."

The door, secured by a chain, finally opened six inches. An older gentleman with unkempt hair, dressed in a plaid housecoat and slippers peered out at them with suspicion.

"I'm sorry if I woke you, Sir," said Ben, who looked down at his pad where he had written the tenant's name. "Mr. Musselman?"

"What's this all about?"

"It's about your neighbor Mr. Parnell who died on Saturday in the park. Can we come in?"

"Show me the ID again."

Ben flashed the badge and held out his ID card. The old man took his time in comparing the picture ID to the man in front of him.

"Who's this?" The old man asked suspiciously, nodding to Gabriel.

"This is Private Investigator Gabriel Ross. He has offered to help me today." The man looked back and forth between Ben and Gabriel before slowly closing the door. Gabriel thought that they had struck out, then after a moment he heard the chain being unlatched.

The apartment had a distinct litter box smell. The man led them to a living room. Heavy dark curtains kept any sunlight from penetrating the old man's cave. The only light in the room came from the TV, which was showing a baseball game. The room, furnished with bulky dark brown leather furniture was depressing. A half-eaten cheese sandwich was sitting beside a can of Budweiser on a cheap particle board coffee table.

"Pretty early for the Cardinals to be playing," Gabriel nodded at the TV.

"Betamax recording from last night. I can't stay up as late as I used to, so I tape it and watch it the next day." It was the Cubs playing at Busch Stadium. "Suppose I should offer you something?"

"Got a beer?" asked Gabriel.

A smile came over Musselman's face, "I'm a Budweiser man. If you want something else, you're out of luck."

"Bud's great." A few minutes later Musselman came back with two cans of bud and a bowl of pretzels.

"Thanks, Mr. Musselman," said Gabriel. Ken Holtzman was pitching for the Cubs. Lou Brock was on first threatening to steal. After the second pitch, Brock broke for 2nd stealing the base easily.

"That darkie sure can run." Musselman took a big gulp from his beer.

"Wasn't even close," said Ben thinking back to what Burnside said about accepting offerings, and conceded that his young partner might have had a point.

"Watch ya want to ask me?"

"We were here the other day, and there was no answer. I was canvassing the building to see if any of the other renters might have any information about what happened to Willy."

"Like what kind of information?"

"Did you know him very well?" Gabriel took a pretzel.

"We watched the odd game together. I guess I knew him well enough to know that there can't be any reason for someone to do that to him."

"The doorman said that he had seen a couple of thug-like characters hanging around. Their picture was on the front page of the paper earlier this week." Ben pulled out a copy of the flyer from his suit pocket and handed it to Musselman.

"Saw the pictures in the paper. I haven't seen anyone hanging around. Just the normal people. Now and then, Willy's family would come to visit. You know, those two girls, the daughter, and her husband."

"So no idea why someone would want to hurt Willy?"

Musselman thought for a moment. Gabriel thought the man was having an internal debate over saying something else. Musselman took a long swallow from his beer. "Nothing comes to mind."

They continued to watch the game, drinking their beer. At the end of the inning, the broadcast went to a commercial and Musselman stuck out his hand, "My Name's Harry Musselman."

Ben and Gabriel shook his hand and thanked him again for the beer.

All of a sudden a Siamese cat jumped up on the coffee table and eyed Ben.

"Whoa! Is he friendly?" Ben asked.

"I wouldn't say friendly. She usually sits where you're sitting. Sometimes this breed can get a little territorial. I wouldn't try to touch her." Almost as an afterthought, Harry said, "Getting back to your question about Willy, there was this one time. Nah! It was probably nothing."

Ben and Gabriel decided to wait for the thought to resurface. When he didn't continue, Gabriel said "Solving a murder is a little like baseball. Sometimes it comes down to inches. In investigating a murder, the slightest little thing can make a huge difference."

Harry didn't say anything right away, but Gabriel figured a burden was weighing on him. The cat meanwhile had discovered Gabriel and was rubbing up against him.

"Budweiser, that's her name. Bud for short. Suppose it's a boy's name, but she don't seem to mind." Pointing at the cat rubbing up against Gabriel, "She don't normally do that. She must like the smell of you."

"I have a cat."

This brought a smile to the old man's face, like having a cat admitted him to some type of fraternity. "It was a month or so ago. I heard voices out in the hallway. You normally don't hear stuff. The walls here are pretty thick. I figured by the sound they were right outside my door. Anyway, I looked through the peep, and I'm sure it was Willy talking to someone. Willy had his back to me, and whoever he was talking to, was standing just out of sight. Willy was talking normally, I recognized his voice. I think the other person must have been whispering because I couldn't make out much. Anyway, the reason it stuck in my craw was I got the impression that Willy was upset. At one point I was going to open the door and break things up. I'm pretty sure they were talking about money. If I had to guess Willy wanted the other person to lend him money or give him money, and the other guy wouldn't.

"Can you remember anything else, even if it's just a word or two?" asked Ben.

"I'm guessing at this point, but I think Willy said something like, you said you would, or you said you could, something like that."

As Ben and Gabriel left Musselman's apartment, they almost ran right into Maven. Ben wondered if the old lady might have been eavesdropping on their conversation. "Hello Ma'am," said Ben, trying to remember if this was Maven or Mabel.

"Nice to see you again Detective." She let her eyes drift to Gabriel, "And who is this cutie?"

"This is an associate of mine, Gabriel this is ...Maven. She lives on the floor, and knew Mr. Parnell."

Gabriel took in Maven, who was wearing a sheer nightie which left little to the imagination. "Nice to meet you, Maven." Gabriel shook her hand which the lady held for an uncomfortably long time.

"Have you found my recipe card?" She turned her attention to Ben.

"No, we did a thorough search of the apartment and nothing turned up." Turning to Gabriel, "I found Maven in Willy's apartment looking for something...a recipe. Sorry Maven."

Maven gave Ben a pouty face. "What have you and your little friend been up to at Musselman's?"

"Oh just finishing the canvas of the building. Still trying to get a handle on what happened."

"I wouldn't put too much stock in what Musselman had to say, he ain't got the sense God gave to a piss ant."

"Where's Mabel?" asked Ben, trying to change the subject. "Mabel's her twin sister," Ben said to Gabriel.

"It's Monday morning. I'm sure she's in bed, hungover. I have to quit asking her how big a slut can you be? I think she's taking it as a personal challenge."

*****

Gabriel drove to downtown Biloxi where they found a taco stand on the corner. "So what's with Maven?" he asked laughing.

"Maven the Raven. At least she was until her hair went white. The police tape was cut when I found her in Willy's apartment. She denies it was her. She said the door was open."

"I think she was listening at the door when we were talking to Musselman. Maybe Musselman wasn't the only one who heard the conversation about money in the hallway," suggested Gabriel. After taking a sip of his Coke, "Do you think that someone killed Willy for the money?"

"Maybe, but I don't understand it. The guy led a simple life. He didn't have much, just some life insurance from when his wife passed. That was invested in a T-Bill at the bank. I saw the paperwork when I searched his apartment," Ben said in between bites of a taco.

"T-Bills can be sold. How do you know he didn't lend that money to someone and then maybe, that someone decided to kill him because he didn't want to give it back?" asked Gabriel.

"That plays but who?"

"The two guys in the sketch...your Sons of Silence guys," replied Gabriel.

"Why would he lend these guys money?"

"I didn't say it was a good theory. Didn't you say Willy worked on the docks? Maybe he knew them."

"So they beat him up in the park, causing the heart attack, and then to hide the financial motive they make it look like a hate crime?"

Gabriel nodded. He had opted against having a taco, the early-mid morning Budweiser wasn't sitting well with him. They were standing in front of Laity and Associates and both looked up at the same time. "You think?" asked Gabriel.

*****

When they opened the door to the lobby, they noticed that the elevator was out of order for maintenance. "What floor are they on?" asked Ben.

"The eighth." Gabriel held the stairwell door open.

"Why does everything have to be on the eighth floor? Willy lived on the eighth floor, this place is on the eighth floor, your office is on the eighth floor." Ben continued to grumble as he started the long climb.

When they got to Laity and Associates, Ben sounded like an asthmatic bulldog as he leaned heavily against the wall.

"Ben you need to start getting more exercise. Maybe just start with some walking."

"Fuck off."

Gabriel opened the double glass doors and walked into the foyer. When they got to the front desk, Jules asked if they had an appointment. Ben, who was hanging back trying to catch his breath, stepped forward and displayed his badge. "I was here the other day, and I need to speak to Mr. Armstrong."

"Is he expecting you, sir?"

"No, we're throwing him a surprise party."

The man seemed put out by Ben's attitude but decided wisely to buzz the investment counselor on the phone. He spoke on the phone for a few moments before saying, "Why don't you gentlemen have a seat? Mr. Armstrong is having a very busy day, but he said he could spare you a few minutes for your 'surprise party.'"

They sat in the waiting area. "This is the second time someone said this guy was really busy. But both times I've been here the place is as deserted as Biloxi Beach during a hurricane. What's more, the phone never rings. What's up with that?" asked Ben.

Gabriel shrugged and picked up a Good Housekeeping magazine off the glass coffee table. "Pretty jazzy decor in here," nodding to the black and white flooring.

"Notice the print on the wall - it's a Picasso."

"Pretty good if you like women with eyes in the middle of their forehead. So who owns this place?" asked Gabriel.

"I did a little research on Sunday. Couldn't find much about the business. The owner's name is Terra Laity. She started the business a few years back. She's clean other than a ton of traffic tickets. Get this, her maiden name is Dactel."

"Terra Dactel?" Gabriel asked grinning.

They were interrupted by the sound of an office door opening and then Morgan Armstong walked quickly in their direction. "Hello Detective, after our conversation at the funeral, I didn't expect to see you again." Ben introduced Gabriel as a special assistant helping on the case. Morgan extended a hand; at close to 6 foot 5 inches he towered over Gabriel.

"Gabriel Ross, I think I've heard of you, weren't you in the papers earlier in the year? That business with the Harrison County Sheriff."

"Yes, that was me. Can we go into your office?"

"Sure, would you like a coffee? An espresso?

This time, both detectives said no thank you. When they were all seated, Gabriel began by asking Morgan to tell him about the firm.

"We're Investment Counselors and represent some large institutional investors helping them take advantage of some market opportunities."

"Institutional investors? What does that mean?" asked Gabriel.

"Companies, organizations....I'm sure you understand the need for confidentiality. I can't disclose anything about our clients."

"Fair enough Mr. Armstrong. Who owns the business?" asked Gabriel, noticing a picture of Morgan with Justyne and the kids on his credenza.

"The business was built by a remarkable lady by the name of Terra Laity. She started it a few years ago, and she's received numerous awards, entrepreneur of the year, business woman of the year, employer of the year..."

"I think I knew a Laity once. Is she from Biloxi?"

"Up north I believe, the name is well known along the coast, though."

"She sounds like quite the dynamo. I would love to meet her."

"She's a pretty busy lady. July is supposed to be a slow month in the investment business, but we've been run off our feet." Gabriel shared a quick look at Ben. "I have a stack of orders that need to be placed, but if you promise to let me get back to work, I can see if she can see you for a quick moment."

Ben pulled out his notebook and made a show of flipping through the pages. "Morgan, last we spoke you told me that your father-in-law Willy had invested the $250,000 insurance proceeds in a T-Bill at the bank." Ben hadn't thought it would be possible for Mr. Extra White's face to turn whiter.

"Is that a question Detective?"

"Let me phrase it differently. Your father-in-law sold his T-Bill and invested, or gave the money to you is that not correct?"

It took Morgan a few moments to answer, "I believe if you actually made notes on our last conversation you will see that it was you who told me that he had his money in T-Bills. I simply didn't correct you. Unless you have a court order than what we do or don't do for our clients is confidential."

"So you're saying your father-in-law was a client of this firm?" stated Gabriel. When Morgan gave him a blank look, Gabriel continued, "Otherwise there would be no confidentiality issue."

Morgan made a move to stand up, signaling an end to the meeting, Ben, however, held up his hand and said he still had another question. "If you prefer we can take you to the station-house."

Morgan sat back down looking visibly flustered. "What?" All pretext of friendliness had left his voice.

"A witness has reported to us that he heard you and your father-in-law arguing in the hallway outside his apartment."

"Arguing about what?"

"Money."

"Your witness is mistaken." After a brief staring contest, Morgan added, "I remember one conversation Willy and I had about six weeks ago. It was about a birthday party that we had been planning for Justyne. I had said I would do something, you know, those pink flamingos you can get to embarrass someone on their birthday...well I forgot. He was upset about it."

Ben nodded his head as if he understood. "Justyne told us that you're going to take care of handling Willy's estate, is that correct?"

"Yes," Morgan said quickly, impatience creeping into his voice. "We've been over this Detective, Justyne does not have my expertise in these matters. Furthermore, I would appreciate it if you would quit harassing her. As I told you Saturday we are all trying to recover from her father's passing."

Ben stood up at that point, and Gabriel could sense that his partner's pot was about to boil over at the suggestion that he was harassing anyone. As Gabriel stood, he put an arm on Ben's shoulder and said, "Thanks for seeing us Morgan, if it isn't too much trouble I sure would like an introduction to Terra."

Morgan got up and left the office saying he would be right back.

While he was gone, Gabriel whispered, "You were just bullshitting about the T-Bill being cashed and the money given to him, right?"

"Yeah, and it worked."

A minute later the door opened, and Morgan took charge of the introductions. "Terra, I promised these gentlemen that I would give them a quick introduction. This is Ben O'Shea, a detective with Biloxi PD, and this little guy," he said with a grin, "Is Gabriel Ross, the famed Private Detective."

Gabriel stood mesmerized by Terra's beauty. Ben shook her hand. He looked over at his partner, "Gabriel?"

Beautiful...her brown eyes draw you in like quicksand. I love brown eyes. I told Rachel I loved blue eyes, but that was a lie. Terra's dark hair tumbled like a veil on her shoulders. She wore a tight fitting black dress that made her look like a bowling pin with boobs.

"Nice to meet you, Mr. Ross." She smiled at the impact she was having on Gabriel.

"Detective O'Shea is the one looking into my father-in-law's death. I've been consulting with them," said Morgan.

Is that Jasmine I smell? That's the same scent Jacqueline used to wear. I could just drown in it, Gabriel thought before focusing on Terra's candy apple red lips.

"Good luck with your investigation Detective," said Terra to Ben. "And what about you Gabriel, are you working on something exciting?"

"Oh....I'm just here to help out. You know do what I can." *She has high cheek bones, I love high cheek bones. I didn't know that until just now, but I am definitely on the high cheekbone team.*

"Well, it was nice meeting you both. Terra handed a business card to Gabriel saying, "If I can be of any help, please don't hesitate to call."

******

The walk down the stairs was much easier. "You could catch flies with that mouth Gabriel."

"Did you see that woman Ben? Did you?"

"She looks like a million dollars. Those tits alone must have cost a couple of hundred thousand. Barbie dolls are more human." When they made it to the bottom of the steps, Ben added, "Gabriel I think you miss Jacqueline so much, you're seeing her in this girl."

"Ben, your eyesight must be going, that girl was gorgeous."

"Gabriel my Dad used to say that women like that fell out of the whore tree and banged every guy on the way down." Ben laughed at his own joke as they went down to the street.

On the walk back to the parking lot Ben asked, "So what did you make of Morgan?"

"Liar, good one mind you, but definitely a liar. See how quick he came up with the pink flamingo story when you asked him about the argument?"

"Yeah, I agree. He was lying. I just don't understand why. The old guy had $250,000. That's not an insignificant amount to us, but when you're dealing with millions, why bother lying? Even if he invested and lost the whole crap load, why not just admit it?

By lying it makes me think he knows something about why his Willy was killed."

"Do you think he's bumping uglies with his boss?" asked Gabriel getting into the VW.

"Hard to tell, you see that family picture on his credenza? Pretty happy family." Gabriel started up the car and pulled into traffic. "Thanks for this Gabriel. I think having you there helped get Musselman to open up. What are your plans for the rest of the day?"

"I don't have any specific plans. Any ideas?"

"Yep, I think if you could control yourself, I'd like to check up on Terra Laity. Are you up for a little surveillance? There's something wrong with that company. Maybe we can get a line on who she meets. You can bring Arnie along and show him the ropes."

"Okay let me get my gear and call Arnie. What are you going to do?"

"I'm going to call Wil Graham and see if there is anything on Laity and Associates. There's a guy named Mike in our Gangs Unit, he was going to check with his team about the Sons of Silence. Think I'll check back with him."

Chapter 40

Once Gabriel dropped him off at his apartment, Ben dialed the number for Will Graham in Jackson. Over the past few months, Ben had stayed in touch with the FBI man and had become an unofficial liaison between the federal agency and the Biloxi PD. Wil picked up the call right away. "Hey, Ben how are you guys doing down there?"

"Pretty good, I'm working a hate crime and some political bullshit at the same time. But making progress."

"Are you talking about that Parnell thing that has caused all the rioting?"

"Yeah, the Coroner decided that Willy beat himself up."

"That would be one way of looking at it. With the Civil Rights Act of 1968, it's a federal offense to commit a crime based on a person's skin color. So another way to look at it would be to say that someone down there doesn't want the Bureau snooping around."

"Was the FBI going to get involved?"

"You better believe it, Ben. I had my marching orders and my bags packed before this was ruled an accident."

"That's interesting Wil. Any idea why the Mayor might not want the feds involved?"

"Only the obvious one that he might be involved in something he'd prefer to have hidden. What do you know about the Mayor?"

"Not much, I think he's a lawyer. I assumed that he was just trying to quell the rioting by making it into an accident."

"That might be right but how is that working out for him?"

"Not too many people are buying the 'he bumped into a tree' explanation. So there were just as many people in the streets last night as before."

"You might want to take a look at Mayor Baxter."

"This might fit in with a theory I'm working on." Ben shared his thoughts about another reason why Willy, in particular, was targeted.

"So the killers just made it look like a race crime?'

"Pretty much." Ben told him about the sketches and the connection to the Sons of Silence."

When Ben was done, Wil said, "If it's not a hate crime, then how can I help you?'

"There seems to be a connection between the old man, his son-in-law and an Investment Company called *Laity and Associates.* I don't have anything concrete, but there is something fishy about that company."

"You think the old man knew something and was going to spill the beans?"

"Like I said, I don't have anything solid, but thought maybe you might be aware of a federal investigation into the company." Ben could hear his counterpart typing.

After a moment Wil responded, "I checked NCIC, and there is no active investigation at the State or Federal level on Laity and Associates."

"Can you check the owner? Her name is Terra Laity." Ben heard more clicking of keys before Wil came back and said she was not the subject of any investigations.

"On second thought can you check the name Dactel. Terra Dactel?"

"Are you serious, her name is Terra Dactel?"

"That's probably why she got married."

Ben waited for a few more minutes before Wil came back and said there was plenty on that name. "Terra Dactel's name comes up as part of an inactive investigation into Frankie "Fingers" Luppino."

"What do you have on him and why is he called Fingers?"

"He's called Fingers because he supposedly likes to cut off people's fingers. He is an associate of Pretty Boy Luccio. Anyway, getting back to Fingers there was an investigation into union activity. I would have to speak to the case agent to find out how Dactel was involved."

"That would be great Wil, I can use all the help on this that I can get. I'm a little out of my depth when it comes to financial stuff. We're going to start doing some surveillance on her."

"In the meantime, there's a guy you should speak to. He's a retired FBI agent named Allen Duffy. He lives down your way in Mobile, he more or less wrote the book on financial crimes."

*****

After the call to Wil, Ben decided to try Mike McShays. The duty officer told him that Mike had left for an appointment with his allergist. It was pollen season, and Mike was sneezing like a hurricane. Ben chuckled and asked that Mike give him a call in the morning.

Ben decided that Gabriel had a point about his need for exercise. Finding himself without a car, he walked all the way from his apartment, 90 feet to the taxi stand so he could take a cab to Twin Thunder.

Chapter 41

Gabriel met Arnie at 7 p.m. in the lobby of the Trade Winds as agreed. Arnie was dressed in dark clothes and carried a flashlight. "I didn't know what else to bring."

Gabriel carried a knapsack, "This has got water, snacks, binoculars, a Kodak camera and a bunch of gadgets that I've used before. "As they piled into the bug Gabriel asked, "Are you all set for your first foray into the world of surveillance?"

"I guess so." said Arnie rolling down the window, "I figure the idea is to get some pictures of Terra and whomever she's meeting with."

"That's ideal, but not always possible. I handled a case where I got the picture, but had to outrun the husband who ended up chasing me down the street half naked." Gabriel put the car in gear and continued, "Most customers want to see pictures, but some would probably be better off just taking your word for it."

Once they arrived at the home, they pulled up about 90 yards from the house in clear view of the driveway. It was a nice Tudor style home with a circular drive and a large magnolia tree in the front. A large NASA sized satellite dish was on guard on the side lawn adjacent to a heart shaped pool. On the other side of the house, they could just make out what looked to be a tennis court.

"They like their toys," said Arnie.

"She seemed to be in pretty good shape when I met her today," offered Gabriel pulling out a couple of magazine from his knapsack. He handed the most recent Time magazine to Arnie, the one with the Three Mile Island nuclear incident. "Just hold it up as if you're reading it. There's still a couple of hours of daylight and someone walking by might wonder what we are doing."

Arnie wondered what would look more suspicious, two men in VW bug sitting in ninety-degree temperatures staring at a house, or sitting there reading magazines. Gabriel held up a copy of Sports Illustrated that had Pete Rose guiding the Phillies. Holding the magazine in front of him, "One of my first cases was a local employer who suspected one of his employees of taking advantage of the sick day policy. I parked outside his house and watched him get in his car. He was wearing his bathing suit and had a snorkel and mask carrying an inflatable duck. The guy looked right at me and then drove down the street. I followed him a little close, and at the first stop sign, he got out and came back to my car and asked what the hell I was doing."

"Have you thought about using a car that might be a little less conspicuous?"

"I've thought about it, and one day I will, but for now this will have to do."

"Maybe we should take my van next time. It has air conditioning and tinted windows, we could stretch out in the middle seat where no one walking by could see us."

"Sounds like a great idea. I wish you had suggested it earlier." Gabriel mopped the sweat from his brow.

"Speaking of husbands, what do we know about him?"

"Not much, I looked up Laity in the directory, and there is a Laity's Welding and Supply. Since there's a gray van in the drive, I'm assuming it's the same guy."

"What if she's in for the night?"

"Surveillance can be pretty boring work. Let's just keep a lookout and be prepared to tail her."

"What if they're meeting in the penthouse of some tall apartment building?"

"Do you know those forms you signed earlier today? They give me permission to hold your legs as you dangle upside down from the roof."

Reaching into his knapsack Gabriel extracted a metal device the size of a pack of cigarettes. "Ben gave me this gadget. It's a tracking device. There's a magnet on one side, and you put it under the suspect's bumper, and it transmits a ping to this receiver. The range isn't great, but it's helped me in the past."

"Is following a car that difficult?" Arnie examined the device.

"Harder than you think, if you don't want the suspect to catch on they're being followed. In the city, you have a lot more cars to give you cover, but you also have traffic lights. I've lost a few because they made the light and I didn't. Out in the country, you have to hang back quite a ways on account of there being fewer cars and it being easier to spot a tail. Probably the hardest part of surveillance, though, is stopping yourself from zoning out and letting your mind wander. Before you realize what's happening, you've lost them. There is also this little gadget," said Gabriel, pulling out a small transmitter the size of a large bobby pin. "You slip this in the ladies purse or clip it onto her coat, and the receiver will pick up everything that's said for about 100 yards. If your suspects go into a coffee shop, you can hear everything that is being said while you sit in your car in the parking lot."

"Were you thinking of using this with Terra?"

"Maybe, let's see what happens tonight. If there's a chance, though, it would be helpful." Gabriel continued to root in the knapsack, this time, extracting a large glass mason jar. "Know what this is for?"

Arnie took the glass jar in his hands, "Pickles?"

"No silly, urine. I have used it many times on surveillance when nature calls."

"Ugh!" Arnie handed the jar back to him.

At 9:30 it started to get dark and one of garage doors in Terra's house opened. They watched as a navy blue Jaguar XJS backed out into the driveway. "Nice wheels," commented Gabriel. Although they couldn't get a good look at the driver, they surmised by the long flowing dark hair that it clearly wasn't the husband. Gabriel waited for the tail lights to dim in the distance before pulling out. The Jag made a quick right followed by a couple of lefts, leading the way to downtown Biloxi. "Laity and Associates is downtown, maybe she's going to an office meeting."

Arnie gave him a deadpan look and said, "Speed up a little Gabriel, I'm losing sight of her in the traffic. In the dark, all the cars look navy blue." They caught up with the car in time to see her pull it into the parking lot of Laity and Associates.

Gabriel parked the VW on the street. Arnie had the binoculars out and watched as she got out of the car. "Did you say Terra was some hot number?"

"Hot? More like scorching hot," replied Gabriel.

"There must be some mistake. The lady that got out of the Jag, who is now going in the building would tip the scale at over 300."

"What?" Gabriel pulled the binoculars away from Arnie. He caught sight of the backside of a large dark haired woman wearing stretch pants and a T-shirt waddling into the building. For a few moments neither said anything, finally, Gabriel spoke, "That's not the woman I met today."

"What do we do now? She could still be meeting someone."

"It doesn't look like the building has security, but I bet she locked the front door behind her." Gabriel drove the car up to the front door, and Arnie got out expecting to find a locked door. It was unlocked. Arnie waived to Gabriel that he should park and accompany him inside. By the time Gabriel had parked and joined him, Arnie nodded to the directory saying, "8th floor, Suite 801, should we take the elevator?"

They debated the likelihood of getting caught in the elevator and finally decided it was safer to take the stairs. Gabriel led the way, racing up the stairs holding the Kodak at the ready. To his credit Arnie, almost twice Gabriel's age, handled the climb with ease. When they got to the double glass doors leading to Laity and Associates, they found the lights off and the doors locked. *Could she have gone to a different floor? I just assumed that after driving to her office that she would be using her own offices for whatever she had planned.* While Gabriel was busy working through scenarios in his head, Arnie walked over to the window overlooking the parking lot. "Oh Boss, isn't that the Jaguar pulling out of the parking lot?"

Chapter 42

Ben was feeling virtuous. He decided to walk from his apartment a full two blocks to the Detective Agency. The light blue sky was clear and looked like a pastel canvas dotted with one or two marshmallow clouds. Despite it being shortly after 8 a.m. there were already walkers and even a few joggers out. Ben decided to reward himself with a beignet and coffee from the neighborhood café.

When he got to the Agency, he turned on the light in the small one room office and saw that Bourbon was patiently waiting on the fire escape. He opened the window, and the cat came in purring and looking for his breakfast. Once Ben got Bourbon squared away, he put a pot of coffee on and went to sit down at Gabriel's desk. Banging his knees into the desk, he let out a yelp and realized that Gabriel was so short he had adjusted the chair as high as it could go. As he was twirling the chair around and around trying to lower it, he picked up the phone and dialed the number he'd been given for Allen Duffy.

The phone rang a half dozen times before it was picked by a man trying to catch his breath. "Hello... Allen Duffy."

"Hello, my name is Ben O'Shea, I'm a detective with the Biloxi PD and Wil Graham from the FBI suggested I call you."

"Yes Ben, Wil called me yesterday to say he had given out my number. Sorry, I'm a little winded, I was out casting off my dock. It's a good time in the morning to catch some bass. How can I help you, Ben?"

He explained the situation with Laity and Associates and what had happened to Willy Parnell, the Coroner's Report, and the conversation that was overheard in the hallway. Duffy listened until Ben was done before asking, "So Detective, you have a quasi-official investigation into a man's death who presumably invested his life savings in this Laity and Associates. Is that correct?" You think that somehow this got him killed?'

"In a nutshell."

"Well, there are a few holes in your theory. Not the least of which is, it goes against type. The people who run these schemes don't usually get their hands dirty. Presumably, your victim didn't like what was happening with his investment and complained. If he had threatened to go to the Securities, the company would have just given him back his money."

Ben thought that he had struck out when Duffy continued, "Let me ask a couple of questions. How long has the business been operating?"

"I believe the son-in-law said three years."

"What do you know about their customers?"

"The son-in-law said they handle mainly institutional accounts. Other than that they didn't want to disclose anything else."

"So what makes you so suspicious?"

"A bunch of things, the son-in-law tried to get me to drop the case, and the owner of the place is somehow connected to Frankie Fingers and an FBI operation into union activities. Other than that, I've been to their offices a couple of times and they say that they're really busy, but both times there hasn't been anyone else there, and the phone never rang once."

"Hmm, that's interesting. Any idea who the Associates are in Laity and Associates?"

"That's a good question. I don't know."

"Probably some numbered company that's owned by another numbered company. Detective, do you know what a Ponzi scheme is?"

"A little bit, but go on tell me what you think I need to know."

"Most of these schemes actually start out being run by totally legitimate companies offering unrealistically great returns. Greedy investors flock to put the money into the company expecting high monthly payouts. Some investments are initially made but the company soon realizes that they can't sustain the high returns. Faced with the prospect of investors pulling their money, they just continue the payments from the capital. Next, word spreads that they're paying such a high rate, and more people want to get in on it. More money comes in, more money goes out with the company producing statements showing the rosy returns. Now if a union is involved, then that's an interesting wrinkle. Funds get deducted from people's paycheck and find their way to the union, and unless the union needs the money for a strike, then this could go on for a long time."

Ben was taking this all in and remembered Justyne saying that Willy had worked as a longshoreman. "So how do these things normally end Allen?"

"Before January, the Dow was down roughly 20%. Let's say you gave them your whole police detective paycheck, all $100 of it. You would be down to $80. But wait, they promised you a 20% return per year, so since they're sending you that money out of your capital you now only have $60. Of course, they send you a statement showing that your $100 has not lost a penny despite the market drop and the distributions paid. So you think you have

$100, but it is down to $60. Now multiply this by millions representing many investors or a big union."

"I could see how the greedy individual investor might get duped, but a multi-million dollar union? Don't they have a Board of Directors that oversees everything?"

"Absolutely but with a union which is being run by a bunch of crooks...."

Ben thanked Allen Duffy for the information and thought that maybe a piece of the puzzle had fallen into place. He wondered how involved Willy had been with the union.

Chapter 43

The following morning, Ben tried Mike McShays again. This time, the veteran Detective answered right away. "Hey, Mike just following up to see if your team had anything to add to our conversation last week."

"You mustn't have got my message. I called your number yesterday, but they told me you were on vacation. Anyway, your partner said he was taking over for you, so I gave him the info."

"Burnside?"

"Yeah, the kid."

"Do you mind repeating what you told him?"

"Wasn't much. No one reported recognizing the faces in the sketch. As for the Sons of Silence, one guy said that there were some guys who were in the Deadheads who patched with the Sons. This guy knows his stuff, but he didn't have anything concrete like where they meet or their names. The only other piece was about the guy that owns Twin Thunder. He goes by Spider, but his real name is Horvat, Ante Horvat. Word on the street is that he's as dirty as a cotton picker's socks. If you want shit done, you go to Spider."

"I was there yesterday on surveillance. I wrote down some plates and was going to run them for warrants. Judging by the look of the people who I saw go into his shop I would bet money that he's dealing."

"You might be on to something, anyway, I told Burnside to give you the message, and that if we could get something on this guy, then we could probably set up a raid."

Ben thanked McShays then dialed Burnside's number and was surprised when Willis answered. "Hey boss, I was looking for Burnside, just something I forgot to tell him."

"Oh, Detective O'Shea! Burnside can't come to the phone right now. He left early. I think it was an appointment with his urologist."

*****

Ben had just gotten off the phone with Willis when the door opened, and a tall black man came in and introduced himself as Arnie Sims. Ben stood up and shook the newcomer's hand, remembering that Gabriel had recently hired him.

"Nice to meet you, Ben, I was supposed to meet Gabriel here to go over some forms and to discuss doing a surveillance job he wanted to do tonight."

Just at that moment Bourbon jumped up and sat on Arnie's lap. "I guess it's welcome aboard, Arnie."

Gabriel arrived shortly after and filled Ben in on the botched surveillance from last night. "I still don't know how the woman we met yesterday could have put on so much weight!" Gabriel said which made everyone laugh. For Arnie's benefit, Ben covered off some of the fine points of detective work. Arnie was a sponge for new information. They finally got around to discussing Laity and Associates, and Ben filled them in on what the retired FBI investigator had to say including the connection to the union.

"I have a cousin who works for the International Longshoreman's Association. I can speak to him if you want, see if Willy had been active." offered Arnie.

"Actually, that gives me an idea," said Gabriel. He explained to Arnie and Ben what he wanted to do.

Dialing the number for Laity and Associates, Gabriel handed the phone to Arnie. When the call was answered, Arnie explained to the receptionist that he was calling from the Brotherhood of Electrical Workers employees and wanted to speak to an investment counselor. Ben had told him to expect Morgan Armstrong, so Arnie was surprised when Terra Laity herself took the call.

"Hi, this is Terra Laity, how might we help you Mr. Sims?"

Without missing a beat, "You were referred to me by some people I know in the Longshoreman's Union. We currently have our funds being managed by an out of state firm, and I was just looking over our returns, and I'm disappointed. With the market doing as well as it is, I would like to see our money work a little harder."

"Our investment funds yielded a return last year of over 22%. How does that compare, Arnie?"

"That's excellent. But how exposed would the union's funds be to risk?"

"To get these kinds of returns consistently, we need to take advantage of some sophisticated investment vehicles like hedges, swaps and forward averaging contracts. But as your partner we manage the risk, we have never lost money for a customer and have returned on average over 20% year after year."

"That almost sounds too good to be true, Mrs..."

"It's Miss Laity, you can call me Terra. Maybe we can discuss this further over lunch?"

*****

"From what I heard, you sounded pretty smooth Arnie," Ben said when Arnie had hung up.

"She wanted to discuss her performance over lunch." Ben and Gabriel had heard Arnie promise to get back to her once he checked on a few things.

"Okay, let's turn up the heat." Gabriel dialed the number Arnie had given him for his cousin in the Longshoreman's Union. When he was put through to Reginald Sims, he handed the phone once again to Arnie, who quickly got caught up on news from his cousin's side of the family. After about five minutes the discussion turned to the reason for the call. "Listen, Reggie, what we're going to talk about is strictly confidential. Are you okay with that?"

"You know me cos, once something goes in the vault....."

Arnie interrupted and said, "You know I work at the Trade Winds right?"

"Sure. You're a janitor."

"Superintendent. I heard some people talking in the elevator. I think they were cops, and they were talking about an investigation involving the Union and their funds."

"Really, what did you hear Arnie?"

"It was probably nothing." Arnie couldn't resist playing this out.

"Nah, come on cos, I won't say a word to anyone."

"Well, it's about the company that manages the money. An outfit called Laity and Associates, I think that was the name. Anyway, the gal that runs it is being investigated for embezzling funds."

When Arnie got off the phone, Ben asked, "Are you sure he's going to talk?"

"Believe me, this guy is so loose-lipped, he reminds me of Steven Tyler."

Chapter 44

Burnside sat in the cruiser smoking a cigarette, watching the people come from, and go into Twin Thunder. There was a handful of bikers hanging out in front of the store. He used his Pentax to take a series of photos. The word from the Gang Squad was that if anyone were going to recognize the people in Ben's sketches, it would be the owner of the motorcycle store. According to Mike McShays, they suspected Spider was the linchpin for a whole mess of illegal activity. The problem was that the information was from sources who were not prepared to testify or provide evidence. The squad had a couple of undercover cops but it was still early days, and little had been achieved. McShays had told Burnside to pass on a message to Ben that if they could get some photos of known felons, this might be enough to get the higher ups interested.

Burnside thought back to the talk with Ben on Monday. He'd felt totally blindsided by the older detective. He wasn't much concerned about what an old fart thought, but he was worried about getting labeled as a problem. Willis was a little hard to read and going to him to complain about his partner might not be the way to go. If he could gather some real evidence about these guys, then that would be something to crow about and wave in O'Shea's face.

Burnside felt anxious. He had taken a dozen pictures of the punks going into the store. Based on the look of the scumbags they had to be buying drugs. They seemed uninterested in the bikes and were only in the store for a few minutes before coming back out. *I probably have enough to get a warrant.* He thoughts about O'Shea and how he had become winded so easily just by climbing the stairs to the nigger's apartment. *He's too old to crack a motorcycle gang like Sons of Silence.*

It was this bravado that emboldened Burnside to walk over and open the door to Twin Thunder.

*****

The owner of Twin Thunder recognized Burnside as a cop as soon as he entered the shop. He excused himself from a couple of customers and slipped into the back to make a quick call.

With Burnside waiting impatiently, Spider returned and proceeded to stall. He liked to ignore people that he thought were trouble until they got frustrated and left. After he had finished with his customers, he turned his back on the cop and started applying polish to one of the bikes. He continued slowly polishing and making the chrome shine, when Burnside said, "Excuse me." He made Burnside repeat himself a few times before he turned around and faced the cop.

Burnside was flashing his shield, "Biloxi PD, you the owner?"

Spider went back to polishing.

"I'm talking to you, shit-for-brains." The cop was doing a pretty good Dirty Harry impression. Spider continued to focus on his work, silently chuckling to himself. He wondered if the kid had the balls. "Listen I need your help here, we're looking for these two."

In one sentence the cop had just proved he was a pussy. Without looking at the flyer, "Listen, kid, I already told gramps that I've never seen them. I don't know them, So fuck off." The cop paused for a moment, obviously uncertain. If he were going to try anything, it would be now. Spider stood up towering over the young cop. "Did you hear me kid?"

"I hear different. I hear you're the front man for a whole bunch of assholes."

Spider walked back to the counter and pulled out the largest monkey wrench in the history of tools. Fixing the cop with a glare he slapped the wrench into his palm. "Last chance kid, fuck off. I can't help you." He watched as the cop turned to leave, Spider felt a little disappointed. As the cop was leaving Spider yelled out to him, "And don't go sit in your little sucky ass cop mobile across the street. It's bad for business."

"I'll be back," said Burnside as he walked out the door.

Chapter 45

Arnie and Gabriel sat once again in front of the Laity home, this time from the comfort of Arnie's 1965 Ford Carousel. Arnie had put in zebra striped seat covers and shag carpeting throughout. "Quite the pad you have here," said Gabriel, fiddling with the camera in the back seat.

"I wonder which Terra we'll see tonight?"

"I called her house this afternoon when I knew Terra was at work. A woman answered with a thick Eastern European accent. I asked for Mrs. Laity. She said she was Mrs. Laity. But it was a much older woman. I asked her if she was the woman that owned the investment company and she said no. She said Terra was her daughter-in-law."

"Well, that solves the mystery of the 300-pound woman...Showtime!" Arnie said as they watched the garage door rise again and the navy blue Jaguar back out. Arnie quickly climbed into the front seat ready to follow the car.

"I think that's the same lady I met on Monday," said Gabriel using the binoculars.

"She drives faster than her mother-in-law." Arnie started the Carousel and pulled out after her.

Gabriel, who hadn't gotten a chance to move up front said, "Look at that, she didn't even stop at the stop sign, what the hell are stop signs for?"

"To look around for cops who could pull you over for not stopping," replied Arnie putting his foot down heavily on the gas to catch up.

Terra sped along the coastal highway heading towards downtown Biloxi. "I'm going to have to stick pretty close to her. Otherwise, I'll get caught with the red lights," said Arnie.

"If you can, try to keep at least one car behind her. There's still daylight, and she might have noticed the van when she pulled out of her laneway."

They continued the hot pursuit right into Biloxi before she slowed down and turned onto a side street.

"She doesn't even signal her turns!" commented Gabriel. Arnie slowed the van as he followed down the side street. Halfway down the street, she stopped. "Right in the middle of the street," cried Gabriel. The street was too narrow for Arnie to get by, so he had to wait. Once again without signaling, she started backing up, trying to parallel park into a tiny space. "She needs to go back to driver's school," Gabriel said. They watched her make three attempts before she finally got the Jag parked a good three feet from the curb. They were caught off guard as she quickly got out of her car carrying a shawl and a purse and walked in front of the van. She smiled at Arnie while Gabriel ducked behind the seat.

"Now she's not only seen the van, but she had a good look at you too." Gabriel opened the side door. "ll get out here and follow her, you go find a place to park."

*****

It didn't take long for Gabriel to get to the corner of Beach Boulevard. He peeked around a building and saw Terra about fifty yards down the block. She was wearing a small black cocktail dress and a pair of what Jacqueline like to call 'fuck me' pumps. Terra seemed to be taking her time looking in the shop windows. For a Tuesday night, there were quite a few people in the downtown bars and patios. Gabriel tried to look cool, taking an occasional look around the corner.

Terra stopped about halfway down the block, allowing Arnie time to catch up and join Gabriel. "This is the restaurant district," Arnie said. "She's probably going to have her meeting in a quaint, romantic getaway." Arnie craned his neck to take a look, "That sure ain't the mother-in-law."

Just as Arnie said that, Terra stopped and turned towards them. Moving with an agility The Three Stooges would be proud of, Arnie and Gabriel darted back around the corner. "Did she see us?" whispered Arnie.

"I don't think so," Gabriel said, counting in his head to ten before chancing another peek. Terra had moved down a few feet and was looking in the window of a restaurant named Picasso's.

"What's she doing?" asked Arnie, who was staying behind Gabriel.

"I think she's going into a restaurant." On his next peek, Terra was nowhere in sight.

"Okay, she must have gone into Picasso's. "Do you know that place?"

"It's a little bit beyond my means. I'm just a lowly janitor."

"Superintendent." Gabriel corrected. "Okay, so here's the plan, we need to get in there and hopefully take a picture or two of the guy she's meeting with. Plus I brought the listening device in case we get a chance to use it."

"How do we take a picture without her seeing us?"

"I've done this before at a strip club down near here. The secret is to just put the camera on the table and point it at her table."

"You took pictures at a strip club?"

"Worked great until they...never mind long story."

"What if she recognizes us?"

"We're just a couple of guys enjoying a nice meal."

Chapter 46

Burnside wasn't upset. He thought he had played that perfectly; he'd spent twenty minutes in Twin Thunder and sent a strong message. He had learned enough in police training to know the danger of going into a confrontation without backup. Only a fool would have tried to take Spider down on his own. Besides he probably had enough with the pictures to prove probable cause and get a warrant. *That asshole will get his when I come back with a dozen cops and shut him down.*

Burnside put the car in gear and made a statement by spinning the cruiser's tires as he peeled off towards the police station. *What a big fuckturd. We're going to pounce on that fucker. We'll go in hot, knocking over his fucking bikes and flashing our guns and badges. We'll handcuff all the customers until we check their rap sheets. The drugs are probably right under the fucking counter. It'll be fucking huge!*

As Burnside got out on the main highway, he saw the traffic was bunching up ahead. *People getting off work.* He decided to go lights and sirens, as he often did when he wanted to get somewhere quick. As he pressed down on the accelerator, he felt the cruiser's steering start to shake. *What the fuck?*

What happened next took place in less than thirty seconds, although witnesses later would describe it as if it took five minutes. The front wheels of the cruiser began to wobble. Burnside struggled to maintain control of the vehicle. He took his foot off the accelerator but realized too late what was happening. Slamming his foot on the brakes caused the right front tire and the right rear tires to come off. The car to veered sideways and hit the curb. Because of the high rate of speed, the cruiser flipped. It went over and over again, tossing Burnside violently inside the car as if he was on a tilt-a-whirl. He was powerless and watched in terror as the cruiser crossed the median and smashed into a Standard Oil fuel truck. There was an eerie pause of less than a moment before a massive explosion lit up the night sky.

Two hours later the flames were still burning.

Chapter 47

Thankfully the owners of *Picasso's* kept the restaurant dimly lit. After waiting for a couple of minutes, Gabriel and Arnie were approached by a gentleman with the worst phony French accent Gabriel had ever heard.

The guy gave them the once-over before asking them for their "nemes."

"Our names?" asked Gabriel.

""Fur zee reserfeshuns."

"We didn't call ahead, are you full?" Gabriel asked looking around. The main dining area was down a narrow hallway.

"Do you want smukeeng?"

It took a moment, and then Gabriel was indecisive, not knowing whether Terra was a smoker.

"We'll have smoking please Messieux," replied Arnie. The fake Frenchman led them down the hallway. The dining room was narrow with a series of booths along the side and standard tables on the right. The dark room was illuminated only by the candles burning on the tables. The owner must have been a fan of Picasso as there were bright pastel prints of cubist art adorning the walls throughout the room.

Showing them to a small table at the back by the kitchen. Gabriel looked around, and out of the corner of his eye, spied Terra seated alone at one of the tables closer to the middle of the restaurant. She didn't appear to have noticed them and was busy reading the menu.

"Excuse me Messieux, we would like to sit over there in those booths." said Arnie gesturing to spots closer to where Terra was sitting.

"Yuoo seeed yuoo vunted smukeeng, su I bruooght yuoo tu thees teble "

"I've been trying to quit," said Arnie with a smile handing the man a $5 bill.

Frenchie escorted them to a booth half way down the restaurant. Gabriel chose to sit with his back to Terra as it was more likely that she would remember him from Monday. The waiter followed shortly after with menus and took their drink orders.

"Hold up the menu and shield your face," suggested Gabriel as Arnie was in Terra's direct line of sight.

"Don't think they get a lot of brothers in here," said Arnie looking at the prices.

"We might as well enjoy our meal, it's an expense. What is she doing now?"

Looking up, "She's drinking a glass of wine and looking towards the front of the restaurant."

"Position the camera on the table facing her." The waiter came back with their drinks and Arnie suggested that they might have to leave early so they would like to place their food order.

"Good idea," Gabriel said once the waiter had left. "What is she doing now?"

"Same as before. Gabriel, are you going to ask me that every two minutes? Wait. The maitre d' is escorting a man, no it's a false alarm. He is showing the guy to the table beside where Terra's sitting."

"How does she look Arnie?" Gabriel asked taking a sip of his Coke.

"What do you mean? You want me to describe her?"

"Yeah."

Arnie shook his head, "She's taken off her shawl; her heaving breasts are spilling out of her dress. Is that what you want to hear?"

"Yeah, perfect don't leave anything out."

"Do you want to change places Gabriel? You sound like a perv. She's put her hair up in a ponytail. Her lipstick is kind of a pink color. She has makeup on, but not too much. Her skin is a little darker than average, maybe a nigger in the woodpile?"

"Does the word nigger offend you, Arnie?"

"Not that much. What matters are what's behind the word. When I was growing up, they called us blacks, but then people got upset, so they started calling us colored. I personally thought that was a step backward. I don't feel I'm a colored man. Then people started calling us Negros. The term nigger or Nigras, as my Grammy used to say, only bothers me when I think the person saying it is trying to put me down."

"What is she doing now, Nigger?"

Arnie rolled his eyes, "Just call me Arnie. She's pouring herself another glass of wine. Oh, that reminds me I have some files for you."

"What files?"

"I've been filling in those new client intake sheets. I started telling people about my new job, and sure enough, we have two new cases. Remember I said half my friends think their spouse is cheating on them. All I had to say was that I was working with the famous Gabriel Ross and that you guaranteed results."

"Way to go Arnie."

"Oh, she's looking at me. I think she's trying to figure out where she knows me from. Now she's getting up, shit I think she recognized me from the van." Arnie watched in horror as Terra walked right by their table, continuing on to the back of the restaurant where the ladies room was located.

The waiter brought out their meals, they had both gone for the filet mignon. They ate in silence for a few moments and then Gabriel got up and nonchalantly walked over to Terra's table. Taking a look behind him, he picked up her shawl looking for a way to hide the listening device. He heard Arnie cough and saw that Terra had started walking back to the table. *Shit!* Gabriel made his way back to their booth by walking on the other side of the restaurant. As Terra approached, he stopped and turned his back, looking at one of the Picassos. It was a tearful oriental woman wearing an orange hat. The woman appeared to be frightened to death. Gabriel couldn't help but see Jacqueline in the painting. The only problem was the third eye at the side of the women's head.

Once Terra resumed her spot, Gabriel slid back into the booth.

"That was close. Wait, there is a tall man who just came in. The maitre d' is walking him back to the dining room. Christ, it's the whitest man I've ever seen."

Gabriel couldn't help but take a quick peak. He watched over the top of the booth as Terra stood and gave Morgan Armstrong a kiss on the cheek. "That's Willy Parnell's son-in- law. Maybe it's a business meeting." Gabriel turned back to face Arnie.

Arnie gave him another deadpan look, "If you say so boss, but the body language would suggest otherwise."

"Why, what are they doing?"

"They're talking, and sitting so close their heads are almost touching."

"Maybe they're sharing a business secret. Keep going, now what are they doing?"

"The waiter came back, and it looks like they're ordering dinner. The waiter is leaving...they're lifting their glasses...they're making a toast."

"Maybe they closed a big deal."

"Maybe, but does that explain the kissing?"

"I guess, maybe...

"Still kissing, I couldn't hold my breath for that long."

"What a bastard!" Gabriel said, thinking of Justyne and the kids. "Next time they do that, I want you to take a picture."

"Are you sure, Gabriel? What if someone sees us?"

"Don't worry, no one will know. I've done it before. What are they doing now?"

"They're kissing again." Giving Gabriel a frightened look, Arnie pressed the shutter on the Kodak. Immediately the dark room was ablaze with a flash that would probably go down in history as the second brightest flash of light.

As soon as Gabriel realized what had happened he took the camera off the table and put it beside him in the booth. Arnie was looking at him with horror as the customers in the restaurant turned in their direction. Arnie shrugged his shoulders in response.

"What's Terra doing?" asked Gabriel.

"They're looking over this way, I don't know if they realize that the flash was our camera. They're whispering. The waiter is back with their food. Now they're laughing, maybe the waiter said something."

"Probably making fun of that guy's accent."

"Waiter's gone, they're kissing again. Forget it, I'm not taking another picture. You must have set the flash to automatic. There is a high-speed film you can get that works in this type of lighting. Plus you need to increase your ISO and widen the aperture."

"From now on you can be our camera man," replied Gabriel.

No more than an instant after he said that, a huge explosion rocked the restaurant. They felt their whole table lift a couple of inches. Almost simultaneously there was a blinding flash of light, like sheet-lightning, easily a hundred times brighter than the flash on the camera. The restaurant erupted in activity with some people hiding under their tables while others ran for the rear of the restaurant. The maitre d' ran out into the street, which looked ablaze with light. He came back in the restaurant moments later, "Sumetheeng bloo up doon zee street. It's zee beeggest flocking bunffure-a I'fe-a ifer seee!"

*****

When Gabriel and Arnie made it out to the street, they could see the flames rising in the night a couple of hundred yards away. The street was chaos, full of people who had left their meals half eaten to check out the fire. No one seemed to know what had happened, so Gabriel ran towards the scene. They came up to a young black man hurrying away from the scene.

"Hey, do you know what happened?" asked Gabriel.

"Yeah, a car flipped over an' slammed into a tanker. Thar's cops all on over the' place." He said looking around nervously. "Ah heard one of them say a bunch of people died includin' a cop." I'm so'ry man ah can't hang aroun', got a couple of bullshit drug warrants."

Gabriel ran the distance to where a couple of patrolmen were setting up crime scene tape. Heat from the fire was making the temperature even worse. From where he stood, he could make out what might have been an unmarked police cruiser. Flames were out of control, whoever was driving would have been burned alive.

"Okay everybody move back," said one of the patrolmen. "There might be more explosions." The crowd reluctantly moved back only to creep forward again moments later. As if on script, there was another loud explosion. It was as though a fist of orange flame had decided to punch its way to the heavens. Windows shattered. Smoke and fire engulfed the cars. Thousands of pieces of glass and steel, a deadly rainfall, showered down on people. The sound of alarms, shrill and deafening, could be heard.

Arnie caught up with him to say that in the confusion they had lost track of Terra and Morgan. Gabriel recognized a police sergeant, who Ben had introduced him to during the William Cooper trial. He caught the man's eye, there was a flicker of recognition. "Gabriel Ross, we met earlier in the year at the Cooper trial." When the sergeant nodded in recognition, "Tell me that wasn't Detective O'Shea in that car.?"

"Nah, it might have been his car, though."

Chapter 48

The call from Willis came in shortly after ten. Ben was nodding off, sitting in his easy chair in his Winnie-the-Pooh pajamas.

"Ben, have you been watching the news?"

"No, I don't even own a TV."

"It's Burnside, he went up in flames."

"Burnside...flames.....Chief it's too late for jokes."

"Not a joke Ben, I 'm down at the scene, and it's horrible. I think you need to get down here. From what I've learned so far, earlier this evening, there was an accident. Burnside's cruiser was speeding, lights, and siren, and he must have lost control, flipping the cruiser and smashing into a Standard Oil truck. The whole thing went up in flames. A couple of other cars were totaled as they got caught up in the blast. If you have a south-facing window, you might still be able to see the flames."

Ben stretched the phone cord to the living room, and sure enough, there was a fire raging near downtown Biloxi. "Oh my God," Ben said. For a moment, there was silence on the line as Ben took in the scene. "Shitfuck! Did Burnside get out? Was there anyone else in the cruiser?"

"No, I'm sorry Ben I know you had your issues, but he didn't stand a chance. In total, we think there are six dead. Burnside, the truck driver and then a bunch of people in the other cars."

"Chief, if he was lights and siren, dispatch will know where he was going."

"I checked. Burnside was off duty. No one had seen or heard from him since he left earlier this afternoon."

"Did any of the witnesses see whether he was in pursuit of another car or ...maybe a motorcycle?"

"I don't know that. You thinking that motorcycle gang?"

"It's possible. I met with McShays earlier. He was to get back to me about this gang. Anyway, Burnside caught the callback and told Mike that he would pass on the message, which was basically all about the guy that owns Twin Thunder. McShays said one of his team thought that the guy might be the front man for a gang. Burnside might have been looking to prove himself after our talk this morning."

"That's a stretch, Ben. Burnside was a little odd, maybe he was on meth or something."

"Ah, crap. I was already feeling lousy about giving him the gears this morning," said Ben. "I'll head over and check things out."

"I'll probably be gone by the time you get here. I have some tough calls to make."

*****

By the time Ben arrived at the scene, the fire trucks had finally put out the last of the fire. A whole city block was cordoned off with crowds of spectators watching as cops, ambulance people and firefighters worked the scene. He flashed his badge and caught the eye of Detective Robbins, who waved him through. "Geez, I'm sorry Ben, if it's any consolation it all happened quickly. Burnside didn't stand a chance."

"Any idea about what he was doing down here?"

"No. Willis just left, but he said to tell you that he checked again with dispatch, and there's no related call in or reports." Ben watched as a forensic team examined the police cruiser. He knew one of the guys and walked over.

"Hey Ned, find anything yet?"

"Oh, hi Ben, sorry about your partner. We're just getting into it, but on first blush, I'd say this wasn't an accident. See that tire over on the median? There are two others that came off the cruiser before the crash. Witnesses are saying that the cruiser was coming from Gulfport traveling east and heading into downtown. Estimates are all over the place, but most witnesses are putting his speed to be at least 80 MPH. People figured he was heading to a robbery or something because no one remembers seeing another car. Judging by where we found the tires, the front passenger tire came off first. At his rate of speed, the car would have been almost impossible to control. Shortly after, the back tires came off one after another. I figure Burnside tried to brake which caused the cruiser to flip. He rolled a couple of times before hitting the tanker truck in the westbound lane. The explosion was enough to incinerate both vehicles as well as two others following behind.

"So three tires came off?"

"Saw this once before, someone loosened the lug nuts enough so that the wheels would just fall off. I figure whoever did this, left the front driver's side alone because they thought Burnside might notice."

Ben looked up and saw a couple of TV vans. "Do the press know about this yet?"

"No, Willis told us to take our time and threatened to castrate anyone who blabbed."

"A homicide," Ben said to no one in particular.

"Well, actually, it's six homicides."

Chapter 49

The previous night's accident and horrific explosions were all over the morning radio stations. So far they were describing it as a fatal accident and saying that it was too early to reach a conclusion on the cause. Ben retrieved the morning paper, which had the fiery crash on the front page. Dana Lorimer's column went so far as to list the number of casualties but stopped short of listing the names of the deceased. Ben knew that before the day was done everyone would be talking about Detective Burnside and that the accident was being investigated as a homicide. He also knew that Willis would be canceling all leave and would be insane after having called the family of Detective Burnside. Before heading into the station he called Gabriel.

Gabriel answered right away, saying he was very sorry about Burnside and that he and Arnie had been downtown on surveillance when the explosion happened. "At first, I thought it was you."

"I think it was supposed to be," Ben explained about the message from McShays, how Burnside was driving the cruiser, and how the lug nuts had been loosened.

"Oh my God! Ben, what can we do?"

"I don't know Gabriel, but I better go to work. I suspect it's going to be a long day."

Gabriel told Ben about the surveillance and that they had a photo of Morgan Armstrong making out with Terra. Ben had a one-word response.

"Bastard!"

"What should I do with the picture?"

"Would you mind playing this out a little? I would love to get a listening device on her, I don't know why, but I think she knows what happened to Willy. There is no way I would be able to get a warrant with just that photograph."

Chapter 50

It was mid-morning when Arnie Sims walked into the office of Laity and Associates. Stopping to talk to the young man at the receptionist counter, he announced himself to be from the United Electrical Union, wanting to see Terra Laity.

Arnie had dressed up in his Sunday best and wore a large Afro wig just in case Terra recognized him from the previous night.

"I'm so glad you stopped by Mr. Sims," she said, coming out of an office. "Welcome to my company, won't you come in and sit down?" Terra was wearing a skin-tight red jacket over a cream colored blouse. Her hair was a river of dark curls cascading down on her shoulders. Arnie could see why Gabriel had thought her attractive.

"Have we met somewhere before Arnie?" she asked as he took a chair by her desk.

Arnie shrugged his shoulders, "I don't think so Terra."

Terra made a show of unbuttoning her red jacket and hung it up on the back of her door. "Do you ever attend those award ceremonies? My firm and I have won so many awards," she said pointing out the plaques on the wall behind her desk, "Entrepreneur of the Year, Employer of the Year that type of thing. Maybe we met at one of those functions?"

Slut of the Year? "I don't think so, I'm sure I would have remembered. Working for the Electrical Union, I don't get to attend too many of those. You have a lovely office, Terra."

"Thank you, Arnie," before sitting down, "Can I offer you an espresso?"

"Only if you make it yourself and join me."

"If you don't mind me abandoning you for a few minutes, I will be right back," she said with a twinkle. Terra brushed past Arnie, letting her hand rub gently on his shoulder, "Arnie, I have a special feeling about our relationship."

You can say that again. Once Terra was gone Arnie got up and circled her desk, looking for her purse. He checked in her credenza and then started to open the drawers of her desk. He found it in the right-hand drawer. From the pocket of his sports jacket, he pulled out the listening device and a tube of Krazy Glue. He had seen an ad showing a construction worker holding onto his construction helmet which had been Krazy-glued to a high rise girder. He dabbed a little bit of the glue on the underside of her leather purse and then held the listening device in place, slowly counting to ten.

He had just enough time to move to the window in Terra's office before she came back in carrying two cups of espresso.

*****

Twenty minutes later he rejoined Gabriel, who had been waiting in the VW. "How did it go?"

"Piece of cake. Have you ever heard the expression she could travel to the moon on a skateboard?"

When Gabriel shook his head, Arnie explained, "It's an old expression that people use to describe people who would do just about anything to get what they want. I'm having dinner with her next week at Picasso's."

"I guess we had better solve this case before she figures out who you are."

"Are you picking up a signal?"

"No, nothing but static. It could be the height is putting the unit out of range or maybe there something about the way the building is built." The two detectives continued to play with the receiver hoping for a signal. "Let's go up to the 7th floor and see if there's a spot we can set up shop."

They took the stairs again just on the off chance of Arnie running into Terra in the elevator. When they got to the 7th floor, they found all of the offices were occupied. Gabriel and Arnie opted for the men's washroom. When they turned the receiver on the first thing they heard was Terra's voice.

"Calm down, it's probably nothing." There was a long moment of silence which led Gabriel to conclude that she was on the phone.

"Last time? I said I would take care of that, didn't I?" Gabriel reached into his knapsack for his tape recorder and hooked it up to the receiver.

"Yeah, he was in today. Another fucking nigger. I think we'll get their business. By the time I was done playing with him, his tongue was hanging out, dragging on the floor." Gabriel raised an eyebrow at Arnie.

"A bribe? I don't think it will be necessary Frankie."

There was another long pause before she ended the call with, "Okay Babe, I'll see you around 8. Albert is an idiot. Get this, he invited his fucking mother to come stay with us. On Monday night she tried to give ME advice on how to handle her son in the bedroom. It made me so ill, I locked myself in the bathroom and wouldn't come out. I ended up sending her to my office on an errand. I don't know who the bigger idiot is, Albert or his mother."

She hung up with, "Later Lover."

Chapter 51

After about five minutes the receiver picked up something else. "Morgan, I just got off the phone with the union guy from the ILA. Something strange is going on. He said that the scuttlebutt around the office was that Laity and Associates and in particular me, were being investigated by the FBI."

"Investigated?" Gabriel recognized Morgan Armstrong's voice. Just then Gabriel heard voices coming into the washroom. He quickly grabbed the equipment and went into one of the cubicles. Arnie made like he was washing his hands.

In the cubicle, Gabriel turned the volume on the receiver down. There were two men, and they seemed to be at the urinal. Gabriel took a peak under the door and could see a pair of brown oxfords and beside him a pair of Italian loafers. He heard one of the men say something and then Arnie's voice saying he thought the guy in the cubicle had a radio.

"Morgan someone must be talking to the cops." There's only a handful of people that work here, and you and I are the only ones that know we've been draining the fund."

"I don't know what to say, Terra, you can't honestly think that I would ever do that?"

"Well, then you tell me, Morgan?"

"I don't know. That cop doesn't believe that Willy died by accident."

"Let's look at this logically. **Your** father-in-law gives you his $250,000 and a few months later he starts questioning his statements and asking questions. **You** said he threatened to go to people he knew in the union. I tell you to just give him his money back, but no that's no longer good enough for **your** father-in-law. Then we have to get our hands dirty because of **your** father-in-law. Next, a little detail about his heart. That would have been good to know. Now someone has told the investment board at the union that the Feds are investigating. Seems to me **you're** the common denominator in all of this."

Gabriel heard one of the guys outside the cubicle whisper 'What the fuck?"

"I would never say anything."

"I'm not thinking about you, Morgan. So Daddy didn't blab to the union, just to his daughter. Now she's snitching to the cops. Didn't you tell me that she and that Detective were meeting? You understand what I'm getting at, Morgan?"

Shit, this is good thought Gabriel. He was hoping that the men would hurry up and leave when all of a sudden the receiver started chattering. At first, it was a ruffling sound, then Terra's sultry voice, "We didn't get a chance to finish what we started last night." Gabriel heard the sound of kissing and then moaning. Gabriel saw that the oxfords, the loafers and Arnie's black dress shoes were now standing outside of his stall.

He heard one of the men whisper that the woman's voice sounded familiar.

"That's it, Lover," Terra said. Then the unmistakable sound of a zipper being pulled down. "Need to do some damage control, Morgan."

Then came a medley of noises from wet sucking to moaning and after that a strange humming sound. This went on for some time and after, Terra's voice asking, "Do you like that baby?"

Gabriel heard the loafer say, "Hey, I knew I know that voice. That's Terra Laity, she works on the 8th floor. I'm sure of it. Hey, who's in there? Are you in there Terra? I thought we were an item?" Loafer started banging on the door. "Come out of there you little slut!"

As Gabriel turned off the receiver and prepared to come out, there was a scuffle between Oxford and Loafer. Oxford was pulling Loafer away. "Let it go, Paul, nothing good is going to come of this. You aren't the only person who's been with her."

After a few more minutes Oxford and Loafer left and Gabriel opened the door, Arnie had a hold of the sink shaking with laughter,

"Oh my God!" Gabriel said.

Chapter 52

The atmosphere in the squad room was like a wake when Ben arrived. As he normally did, Ben went to Willis' office. The door was open, but his boss was on the phone. It sounded like Willis was getting an earful from the Mayor.

When he got off the phone, Willis said, "How the hell are you this morning?" Ben nodded, which led his boss to ask, "Have you seen the fucking news? We're a national story."

"The papers are still saying it was an accident."

"That'll change today, some cocksucker out in that squad room is probably blabbing as we speak, laying out the whole thing for a reporter. I can picture tomorrow's headlines, 'Cop investigating racial murder, burns to death...sources say it was fucking murder.'"

"They don't use the word fucking in the media."

Willis didn't crack a smile. "You realize that was your car. That could have been you. What the fuck are we going to do Ben?"

Ben shrugged.

"You think Burnside went out to that motorcycle shop by himself and did something stupid?"

"It's possible, he might have wanted to redeem himself."

"Don't take this the wrong way Ben, but in a way, this is all your fault."

"How do you figure that?"

"It was you that kept digging when the Mayor and everyone else was willing to say it was a misadventure. It was you at the press conference telling people about the sketches in the paper."

"Shit, Chief I already feel crappy about Burnside. Maybe you're right, we should just let these guys take over the city, let them kill whoever they want."

"Don't get sarcastic with me."

"How did the family take the news?"

"They were upset obviously. The real anger came when they told the uncle, Mr. Congressman. He called the Mayor right away demanding a full investigation and alleging that with all the rioting down here, we must all be incompetent."

"Maybe we are incompetent."

"FUCK OFF BEN, what are we going to do?"

"I was staking out Twin Thunder myself on Monday afternoon, and I would give my right nut if this Spider guy, the owner, isn't dealing drugs. Further, I copied down some plate numbers of some of the customer's bikes. I had them run, and at least 3 have warrants and are known felons. I think this is enough for the DA to get a friendly judge to sign off on a warrant. We get the deputies involved because it's in Gulfport, but we hit that place hard and throw a bunch of them in the tank. Hopefully, one has something to say."

"Let me think on that. Give me everything you have, and I'll talk to the DA. Where are you going to be today?"

"I have a couple of things to run down on the Willy Parnell case. Don't ask me how, but I have a photograph showing that Willy's son- in-law was doing the happy dance with his boss."

"Bastard."

Ben left Willis and called Justyne Armstrong to ask if she would be willing to talk. He made an appointment to meet her for coffee.

His next call was to Gabriel at the Agency. As soon as Ben said good morning, his young partner spoke up excitedly, "Ben, you won't believe what we have for you. We have a recording of Terra discussing Willy Parnell's death in a way that more or less implicated her and Morgan Armstrong."

"Really?"

Gabriel filled his partner in on the listening device and how Arnie had planted it under her purse.

"When can I get a copy of that?"

"It gets better, we have her half of a phone conversation with someone named Frankie, talking about a union embezzlement scheme."

"Frankie? Did she actually call him Frankie Fingers?"

"Just Frankie and just her side of the conversation. She's meeting him tonight, so we're going to tail her again. You'll have to listen to it yourself and see what parts you can use. But like you said, it might be enough to get her to talk."

"Fantastic Gabriel, we could use some good news around here." Ben filled him in on the plan to raid Twin Thunder. "I should hear back from Willis this morning. He's pretty desperate to show that he's doing something."

There was a pause for a moment before Ben continued. "I told Willis about the picture of Morgan and Terra, and he's going to want to see it. As for you, I want to keep your involvement secret, so I'll let him believe that I took the picture.

"That's fine. How are you going to explain the tape?"

"I'll have to come up with a really good story. I'm meeting Justyne Armstrong at the Friendship Café in fifteen minutes. I told her to come alone and not to tell her husband. Why don't you join us and bring the tape."

*****

Tweedy gave Ben and Gabriel a big smile when they came in and showed them to their usual booth. Ben told her they just wanted coffee and that a young woman would be joining them.

Once Tweedy left them, "Are you going to tell Justyne about Morgan and Terra?" asked Gabriel.

"I don't know, let's play it out and see how she is."

Just then Tweedy came back with Justyne Armstrong. Justyne had more makeup on than usual, and it looked like she was trying to cover up a bruise on her right cheek. "Hello again," she said as she slid into the booth beside Gabriel. "Why didn't you want me to tell Morgan that we were meeting?"

"Did something happen Justyne, it looks like your face is bruised?" asked Ben.

"It's nothing Detective, I'm so clumsy. I walked right into an open door."

"The girls at the sitter?"

"Yes, now are you going to tell me what this is all about?"

"We are investigating your husband's company. There are some things that don't add up."

She looked shocked and after a moment, "Is Morgan in trouble? Does he need a lawyer?"

"We're still looking into things, but something came up that maybe you could shed some light on."

"Morgan hasn't done anything wrong."

"When's your birthday Justyne? asked Gabriel.

The question caught her off guard. "It's in November. November 25th."

Gabriel shared a look with Ben, who then nodded. Gabriel told her what Musselman had said, and that Morgan didn't deny the argument, but said it was something to do with her birthday.

"So he lied about having an argument with my Dad." She thought about it for a moment, "Wait you guys don't think Morgan did something to my Dad do you?" Her voice showed her stress level was rising.

"When we talked to him, Morgan admitted that your Dad's money was with Laity and Associates. Did you know that?"

"No, Dad said his money was at the bank."

"Where was Morgan last night?" asked Gabriel, looking at Ben.

"He said that he had a meeting with a client. He was home around 11, and he told me that the meeting was cut short because of the big fire."

Gabriel reached over and put his hand on her arm, "Justyne, I know you've been through a lot, but Morgan's lying. I know he is, just like I know you didn't walk into a door. Want to tell us what really happened?"

Gabriel thought she was going to get up and leave, but in the end, he saw a small tear hit her cheek. "He's been so busy at work...."

"That's another lie Justyne. When did he hit you?" asked Ben.

For a while, it looked like Justyne wasn't going to say anything and then, "The night before last we got into an argument. It kind of came on all of a sudden. It was stupid. He told me that you had gone to see him and were asking a lot of questions. I defended you and said that I needed to get closure about what happened to Dad. That's when he called me stupid and hit me. He apologized right away, I don't think he meant to hurt me. I was just happy that the kids weren't there to see it."

Ben looked at Gabriel, who shook his head. He turned back to face Justyne. "I don't at this point suspect Morgan of having done something to your father, but I'm positive that he's been hiding stuff from you, and from us. I expect that things will come to a head very soon, and you may see more stress. Can you find an excuse to get away with the girls, maybe visit a relative?"

"He would be suspicious. He...he'd think I was running away from him."

"Think about it, Justyne. The department would even pay to put you up in a hotel somewhere."

"This has been a lot to throw at me. Let me digest this, and I'll get back to you."

Chapter 53

When Ben walked back into the squad room, Willis was holding court practicing his four letter curse words in front of a combined group of Deputy Sheriffs from Harrison County, the Gang Task Force and a bunch of Biloxi's finest.

When he spotted Ben, "I'm glad you're here. This is Detective Ben O'Shea, he'll be leading the raid." When he noticed the confused look on Ben's face, "We have the warrant to search Twin Thunder for any evidence relating to either narcotics or affiliation with wanted felons. I spoke to the Mayor, and he wants to have the raid in time to hit the next edition of *The Herald*. Ben, you've been inside this place so tell us how you think we should play this."

Ben nodded reluctantly, thinking that things were moving too quickly. He moved to the chalkboard and started drawing a diagram of the property. "From my surveillance, this the rough shape of the building. There is usually a half-dozen customers in the store. The store has a parking lot in front of the premises with about a half dozen Harley's on display. Once you go in the door, there are more bikes, and at the back of the shop, there is a counter and a cash register. This is probably where you will find Spider, who is the big guy that owns the place. Be careful, I suspect he has weapons under the counter. Beyond the counter, there is a curtain leading to a storeroom, and probably a garage. I suggest we go in quiet and secure the front and back doors. We go in, serve Spider with the warrant and keep him from going for a weapon. As for the other people in the store, let's make sure no one leaves until they've been cleared for warrants. The warrant allows us to do a search of the premises for drugs and other evidence that might relate to gang activity as long as it is in plain sight."

Chapter 54

Gabriel went back to the office and was sitting with Arnie going over the new customers that had agreed to hire the Agency. "This is fantastic Arnie, when would you like to get started?"

"I told them that I would start the process, but that there were a couple of cases that we were still finishing up." They were interrupted by the phone ringing. It was a very agitated Ashley Loewen. "Can you slow down and repeat that Mr. Loewen?" asked Gabriel.

"The Congressman has received another letter. Some kid rode right up to the front door, and hand delivered the fucking thing."

"Alright."

"It's a ransom demand," Ashley shouted into the phone. "Whoever it is, they want their money tomorrow night. That doesn't give the Congressman enough time. Plus he has a function scheduled. You were supposed to make this problem go away. What have you accomplished?"

"Settle down Mr. Loewen, I have been working the case, and I was closing in. Yesterday I got a physical description."

"Physical description? Who is it?" Gabriel could feel the panic through the phone lines.

"The lady who you said it was. Dark hair, maybe a little older than Rogers thought, but he obviously ... got the better look." There was silence on the line, and Gabriel quickly asked anticipating another outburst, "Who touched the envelope?

"I did, the Congressman, Charlie, the fuckin' kid and presumably the people responsible."

"What does the note say?"

"I told you they want the money tomorrow night."

"Specifically Ashton."

"It's Ashley."

"Whatever, read it to me."

"It's in the same cut out block letters as the other one. It says,

'Enjoy the pictures, they'll be sent to the newspapers on Friday if you don't follow instructions:

1) Drive 9 m North of Town on 27

2) When you get to the sign for the Salem School District, take the next left. Gravel road into the trees.

3) Large clearing - park car & get out

4) Take the walking path through trees

5) Bring bag with $1,000,000 in small unmarked bills

6) Come alone at 11:30- I will be watching. No police no tricks.

7) 200 ft. from clearing find garbage can with yellow X

8) Put Bag in can, go home.

9) Do as I say and get pictures Friday.

"That's it, Mr. Ross."

Gabriel had Loewen read through the instructions a second time. Not because he needed to, he just wanted to irritate the man. "Quite a detailed list. I'll be by tomorrow to pick up the letter."

"Mr. Rogers can't possibly come up with this much money by tomorrow. It's out of the question."

"I didn't say he should. The ransom demand suggests to me that we're dealing with an amateur. They've probably never done this before."

"What do you mean?"

"It said a million in small bills?"

"Yes, small bills, unmarked."

"Okay Ashford, let say half in tens and half in 20's. That would weigh conservatively 165 pounds, not including the weight of the bag. It would take two strong men to carry the bag 200 feet. Rogers wouldn't even be able to drag it ten feet. This is what I want you to do..."

Chapter 55

Ben gathered his squad down the block from Twin Thunder and went over the instructions again. Each member of the squad had a bullet proof vest, a battle helmet and carried stun grenades and a semi-automatic assault rifle. He assigned two teams to go to the neighbor businesses to warn them to stay inside. Two other teams were dispatched to block the streets. Ben would be giving the go-ahead for the coordinated raid on what Willis was calling "Operation Thunder."

Once everyone was in place, Ben radioed the teams that they were going in. Ben led six officers on foot through the parking lot and gestured to two of the teams to go around to the rear door. Ben and the other 4 officers approached the front. A Japanese couple was outside looking at the Harleys and noticed the cops with their swat team uniforms. When they became animated, Ben gestured for them to be quiet and to move away.

Ben opened the door to the store. Taking a quick look into the store he saw a handful of people looking at bikes. Spider was at the counter selling a saddle bag to a customer. He looked up as soon as the bell over the door signaled a visitor.

"What the fuck is this?" he yelled out, seeing Ben enter followed by the other cops.

"This is a raid, everyone on the ground. Biloxi PD, we have a search warrant."

Spider ignored the command as did his customer. There were grumbles from the remaining customers as they got down to the ground. While one cop watched the door, the other three went to secure the customers. Ben, holding his revolver steady, approached the counter and repeated his command to get down. While he was staring Spider down, the customer made a break for the curtains behind the counter, carrying the saddlebags with him. Ben didn't want to let Spider out of his gunsight, so he radioed that they had a customer running for the back door and hoped the team there

All hell broke loose. First, there was what sounded like a firecracker followed by a scream, then the dakaa-dakka fire of a semi-automatic. Ben watched Spider's eyes as he contemplated going for what Ben later learned was a shotgun under the counter. Ben had his 38 special pointing at the man's forehead, "Please go for it."

*****

When the dust had settled on the raid, one deputy sheriff had taken a bullet to his vest and the guy with the saddle bags was dead. As he fell, he dropped the bags, spilling about 2 grand worth of meth. The remaining customers were eventually released, except for one who had outstanding warrants for dealing narcotics. Spider, with a smug look on his face, was handcuffed and taken downtown. They retrieved Spider's shotgun and the handgun the customer had used to shoot the deputy. After an exhaustive search of the store all they came up with was the meth that had fallen out of the saddle bags.

Chapter 56

Ben sat across from Spider in an interview room...." You're in a lot of trouble Mr. Horvat." Ben looked down at the file they had put together on Ante Horvat. "You were first arrested for burglary at age 16 in 1962. You were sent to live with your Aunt because your parents refused to have you rejoin the home. Aw shucks, that's rough Ante. Little Ante living with Auntie."

"Then you ran away and resurfaced a year later, arrested for assault. This led to 2 years in juvie. Once you got out, you went off the grid until you were arrested again in 1969 for burglary. When you got out in 1973, you joined the Hells Angels Motorcycle Club. During the next 4 years, you were arrested for assault, drug trafficking, and rape. You were busy Ante! The charges were all dismissed for lack of evidence. Beautiful, I bet Mr. and Mrs. Horvat are very proud." Spider just leaned back smiling, his legs shackled to the floor. "We have the meth from the saddle bags."

Spider shrugged, "Not my saddle bags. I don't make it a rule to search each person who comes into my shop."

"We both know you sold him that meth." Spider gave a disinterested look and asked for a cigarette. "Tell me about the cop that was killed last night?"

"You mean in the fire? Saw that on the news. They didn't say it was a pig roast."

"We have confirmation that he was in your shop yesterday." Ben lied.

"That so? Maybe he wanted to buy a bike."

"I know that you're running drugs out of the store. What's more, we have information that you're involved in a huge criminal conspiracy."

Spider gave Ben a bored look, "Listen peeg, did you find any drugs in the shop? No? Then fuck off." When Ben didn't answer. "You didn't find anything cos there's nothing to find. Charge me and let me make a call, or let me go. Either way, I'll be out of here before you can say little Benny peeg fucker."

"We're running your phone records as we speak. Do you think we might find a call or two to those Sons of Silence creeps?"

"The only person I ever call is your mother. How is that little slut?"

"We're also running that shotgun against a couple of unsolved cases. Maybe we'll find a match."

"Maybe you can kiss my ass."

"We're going to hold you as a material witness. This is Mississippi, I can hold you as long as I want. It's a dangerous world out there Ante...it's for your own protection."

When Ben left the interview room, he saw that Willis had been observing from the two-way mirror. "Little Benny pig fucker? That's a new one."

"If we had some leverage, something to charge him with then, I bet he would sing his heart out."

"Yeah? I doubt it. Nice try with the material witness thing, but any judge would throw it."

"Remember that case up in Washington County? They kept the woman for 36 days in jail just because she could identify the suspect."

"The difference was that they had a suspect in custody, we don't."

"Do me a favor let's keep him around for a while, I'll have another go at him."

Chapter 57

Gabriel brought special equipment to the surveillance that evening. When Arnie drove up to their normal spot in front of Terra's home, Gabriel pulled out the receiver for the listening device. All they could pull in was static. "It has a range of 100 yards, but we're well within that. Maybe they're in another part of the house. Gabriel reached into the knapsack again, pulling out the .38 special that Ben had given to him back in February.

"Whoa, what do we have here?" said Arnie taking the black revolver.

"Ben gave it to me. He took me out to the shooting range to show me how to use it. I'm afraid I wasn't very good. I haven't had occasion to use it yet." He started to tell Arnie how to aim the gun and to gently squeeze the trigger, but then looked over at Arnie, who had already spun the chamber and emptied the cartridges by dry firing out the window.

"Wait do you know about guns?"

"Son, I ain't some Yankee from up north. I got my first gun when I was 12. I have about a half dozen guns in my safe at home. My favorite is a Heckler and Koch P11. But my prize possession is a Colt 1851 that my great grandad took off an officer of the Confederacy. If I knew we were going to play with guns, I would have brought one."

They discussed the plan for handling the ransom drop, and Gabriel said, "I'll leave you at the site early so you can watch as I do the drop; I'll be disguised as Rogers."

"Isn't Rogers a tall man?"

"Yeah, I'll think of something."

"Have you ever been 200 hundred feet in a Mississippi forest at night?"

"No."

"You ain't gonna see much. I imagine that the blackmailer will be using a flashlight, but we can't very well do that and expect them not to see us. There's an army surplus store in Gulfport, let me do some shopping," Arnie offered.

They were interrupted by sounds coming out of the receiver. First, they heard a man's voice. "Where you going?"

Then Terra Laity's voice, "The usual, another meeting with an important client."

"Why do you have to dress like that?"

"Oh, Bert, dressing like this is all part of the game. Don't ask me any more stupid questions. Have you thought about my offer?"

"I don't want a divorce."

"You won't have much choice. We don't love each other anymore so why keep this up? You have your business, and I've offered you an attractive settlement."

"I don't want your money," the man's voice was clearly agitated.

"Fine. Why don't you just leave and go find a woman like your mother? You know the one with all those special moves she wanted to teach me." Terra started to laugh hysterically before adding, "You're a fool."

There was the sound of glass breaking and then a door slamming. Then a few minutes later at 7:45 Arnie and Gabriel watched the garage door go up, followed by the Jaguar being backed out into the lane.

They heard music over the receiver. She was listening and singing along to *Le Freak* by *Chic*, "At least she's got good taste in music," said Arnie getting into the front and putting the van in gear.

Arnie raced to keep up with the Jag, "She's in a real hurry tonight." After following her for twenty minutes and almost losing her twice, they saw the Jag's taillights come on as she turned into a driveway in North Gulfport.

"No signal light for the whole trip!" said Gabriel in disgust. Arnie pulled the van to the curb about five houses down from where she turned.

"Pretty nice house, my guess would be that this is the Frankie Finger residence," said Gabriel, climbing into the front with Arnie. They heard the car door slam and watched as Terra walked right up the lane. She had her purse in her left hand and was wearing another dark dress and showing lots of cleavage. They heard a doorbell and then moments later the rough, gravelly voice of a man. They watched as she went into the house.

"Hey baby, you look fantastic!" said the man. There was some ruffling noise and then a series of *ums and ahs*. "Want a drink baby?"

"Come here Frankie, it's been a while."

"Wait! Did you find out what's going on with the cops?" Gabriel raised an eyebrow and looked over to Arnie.

"I talked to Morgan. If anyone is talking to the cops, I would bet it's his wife. I told him I would take care of it."

"We gotta a nice little thing going on here Babe. There's no reason we can't keep this going. We're all making some nice bread with this little scam of yours."

"It was your genius, Frankie. What about the union?

"There's talk about asking for an external audit. I'm going to have to work on a couple of people, see if I can't persuade them to drop it."

"If an auditor was to come in now it wouldn't take long to find out the securities are about $2 million shy."

"Wow," said Arnie to Gabriel, "We have to get this to Ben. We have Terra Laity on tape admitting to defrauding the union. What's more, I would say that Justyne Armstrong might be in danger."

For the next 30 minutes, Arnie and Gabriel continued to listen for any other incriminating evidence. They both grew embarrassed at the sounds coming from the receiver. When finally there was a lull punctuated by loud snoring, Gabriel said, "There goes another branch on the whore tree. I feel sorry for her husband. Have you ever been married, Arnie?"

"Nah. Came close a couple of times. But no, I value my space. How about you?"

"Once up in Detroit, but I went through what I call a Pinto divorce. I got a job working for Ford; things were looking up, and I married my high school sweetheart. Then Ford came out with the Pinto, and that's when everything fell apart."

"What do you mean?"

"Well the Pinto was such a piece of shit, you know "Found on Road Dead," "Fix or Repair Daily,"... getting lots of bad press. The company had made a large investment, and it was going south. I got fired mainly because I refused to drive one. When I broke the news of my firing to my wife, she responded by telling me she wanted a divorce. You see, she had been spending a lot of 'quality' time with the mechanic. The guy that fixed her Pinto."

They had followed Terra back to her house shortly after midnight and decided to call it a night. Once Arnie pulled up the Trade Winds, Gabriel suggested that they head to Tylertown for the ransom drop after lunch to give them enough time to examine the note and brief the Congressman.

When Gabriel unlocked the door to his apartment, he heard the phone ringing. When he picked up the extension all he could hear was the sound of a woman crying.

"Who is this?"

In between sobs, "It's Justyne...I think they're here...I called Ben, but there's no answer...can you come? Please?"

Chapter 58

It had been a long week for the girls. Long week for everyone. When Justyne spoke to Morgan about taking a little vacation with the girls, he surprised her by quickly agreeing, and suggested they leave right away. Added to what the Detective had said about being in danger made her want to get away as soon as possible. The thought of those two creeps figuring out that she was the one that identified them for the sketch artist made Justyne's heart race.

Get a grip girl. The girls hadn't been out to visit her father's sister for a couple of years. Her farm house north of Pascagoula was only a forty minute drive. *Things will be better after a good night sleep. No, don't be a fool. There is something wrong, seriously wrong. Morgan is a good man, a good father who loves us. But what would make a good man yell at his kids just because they wanted his attention? What would make him hit me? All I did was ask a question about my father's death. Could he be having an affair?* The thought had occurred to her a couple of times lately. Too many late night meetings with clients. *What about that vial of white powder I found in his sports jacket when I was looking for change for the paperboy?* She didn't have the courage to ask him about it. To ask if he had been taking drugs.

The traffic east on Highway 90 was heavy, and her eyes constantly checked the rearview mirror, paranoid that they were being followed. A car with tinted windows was following too close. A bald man in a pickup truck driving in the next lane was looking at her. She subconsciously sped up. The girls had been quiet for the first part of the drive but now, maybe sensing Justyne's nerves, were starting to get revved up.

Holding up her Miss Piggy puppet over the front seat, Cicely in her theatrical voice, "My God cab driver, when are we going to get to Aunt Sissy's? Can't you go any faster? My fans await!"

"I'm going as fast as I can Miss Piggy," Justyne replied.

Not to be outdone, Miriam and the Cookie Monster made an appearance speaking in a gruff voice, "We need to stop for Cookie break."

"I'm sure your Great Aunt Sissy will have some fresh baked cookies Mr. Monster." Thankfully they were getting close to the exit off the highway.

Out on the country highway the traffic thinned out, and all that was behind her was a couple of motorcycles. Justyne allowed herself to relax for the first time since they'd left the apartment.

*****

"My Lord look at these children. Miriam, Cicely it is so wonderful to see you," said Aunt Sissy, standing on her porch and giving each of her great-nieces a hug. When she was done making a fuss over the girls, she opened her arms and gave Justyne a big hug. "Welcome child."

Justyne returned the embrace, a tear falling to her cheek. "Oh, Aunt Sissy it is great to see you, it's been a terrible week."

"Don't you cry now darlin' you're safe here." Holding Justyne back with her arms extended. "Oh my! What happened to your face child?" Sissy's tone suddenly became serious.

Justyne looked at the girls.

"I made a whole mess of chess square cookies, they're in the kitchen, why don't you go help yourself?"

The kids scrambled noisily into the house. Once they were gone Aunt Sissy said, "I thought there might have been trouble when you said Whitey wasn't coming with you. Did he hurt you dear?"

Justyne was about to answer when she saw that her Aunt's gaze had shifted to the front of her lane. "Are they your bodyguards?"

Justyne turned and saw the two motorcycles and riders parked at the end of the lane looking up at them. "No, I don't know who they are, but I'm scared."

Aunt Sissy went in the house and came out carrying a shotgun. "I may be 86 or thereabouts, but I'm not too old to put some buckshot into those two." The lane was approximately the length of a football field and the two riders were just sitting on their bikes revving their engines. As if on cue one of the riders removed his dark face shield helmet. Even at that distance, Justyne recognized him as being one of the men in the sketch.

"Oh, my God, Aunt Sissy - we need to call for help. Those are the men that killed Willy!"

She had no sooner said that when her Aunt fired a round of buckshot over their heads. The men continued to stare at the house. "There's a phone in the house, call the sheriff. Go on girl."

Justyne ran into the house, looking for the phone. She finally found a black rotary dial phone in the front room and tried dialing "0" for the operator, but got nothing. She remembered the business card that Gabriel Ross had given her and fished it out of the pocket of her jeans. It was late, so she dialed the home number. It rang 3 times before Gabriel came on the line. In between tears, Justyne blurted out what was happening and gave him the address.

She told him to come fast but then realized that the line had gone dead.

Justyne heard another gunshot out on the porch and ran outside, followed by the girls. "Get inside girls." yelled the old lady. The girls started crying as they watched their great aunt reloading.

"What happened? The phone went dead."

"One of those crackers was climbing up that phone pole, so I took a shot at him. I guess the old eyesight is not as good as it used to be."

"I couldn't get through to the Sheriff, but I called a detective in Biloxi."

Sissy was staring at the men, clearly contemplating taking another shot. "It's gonna be dark soon, that's when they'll come. You need to get those girls to safety."

"I'm not leaving you here," Justyne said with determination.

"Nuthin' gonna happen to me, just don't want you to see me blasting holes in those honkies who killed my little brother. Go on go out the back door and hide in the loft of the barn. Cover the girls with straw and tell them to not make a sound."

Taking a final look at the two men at the end of the lane, Justyne ran back into the house to get the girls.

*****

Gabriel drove the VW as fast as he could. He wished he had some way of contacting the Jackson County Sheriff. It was getting dark, and he worried that he would arrive too late. He reached over to his knapsack on the passenger seat, pulling out his handgun.

*****

Justyne gathered the girls and practically dragged them to the barn. They climbed up the wooden ladder to the loft. "Girls I want you to do something for me. I going to cover you both up with hay, and then you have to be very, very quiet."

"Mommy I'm scared," said Cicely.

"I know you are, so am I. Now keep really, really quiet. They heard another shotgun blast coming from the house, followed by another shot that sounded like it came from a smaller gun. Once Justyne had covered the girls she hid behind two hay stacks. At the last minute, she grabbed for something to use as a weapon. There was no sound coming from the direction of the house.

Justyne was saying a silent prayer for her Aunt when she heard, "Hey nigger lady, you hoo nigger lady." The sound was coming from the house. "Come out come out wherever you are." The man calling to them had an accent. "I hear you like white men, nigger lady. Come out, I have something for you."

Her mind was racing, *there was only one voice, does that mean that Sissy shot the other.one? Did they follow me out here or had Morgan already told them where we were going?*

"Hey nigger lady, nigger lady come out, come out. If you come out, maybe I won't hurt your girls".

She tried to summon her courage, the voice was getting closer. *He's probably figured out that we are hiding in the barn. Should I wait here for him to find us? I can either hide here or maybe I should make a run for it and lead them away from the girls.*

*****

Branko was pissed. The old lady had lain in wait, sitting in the dark in a rocking chair with a blanket covering her.

"Hold it right there," she'd said. "What do you boys want?"

Juraj was angry at being shot at and had continued to approach the porch. He climbed the steps and was a foot or two away from the old lady when her shotgun blast blew a hole in his chest, knocking him right off the porch. Branko didn't waste time pulling out his gun and putting one in the old lady's forehead.

Branko bent over his brother and knew he wasn't going to make it. He reached into Juraj's pocket and took his identification. After a quick search of the house, he figured that the woman had run to the barn with her two brats. As he made his way to the barn, he called out to her.

*****

Gabriel got to the address and turned down the lane. The darkness of the house gave him a bad feeling. He parked in front of the house, the headlights picking up a body on the ground. He got out of the car holding his gun in front of him. The stiff on the ground was one of the guys in the sketches. He had a hole the size of a tomato soup can in the middle of his chest. Gabriel climbed the stairs to the porch and saw an old lady in a rocket with a bullet hole in her forehead. "Shit, this can't be good."

*****

Branko was almost to the barn when he heard the car and saw the headlights coming up the lane. The car sounded loud ...

maybe more than one. He left his bike down by the road, so he decided to go through the cornfields.

***** *

It was a small farmhouse, so it didn't take Gabriel very long to clear. He went out the back door and saw the barn. He snuck across to it, trying to figure out what might have transpired. His guess was that the old lady had shot one of the brothers before the other got her. Justyne's car was parked in front. Did the other brother have Justyne and the girls?

***** *

Justyne heard someone enter the barn. It was pitch black. She could hear someone else's breathing. She was worried her heart was going to leap out of her chest. She had her weapon, and if she sensed the man starting to climb the ladder to the loft, she was going to drive the pitchfork through his scumbag heart. *The breathing is getting closer. It won't be long now.* She tried to psych herself up. *Fucker beat my father to death, fucker probably killed my aunt, fucker wants to kill my girls.* Getting close now.

"Justyne are you in here?"

"Gabriel is that you?"

"Yeah where are you?"

She ran to his voice and then hugged him. "Thank God you called out, I was going to skewer you like a shish kabob. Wait, where are the bad guys?"

"One's at the house. I think your aunt put a hole in his chest."

"My Aunt Sissy?"

"I'm sorry Justyne, the other one must have killed her." They heard the sound of a motorcycle starting up and heading south. "That's probably him."

"Cicely, Miriam, you can come out the cavalry is here to rescue us."

Chapter 59

Gabriel drove Justyne and the kids over to a neighboring farm and asked them to call the sheriff. Before they knew it, Aunt Sissy's farm was lit up with cruisers and ambulances. It was well into the early hours of the morning before he brought Justyne and the girls into the Good Night Motel in Ocean Springs. He was familiar with the motel, having hidden out there with Jacqueline when she was being pursued by her husband.

It was after 8 a.m. by the time Gabriel arrived at his apartment and opened the door to a ringing phone.

It was Ben. "I got a call from the Jackson County Sheriff, you must have given him my name. Sounds like you had a rough night."

"You can say that. I stashed Justyne and the kids at the Good Night and just got home. The good news is you only have one bad guy to worry about now."

"Yeah, the Sheriff said he had no ID on him, so we aren't any further ahead in finding the other guy. The Sheriff is running the serial numbers of the Harley that was found in a ditch. Maybe something will come from it."

They discussed what happened for a while before Ben suggested, "Listen, grab some shut-eye, but not too much, there's something I want you to do."

Thankfully Gabriel was able to sleep a couple of hours before the ringing phone woke him up. "Sorry to wake you Sleeping Beauty," Ben said. "But I thought I had better call you. Things are happening that you should know about."

"Right...uh Tylertown, the blackmail thing. It's all coming back to me."

"Have a quick shower and then go to the corner and get a coffee and today's Herald, then call me back."

*****

There was a paper box at the corner, and Gabriel threw on some jeans and a t-shirt and headed out. When he got outside, he saw that the morning was already colored by a red sky. He hadn't heard the forecast but was always told that red sky in the morning meant a sailor's warning. He got to the paper box and could see through the glass that their main story was about Tuesday night's crash and fire. Inserting a couple of coins, he grabbed a paper and sat down on a bench to read.

Below a color photo of Burnside's cruiser going up in flames was Dana Lorimer' story.

Cop Killer on the Loose

Dana Lorimer

Police today raided a local Gulfport business based on the belief that the proprietor, a former Hells Angel, was implicated in Tuesday night's crash that killed 6 people including Detective Oliver Burnside. Gulfport Medical Examiner James Tifton issued a ruling early Wednesday afternoon that Detective Burnside's car had been tampered with, causing the Detective to lose control and hit a tanker truck. Detective Burnside was part of a team investigating the unfortunate death of local resident Willy Parnell a week ago at Hillier Park. Asked if there was a connection between Parnell's death, which was ruled an accident, and what happened to Detective Burnside, Chief of Police Willis said that nothing was being ruled out. Asked about the outcome of the raid, Willis stated that investigators were still looking at the evidence, and an unspecified amount of crystal methamphetamine had been recovered. Michael Grainger of Pass Christian was shot during the raid after he fired on one of the Harrison County Deputies in an attempt to flee.

When this reporter asked about the connection between the individuals whose sketches were first reported in Wednesday's edition, Chief Willis said that there was evidence linking the hunt for the two men and the motorcycle store run by the former Hells Angel.

The reporter had included a reprint of the sketches asking readers to call the tip line set by the Biloxi PD. There were numerous follow-up stories and pictures throughout the paper including a feature on the growing problem with motorcycle gangs along the Gulf Coast.

Running back to the apartment Gabriel called Ben. "I read it. Is there more than what's in the paper?"

"Just that we are holding Ante Horvat, better known as Spider, as a material witness; and he's a real asshole. Willis told me that if we can't come up with something to charge him with, then we have to kick him loose."

"What about the drugs?"

"The guy that got killed had the drugs in a saddle bag when he got shot. I suspect he bought the stuff minutes before we arrived but since we couldn't find anything else the DA doesn't think we have enough."

"I have some stuff to bring you up to date on. I'm not sure where this all fits, but some of it I think might be related to Willy Parnell or this Spider guy." Gabriel told Ben about last night's surveillance at Frankie's house and that they had Terra Laity on tape admitting to a $2 million dollar embezzlement and also suggesting that she might be involved in what had happened to Willy Parnell.

"Wow. And last night these scumbags went after Justyne. I listened to the tape you gave me yesterday; Willis is playing it for the DA this morning. I know it isn't admissible, but it sure gives us some ammunition. With what you got last night and the connection to Frankie Fingers, I know we have enough to at least bring Terra in for questioning."

"Did Willis ask you how you managed to get the tape?"

"I told him he didn't want to know and for now, he's smart enough not to ask any more questions. Can I swing by and get that tape?"

"Sure, why don't I meet you at the agency at 11:30? There is something else we should discuss."

Chapter 60

It was just past 11:30 when Arnie, Ben, and Gabriel started listening to the tape. "This is going to break this case wide open," said Ben. "We should be able to get a court order to tap her phones. She's cheating on her husband with Morgan and cheating on Morgan with Frankie." He shook his head.

"Don't forget about the reaction from Mr. Oxford and Mr. Loafer outside the stall."

"Oh, my God, I feel bad for the husband. Do you think he has any clue?"

"He must," said Arnie. It's probably one of those 'I know that you know that I know what you're doing'....but it's easier to deny it to yourself rather than get in a big fight."

Ben just shook his head again. "Gabriel you said on the phone that you had something else to tell me."

Gabriel pulled out the picture from the *Herald* of Burnside's burned-out car with the tires in the foreground. He then dug out the picture of Esther Rogers' fatal car accident. Once again the tires were in the foreground. "This second picture is of

Congressman Rogers' wife who died in a car crash back in June. Notice anything?"

Ben and Arnie huddled over the two pictures. It only took Ben a few moments to see it. "Someone tampered with her car!"

"Looks that way to me, just loosen the lug nuts and watch the car crash. It's not infallible, but it's pretty suspicious. We'll call them the Lug Nut Killers."

"The congressman?" asked Arnie.

"Are you thinking that Congressman Rogers arranged the accident, maybe with the same people that killed Burnside?" Ben finished Arnie's thought.

"Let's not get ahead of ourselves. There's also the aide Ashley. He gives me the creeps. Arnie, maybe when we go up there this afternoon you can give me your assessment."

"You're going up there?" asked Ben.

Gabriel told him about the ransom note and the plan for the evening.

"I'd like to go with you. I know you have Arnie, but just to be your back up."

"I appreciate the offer, but for now, I want to stick to the agreement I signed. We should be able to handle it."

"Speaking of that," said Arnie, "I went shopping this morning at that Army Surplus store I was telling you about." Arnie reached into a paper bag and extracted two pairs of night vision goggles. "These are leftovers from the Vietnam War. They're called PNV Tanker Goggles. They use ambient light to magnify what can be seen in moonlight approximately 1000 times. I checked, and there'll be a half moon tonight. They've come out with newer models that are much better, but we would have to order them. If we're lucky, these will allow us to see the blackmailer, maybe not clearly but at least recognize their shape."

"That's great Arnie," said Gabriel, examining the goggles.

"The only concern I have Gabriel, is how a 5 foot nothing guy is going to pull off looking like a much taller Congressman Rogers?" Arnie asked.

"Piece of cake," Gabriel said. "I did some shopping myself." Reaching down to a bag he had tucked under the desk, Gabriel brought out a pair of 6-inch men's platform shoes that were painted with the American stars and stripes. "What do you think of these?"

Both Arnie and Ben started laughing. "Where the hell did you get those?" asked Arnie. "They're just about the ugliest thing I have ever seen."

"At a shoe store down the street, they were left over from Independence Day."

"Actually I kind of like them. Maybe I could wear them to a staff meeting one day...add a touch of character," said Ben. Gabriel and Arnie took a look at him wearing his checkered seersucker pants with a lime green blazer and burst out laughing.

Chapter 61

Laity's Welding and Supply Company was located in the industrial part of Gulfport. Ben took in the building from the front seat of his new cruiser and planned his approach. The building looked like a remodeled service center with abandoned cars and parts scattered around. A large service bay was open, and Ben could see someone working at a table. As Ben got out of the car and approached, he noticed that the man was almost as wide as he was tall. He had a dark faceplate and sparks were flying as he worked on what looked like a crankshaft.

It took a couple of minutes, but the man finally sensed Ben's presence. He turned off his torch and raised his face plate. Ben saw a balding man with a friendly smile looking back at him.

"Good morning. I was looking for Mr. Laity, my name is Ben O'Shea from Biloxi PD."

"It's Alberto," said the man, extending his hand.

"Are you the owner Alberto?"

"Yes, all that you see belongs to me.... and the bank." There was an informality about the man that Ben liked.

"Alberto is an Italian name isn't it?"

"Yeah, my mother is a Fanucci she married my dad, he's the Laity."

"It looks like you're pretty busy Alberto, so I'll get right to the point. It's about your wife, Terra."

Alberto rolled his eyes as if to say, 'What now?' "Yeah, what did she do?"

"Her name came up in an investigation, and I thought I could get a bit of background from you."

Alberto's response was to pick up a hammer and start banging loudly on the work bench. After a few hits, "My mother she says she's a slut. Terra wants a divorce, says she doesn't love me. I don't know if she ever did."

"Do you know anything about her company, Laity and Associates?"

"Not much, she tried to explain it to me. I said 'so you're a broker' and no, 'she's an Investment Counselor'." Alberto used air quotes. "I keep calling her a broker just to piss her off."

"Any idea who the Associates are?"

"No, and I don't want to know. Probably these people she meets with at night."

"How did you two meet, Alberto?"

"In a bar." He grinned, and they both started laughing. "That's where you meet girls like Terra. She played the innocent farm girl while I paid for her courses. But I think I knew deep down that she was not what she made herself out to be."

"And what is she, Alberto?"

"She's the kind of woman that wants everything. If you have something that she wants, watch out. She'll do whatever she has to do."

"So she grew up on a farm?"

"Yeah, she talked about it once. She's from a place called Lula up north in the state. Farming country. You know her name maiden name is Dactel. She has nothing to do with her family. I tried calling up there once, her father's name is Redak. I guess I was wondering who would call their kid Terra Dactel. I left a message, but they never called me back."

"Listen, Alberto, I wonder if we could help each other..."

Chapter 62

Ben found a telephone number for a Redak Dactel on Route 6, Lula Mississippi and gave the number a try. The call was answered by what sounded like an old man with a heavy accent. "Hello, my name is Detective Ben O'Shea from the Biloxi Police Department. I'm calling to speak to the parents of Terra Dactel."

"Yes, what is it about?"

"Are you her father?"

"Yes, my name is Redak, but our daughter is gone she live away."

"Mr. Dactel, your daughter lives in Gulfport Mississippi."

"Oh...if you know where she is, why are you calling?"

"Her name came up during an investigation we were doing, and I thought I would call and get some background information."

"She left home and stole from us. We have not heard from her for five years. No card, no letter, nothing. We got a call two, maybe four years ago. A man left a message to say that he was marrying Terra and wanted to talk. We never called him back."

"I'm sorry to hear that Mr. Dactel."

After a moment of silence, "Is she in trouble?"

"Maybe, what was she like growing up?"

"Just a minute," Ben could hear mumbling in a foreign language and then a woman pick up the phone and spoke, "Our daughter is estranged from her family. She stole from us and ran away. She has not gotten in touch with us, it's been almost 5 years."

"Am I speaking to Mrs. Dactel?

"Yes. What else do you want to know?

"What kind of a child was Terra?"

There was a long sigh and then a pause before Mrs. Dactel spoke again. "She was a troubled girl. She was pretty, but never pretty enough. She entered the beauty contest at the high school and won. People say that another girl should have won, but she had an accident. Her father always said Terra was lazy because she didn't want to help on the farm. I don't think she was lazy, she just didn't want the life that we had. We are simple farmers, she wanted more." There was more background talk and then she said, "My husband said she is ambiciozan, you would say ambitious, but not in a good way."

"Do you think she would ever hurt anyone?"

Again there was another pause on the line before she said, "The incident. Things were hushed up, but this other girl was raped a week before the contest. They arrested the boy, he claimed he did it for Terra." After a moment she added, "She was a very bad influence on her brother."

"Her brother? How many children do you have?"

"We have none. When Terra left, she convinced Marko to leave a couple of months later. The difference was that we had no more money for him to steal."

Chapter 63

It was close to 4 p.m. when Gabriel pulled the VW into Congressman Rogers' circular drive. The sky had clouded over, and the weatherman had promised a downpour starting later that evening.

"So this is how rich folk live." Arnie looked up at the antebellum mansion.

"Let's leave our gear in the car for now and go in and meet the man." Once again Charlie bounded down the steps ready to open their door. "Hello Charlie, watch this!" Gabriel made a show of turning off the ignition. "No engine rattle! And look at this," he said getting out of the car, "No creaking noise. You're a master. Thank you."

"No problem suh, glad I could help." Arnie got out from the passenger side. "Charlie, let me introduce you to my colleague Arnie Sims. Arnie, this is Charlie, the Congressman's chief caretaker and jack of all trades."

Arnie walked over to the man and shook his hand, "Nice to meet you, Charlie. I work as a superintendent and jack of all trades at the Trades Winds Apartments in Biloxi so I can relate. I'm now working part-time helping Gabriel."

"Well that's mighty fine Arnie, I'm honored to make your acquaintance." Turning to Gabriel, "I believe the Congressman and Mr. Loewen are quite anxious to see you about something. They've asked me to rush you all into the house straight away."

"After you then." As the three men walked up the long stairs leading to the door, Gabriel continued to sing Charlie's praises to Arnie, "The car used to rattle on for a good minute after I turned it off."

"Why thank you suh, does Mr. Loewen know that you are bringing Mr. Sims?"

"No, it's a surprise, but don't worry, he'll get over it."

Charlie chuckled as he escorted the detectives into the front hall.

"Impressive," said Arnie, looking around as Charlie knocked on the Congressman's open door. "Mr. Congressman, Mr. Gabriel Ross, and his associate Mr. Arnie Sims."

Loewen was seated with his back to the door. "It's about time.....," he said, stopping when he turned and saw Arnie. There was a moment of indecision as both Rogers and Loewen looked from Arnie then to Gabriel for an explanation.

"As discussed gentleman, I will be doing the drop tonight, and I intend to apprehend the blackmailer. Since we are probably only going to get one chance at this, I have brought a senior associate of my Detective Agency, who will ensure that the suspect doesn't get away."

This seemed to calm Rogers. Loewen, however, continued to stare at Arnie with his mouth open.

"Can I see this latest letter?" Gabriel's question seemed to break Loewen's spell.

Rogers circled his desk and extended a hand to Arnie. "Welcome to the case Mr. Sims, I presume your boss has appraised you of the need for confidentiality?"

"Yes sir, I have signed a declaration to that effect."

Loewen walked over to a side table and picked up a letter, handing it to Gabriel. After reading through it, Gabriel handed it to Arnie. "It indicates that photos were enclosed. Can I see them?"

"The blackmailer must have neglected to include the pictures. The envelope just had this ransom note."

Bullshit. Gabriel decided to take Loewen's chair and gestured for Arnie to sit down. "So really? You're saying, Ash, that the blackmailer just happened to forget the pictures, the very thing he is blackmailing the Congressman about?"

"Yes," repeated Ashley.

"Well, how do you know there are pictures then?" asked Gabriel incredulously.

"Because we saw the first one, the one Congressman Rogers burned in the fireplace."

Gabriel shot Arnie a look and then noticed Rogers looking down at his shoes. *This guy looks at his feet every time Powder Puff tells a lie. Better than a lie detector.*

"I understand you told Ashley here that you wanted a duffel bag, and that we were to fill it up with monopoly money?" asked Rogers.

"Yes, the blackmailer didn't specify US dollars. He just wanted small bills totaling a million. Besides, the way this government is managing our finances it will probably be worth....," Gabriel stopped suddenly, remembering he was talking to a sitting US Congressman.

"Fine, I couldn't have raised anywhere near that amount. Esther's accounts are still frozen in probate. I did put together the $5000 you requested. What's that for?"

"To sprinkle on top in case, he looks in the bag. Can I see the bag?"

Ashley got up and opened a closet, dragging out a US Marine canvas duffel bag stuffed with pink, blue and yellow funny money.

Reaching into his pocket for the tracking device, Gabriel turned it on and slid it into the canvas bag. "Now let's go through this. The blackmailer is expecting you to do the drop, so I'll need to drive your Mercedes. I'll leave the keys to my bug in case you need to go out." Gabriel said with a smile. "I'll drive Arnie to the drop point roughly an hour before the appointed time. He is equipped with night vision goggles and will set up in a location where he can observe. I'll follow along at the appointed hour and will bring the duffel bag as instructed. After putting the bag in the garbage can, I will leave in the Mercedes."

"I think I should go," said Loewen. "To protect the Congressman's interests."

"Ashley old boy, we've already been over this. I will be doing the drop and Arnie will be my back-up. Besides, the duffel bag would be too heavy for you. Now let me continue. After leaving in the Mercedes, I will drive down the highway just in case I'm being watched. I will be in touch with Arnie this whole time by radio. After about ten minutes, I will hike back to the drop point and hook up with Arnie using the night vision goggles. Once we follow the blackmailer to a location, we intend to subdue the individual and secure the photos and negatives.

"What are you going to do with the blackmailer?" asked Loewen.

"Tell them they were naughty, and that I'm going to have to tell their Mommy."

Ashley was growing exasperated with Gabriel. "Can you be serious here? How will you know that they don't have other copies or accomplices?"

"Because I'm going to ask them nicely. Remember it was your condition that the police not be involved. I can't very well call the cops now."

"Mr. Ross, you are barely 5 feet tall while I'm over 6 feet. Do you really think the blackmailer is going to be fooled?"

"I can act taller. Plus don't forget it'll be dark. He might have a flashlight, but my guess is that he won't want to give away his position....and I have a secret weapon." Gabriel said flashing a smile at Arnie.

"What is that? asked Ashley.

"Well, Ashburn old pal that's why it's secret."

Chapter 64

At around 10:30 that night, Gabriel turned off Highway 27 and drove the Mercedes onto a narrow dirt road bordered by loblolly pine trees. After a couple of minutes, he came to a deserted clearing. There were no signs, but through his headlights, he could see a trail approximately five feet wide that led into the wooded area. "What's this place, Arnie?"

"Don't know if it has a name. My guess is that people use the trails for hiking. It's probably also used by deer hunters; lots of whitetails around these parts." Gabriel turned off the headlights, plunging them in total darkness. "I can't see a thing."

"Once your eyes adjust, you'll be able to see shapes in the moonlight."

"We have a little bit of time. We should check the equipment." Gabriel had brought his knapsack while Arnie carried a red nylon shoulder bag. Gabriel reached into the bag pulling out a pair of Motorola push-to-talk walkie-talkies. "Let's check these out." They set the units to the same channel, "Come in black dog, big pussy here do you read me? Over."

Arnie rolled his eyes, "Black dog? I ain't no black dog."

"You're supposed to say over."

"Alright Gabriel, they work. Let's try out the night vision goggles." Arnie pulled out the bulky goggles and showed Gabriel how to put them on.

Once Gabriel turned on the goggles, his vision was bathed in a weird green haze. He could make out the trees and the path. "Cool."

"The one major drawback to these is they are kind of heavy and if someone shines a bright light on you....well you might go blind."

As Gabriel put on his platform shoes, Arnie started to laugh. "Good thing it's dark out there. If I saw you coming towards me wearing those shoes, I would either die laughing, or I'd be scared to death."

Next Gabriel then pulled out his 38 special and checked the ammo. It was Arnie's turn for show and tell and he pulled a Heckler and Koch P11 out of his bag. "All loaded and ready for trouble. I also brought this." He held out a Civil War Colt 1851.

Taking the old gun in his hand, Gabriel was surprised at how heavy it was. "Does this even work?"

"Absolutely I keep it oiled and cleaned. It's as good as new."

"So you should get out now and set up your observation area."

'One final thing," Arnie said as he got out. "When you come back try to stick to the path; if you see a branch on the ground, and it moves, best you don't pick it up, lots of cottonmouths around here." Arnie put the night vision goggles on and slipped out into the night.

After a couple of minutes, Gabriel started up the car and drove back to Highway 27 to wait for the drop time.

Chapter 65

Terra looked at her husband with disgust. *You'd think the beast would shower to get the grime and stink off of him after work. And he wonders why I don't want to have sex with him. Since I married Bert, he's put on over 100 pounds and lost most of his hair. The man has no self-control.*

She allowed her thoughts to drift to last night and Frankie. She could almost smell his cologne, feel his caress, feel his power. The situation with the FBI was troubling. She hadn't heard what had happened last night with Morgan's wife. *I bet she already told that fat cop about her father's suspicions.*

The phone rang. Terra reached back and picked up the receiver off the wall. It was a man she didn't recognize, asking to speak to Alberto Laity. *Who could this be? No one ever phones for him.*

"Is there any more pasta?" Alberto asked, showing no interest in who was on the phone.

"No just what's in the bowl," *You fat pig.* "There is a man on the phone for you. I'm going to have a cigarette." She knew Bert disapproved of her smoking as much as she disapproved of just about everything about him.

Terra went into the front hall where she had left her purse and took out a pack of Virginia Slims. She lit one up and took a long drag, letting the smoke fill her lungs. *I wonder who that was. Maybe someone from the shop? Did Redak finally get a lawyer?* She threw the pack back into her purse, which caused it to tip over off the table, turning upside down on the floor. She was about to go back to the kitchen and eavesdrop on Alberto's conversation when she noticed something stuck to the bottom of her purse. *What the fuck is this*? There was something glued to the bottom. It was small, the size of a nickel with a wire extending about three inches. She tried to rip the thing from her purse, but it wouldn't come off. She held the purse under a lamp and looked at the object. Suddenly she realized what it was. *The fucker's been listening. Well fine, I hope he enjoyed listening to Frank fuck me. Wait a minute, how long has this been on here? Did I say anything that might come back to haunt me? Would Bert give this to that cop?* Terra swayed in the sudden grip of anger. She went back into the kitchen and saw Alberto was off the phone and back to his food. She stood over him, "Here you want more to eat? Eat this, you disgusting pig!" She threw her purse at him.

Alberto looked up at her and said "What? Why did you do that?"

"You're disgusting. Only a pig would let himself go and wallow in the mud, and then be surprised when his wife sees other men." She screamed at him.

Alberto got up from the table and said, "I heard Terra, I know what you have been doing. Mama is right, you're nothing but a whore."

She could see his eyes harden with hate, something that she hadn't seen before. She saw this, moments before seeing his big fist smash into her face.

Chapter 66

Gabriel returned to the clearing a little bit before 11:30 and parked the Mercedes near the path. He pressed the talk button on the walkie-talkie, "Black Dog come in. Come in Black Dog, over."

"Shush," came the reply, "there's something out here. I can't see them, but I hear something."

""Ten-four, starting to rain. I'm leaving with the duffel bag now, over."

Gabriel turned off the ignition and shouldered his knapsack as he got out. He opened the rear door and pulled the duffel bag towards him, deciding to forego the goggles just in case someone was watching. He tried to carry the duffel bag but ended up dragging it into the woods. The rain was starting to fall in heavy drops the size of pomegranates. Gabriel strained to drag the bag down the path. *If there was someone out here watching, they might not be able to see me, but I'm sure they could hear me.* He had gone 20 feet when it got appreciably darker. He could barely make out the path. The trees were blocking out the moonlight. His pace slowed. The platform shoes didn't help, and he almost lost his balance. Gabriel stopped to catch his breath, and he thought he heard something off to the right. In the moonlight, the trees all looked like bears. Arnie didn't say anything about them, but he knew that there were black bears in Mississippi. He tried to pick up the pace. It took another ten minutes to travel the remaining distance to the trash can. He could have easily missed it, but someone had placed the can directly in the middle of the path. He heard more rustling, a twig snapping. Something was definitely out there watching. Gabriel summoned all his strength to lift the duffel bag up, making 4 attempts before he could raise it high enough to put it in the bin.

Breathing heavily, Gabriel headed back the way he'd come. The trip back was faster, mainly because he wasn't dragging the duffel bag, and partly because he kept imagining a bear jumping out every minute. When he got back to the clearing, he wasted no time in getting into the Mercedes and heading back to the highway.

Chapter 67

Terra lay on the kitchen floor in shock. Her nose hurt, and she felt blood drip on her cheek. Her husband was standing with his back to her looking out the kitchen window at his precious fuckin' garden. She thought back to when he'd first told her he wanted to grow their own vegetables. *He actually wanted me to look after it....get down in the mud to plant the seeds he had bought. I had enough of that growing up.* To Terra, vegetables came in a bag and were frozen.

Look at him he's not even checking to see if I'm alright. While his back was still turned, Terra struggled to get up. She staggered to the counter and selected the biggest fucking knife in the block. She moved quickly, raising her arm and lunging. At the last minute, he must have sensed the movement, and he turned towards her. She screamed like a banshee at him and pulled the knife down towards him, preparing to drive the knife into his black heart.

That's when he punched her again.

Chapter 68

Ben had just finished a *Swanson's Hungry Man* dinner when the phone rang. It was Willis. "Ben, do you know someone by the name of Alberto Laity?

"Yeah, that's Terra Laity's husband. Why what's up?"

"I just got a report that an Alberto Laity phoned 911. Patrols have been dispatched to a domestic disturbance. This Laity guy said his wife tried to kill him. Apparently, his wife found a listening device on the bottom of her purse and went berserk trying to kill him with a butcher knife."

"My God! Is anyone hurt?"

Willis knew his detective well enough to pick up something in his reaction. "Ben, is there something I need to know here?"

"No."

"Well, he's saying it was self-defence. She might need a surgeon to fix her broken nose. He's currently sitting on her. Ben, I was thinking about how you might have acquired that recording. You might want to get over there."

"Give me the address."

Chapter 69

Gabriel left the Mercedes along the highway and put on his night vision goggles and started walking back to the clearing. As he neared, his walkie-talkie went off.

"Gabriel ....it's Black Dog. Where are you? Over." Arnie whispered.

"It's Big Pussy.....I'm just coming up to where I left the money."

"I'm about 200 yards ahead of you. I'm following someone. He's got the bag and is moving at a good clip, carrying the bag on his shoulder. I don't want to take the risk of this path leading to another clearing and a getaway car, so I'm going to try to keep him in visual contact."

"Okay Black Dog, if there's a car you might need to take them down. I'll try to catch up, over." The walk back to the trail wearing the platforms hurt his feet, and he realized too late that he should have changed back into his regular shoes. About 5 minutes later after falling twice, the path started to gently rise through a stand of pine trees. Gabriel heard movement up ahead and saw what looked like a light. He slowed his pace and thumbed the radio whispering, "Black Dog come in, come in Black Dog over."

"I see you, Gabriel. I've stopped about 100 yards ahead of you. There's an old wooden cabin with a light on. Our guy went in. Over."

Gabriel continued along the trail, slip-sliding in the mud. Rainwater was dripping down his face. He eventually saw Arnie kneeling behind an oak tree. What Arnie had called a cabin was little more than a shed about to fall down. The roof was bowed in the middle giving it the appearance of a well-worn saddle. There were two windows that looked out the front at the path. "Have you seen anyone else?"

"No, but that light on the porch was on before the person carrying the bag went in."

"I'm going to crawl my way to the cabin and peek in the window. Have that gun ready in case they see me." Gabriel crept along the tree line as quietly as he could, keeping his eyes fixed on the front door. He'd be a sitting duck if all of a sudden the blackmailer came out. He made it as far as the wooden porch and crawled up to the nearest window. Kneeling, he took a quick peek. What he saw shocked him. It was a man sitting in a rocking chair, the open duffel bag on the floor in front of him. Monopoly money spread all over. He had a shotgun cradled across his lap.

"It's okay Arnie, Come on up," Gabriel called.

Chapter 70

Ben used lights and sirens as he rushed to the Laity's house. When he got there, he found a black and white in the driveway. The front door was open, and the sound of a woman crying came from what he assumed was the kitchen. Pulling out his service revolver, he called out, "Police."

"In here." A man's voice called from the kitchen. When Ben looked into the room, he saw an officer talking to Alberto, who was sitting at the kitchen table. Terra was lying on the floor, her hands cuffed behind her.

When she saw Ben she yelled, "Get these handcuffs off of me. That fat fuck over there assaulted me. He tried to kill me."

The cop turned to Ben, "The husband said she came at him with a knife, and he had no choice but to put her down. I secured the scene." Ben looked down at Terra, who was glaring at him. She had a broken nose, what looked like a black eye, and a puddle of blood around her that was going to leave stains on the linoleum.

Terra tried to get up, but Ben put his foot on her back pushing her back down. This brought on a whole new rash of obscenities. "What the hell are you doing? I'm very good friends with the Mayor."

Ben turned to the patrolman, "Take her downtown and charge her with attempted murder. Make sure they hold her until I get there."

Once the cop pulled her up and led her out, Alberto handed the purse with the listening device to Ben. "Thanks for the call. I knew she was a whore, but now my lawyer will have the proof."

Chapter 71

Gabriel opened the door with his gun drawn, Arnie following close behind him. Charlie looked up and saw them. He made a gesture of greeting but made no move with his shotgun.

Gabriel looked down at the duffel bag and asked, "Charlie, were you the one who was blackmailing the Congressman?"

Charlie nodded, his face expressionless. "He needs to pay for what he did."

"What did he do? asked Arnie softly. Gabriel already knew the answer. In response Charlie unbuttoned the breast pocket of his denim shirt, extracting a bunch of folded papers. Gabriel took the papers from him and began to read aloud.

My name is Esther Burnside Rogers, and if you are reading this, then I guess I am already dead, murdered by my husband,

Being of sound mind and body, I leave all of my worldly possessions to my two children to be managed in a trust by my faithful servant Charlie Benoit until they are of legal age.

Looking back at things I think I made a mistake getting married as a teenager, to someone who turned out to be a different man than I had thought. Dad saw him for who he truly was, but I was blinded by teenage love. While Dad saw a manipulative, fast-talking huckster, I fell in love with a handsome, ambitious, and confident man.

Maybe if Dad hadn't been so adamant and if I wasn't so rebellious then life would have turned out differently. In 1950, I married the catch of a lifetime. Emmett went to enlist as the Korean War had begun, but seeing as he was a married man he didn't qualify. So he came home and said he was focused on public service as a career and as a way to help his country. It was during the war that Cassandra was born. A couple of years later we had Toby. The perfect family.

While I was having babies, Emmett concentrated on politics. He started spending more time at party functions, meeting big shots and traveling the state speaking to whatever group was willing to listen. His pitch was all about a return to Christian values. Wholesome families believing in God, Country, and the Republican Party.

During his first campaign for Congressman, I stood by his side. It was exciting, and I was proud to be Mrs. Emmett Rogers. While he shuttled back and forth from Tylertown and Washington, I settled into the task of running the household and raising our family.

It wasn't until the second campaign that things started to unravel. He hired Ashley Loewen to help run his office and his second campaign. Loewen suggested that I lessen my involvement in the campaign, to free me up to keep the household affairs in order. During that time I found Emmett to be short-tempered and impatient. He had little interest in Cassandra and Toby except when Ashley arranged a photo opportunity. It was around this time that I stopped believing the hype. He was no Ward Cleaver and our life wasn't an episode of Leave it to Beaver.

I guess it's understandable that we became less intimate. I'm told that couples often do over time. At the time, I believed this was the product of his busy schedule and the stress of running a campaign. I didn't suspect him of having an affair until after the second election. He started sleeping in the guest bedroom, telling me that he didn't want to wake me as he tossed and turned worrying about the plight of his constituents.

In January of this year, I had enough. I asked him if he still loved me. 'Of course, I do,' he lied. I pleaded with him to simplify our lives, spend more time with the kids, do some traveling when school let out for the summer. I still remember his reply, 'You know Esther that's a fine idea. Thank you for sharing it with me. Next year is an election year, and I have a lot of work ahead of me. But I'll give it some thought.' Blah, blah, blah.

Things got worse after that. He became even more distant. Finally, I snapped, 'Are you having an affair Emmett?' I asked him. 'Of course not honey. I'm sorry Esther, I have been selfish not thinking enough about you while I do all this traveling. Why don't you hop on a bus and hightail it out of here? Just go.'

I now believe that our marriage is no more than a convenience to him. His bible thumping electorate would never re-elect a man from a failed marriage.

Then in April of this year, I heard something I wasn't meant to hear. I heard him on the phone talking about meeting someone. They were making plans to spend time together during the GOP conference being held on the Mississippi Queen. 'Wear something sexy,' I heard him say. Even though I had more or less written off our marriage at that point, hearing him say that to another was like plunging a knife into my heart.

This time, I went to him and demanded a divorce. I was going to go see a lawyer who would draft documents giving us joint custody of the children. He just laughed at me. 'If you want a divorce then you can have one. The condition is that you leave this house immediately and give up any claim to the children and the money in our accounts.'

I told him to rot in Hell. Most of that money was an inheritance from when my dad passed. I didn't sleep that night, my *anger growing and feeding on itself. I needed leverage, something to get him to accept the divorce with both of us getting what was ours. The people who would be on board the steamboat would be boarding in Vicksburg. Before it was due to sail, I told my husband that I was going to visit a friend from high school. He never even asked the friend's name. When I got to the docks, I found a woman who in return for some cash agreed to help me surprise my husband. She let me on board and unlocked my husband's cabin for me.*

It was a big cabin, nothing but the best for a two-timing Congressman. I got there early so I settled into an easy chair and prepared to wait. I hadn't fully made up my mind about how to handle the surprise. Should I jump out of the armoire when they were in the throes of passion? Should I hide on the balcony and get proof of his adultery and threaten to send the pictures to the press? I must have dozed off sitting in the easy chair. I awoke to the sound of someone rattling the doorknob. Whoever it was, was having difficulty with the lock. That gave me time to slip onto the balcony. It was dark that night, and unless they came outside, then I would be safe.

My husband eventually opened the door. Behind him was Ashley Loewen, who went straight into the washroom. My husband sprawled out on the bed. At that point, I figured that Ashley was merely making sure that my husband, who was clearly drunk, had made it back to his cabin safely. It occurred to me that my husband might be too drunk to perform and that my plan would be for nothing. Then it occurred to me that he might draw the drapes, obscuring my view. I could be stuck out on the balcony for a long time.

What happened next will be an image I will never forget. Ashley came out of the washroom. He was wearing a red and black satin corset and bustier with fancy garter belts. I almost threw up over the side of the boat as I watched him approach the bed and kiss my husband. I can't possibly describe what happened over the next 90 minutes. That is why I am leaving these disgusting photos of my champion, the Mississippi Queen.

When Ashley went back to the washroom, I saw my chance to get out of there. I could hear Emmett's snoring. I quickly left the balcony and made my way out of the cabin. As I left the cabin, a maid saw me and said good evening. The boat docked the next morning in Natchez, and I was able to get off. I took a bus back to Tylertown.

When my husband came home from the cruise, I found my emotions somewhere between pity and disgust. Here he had a family and threw it all away. I think there was a small part of me that still cared for him, and I had no desire to ruin his career and his life. Maybe that's why I tried one more time for the divorce. This time, I offered him $100,000 if he would just leave and sign the papers. Once again he laughed at me and said he would have everything. A couple of days later I approached Ashley Loewen. I asked him to use his influence with Emmett to give me the divorce.

He listened to me and suggested that I wait until after the election in 1980. He promised he would speak to the Congressman. I told him that I had no intention of waiting and that he was to make it happen, otherwise, I would have a story to tell that would rock the nation.

It was his look that prompted me to write this letter and to take Charlie into my confidence.

Chapter 72

As Gabriel finished the letter, Charlie took a stack of photos out his other pocket and handed them to him. The first had Rogers on his knees performing oral sex on Loewen. "Ew." Then there was one of Loewen performing anal sex on Rogers. "Ew, Ew." Gabriel fanned through the rest of the pictures, each displaying the two men taking turns performing various sex acts on each other. All of which Gabriel was sure were illegal in Mississippi. Gabriel shook his head and handed the photos to Arnie.

Arnie had started to look through the photos when the door to the cabin burst open. Ashley Loewen stood in the doorway brandishing a snub nosed .38. "Everyone stay still and put your guns on the floor."

Gabriel nodded to Arnie, and they both put their guns on the cabin floor.

"You too Charlie, put that shotgun down." When Charlie put the shotgun on the floor, Loewen turned to Arnie, "Now give me the pictures."

Arnie carefully handed over the pictures. A smile flashed across Loewen's face. "That was a pretty good story you were reading Mr. Ross, hand it over." Gabriel handed the letter to Loewen, thinking he needed to rush the gunman. There was too much for Loewen to lose, to leave this many witnesses. "What the fuck are you wearing?" Loewen looked at Gabriel's platforms, all covered in mud. Gabriel looked down at his pants which were a good six inches too short.

"Picked them out of your closet, Powder Puff."

"Hahaha, that's funny. Too bad about Esther," Loewen's face went serious. "Had she taken my advice and just gone away then she'd still be alive."

"What happened to her?" asked Gabriel, inching closer.

Loewen waived the gun at Gabriel, "I contacted someone I knew and arranged for her to have a little accident." He had no sooner got the words out of his mouth when Charlie charged him, rage in his eyes. A loud noise resounded in the cabin as Loewen fired the gun point blank into Charlie's chest. The old housekeeper let out a cry and dropped like a sack of potatoes, blood creating an ever enlarging red circle on his hunting shirt.

Another huge blast filled the small cabin, knocking Loewen backward against the cabin door. Gabriel looked over at Arnie, who was holding the Colt revolver. Moving quickly to Charlie, Gabriel grabbed a blanket and tried to staunch the wound.

Arnie kicked the revolver away from Loewen and retrieved the pictures and papers. Loewen was whimpering, holding his shoulder, seeing the blood. "You'll live Loewen, I just winged you," said Arnie.

"We need to get to a phone and call for help, Charlie's losing a lot of blood."

Arnie took a look at Charlie's wound and shook his head at Gabriel.

"I ...let her down," Charlie struggled to get the words out. "I promised her daddy that I would look out for her." He coughed up a load of black blood, "I didn't want the money. Just wanted him to ...quit."

Gabriel nodded that he understood, "None of this is your fault, Charlie. We'll make sure that people pay the price." Moments later Charlie closed his eyes for the last time.

"Okay, Loewen quit your blubbering. We saw you murder Charlie, what's more, you admitted that you had someone kill Esther, plus we have her letter and these wonderful pictures. What should we do with all this, Arnie?"

"I think Ashley here is just a patsy. How much did Rogers know about the accident?" Ashley had stopped moaning but wasn't talking either.

"What do you think Arnie? Should we call an ambulance or maybe just wait until the morning?" Gabriel looked down at Ashley.

"Have you ever seen a Mississippi sunrise in the woods?" Replied Arnie.

"No, can't say that I have."

"I need an ambulance," cut in Ashley. "I'm going to bleed to death."

Arnie ignored Loewen, continuing, "It's one of the truly special moments, the sun shining its rays through the trees, the birds chirping..."

"Listen, Rogers didn't know about anything. He's too self-absorbed. He has no clue, if it weren't for me, he wouldn't even be a Congressman."

"What about the person who you arranged the accident?"

"I can give you them, but you need to protect me."

Chapter 73

They helped get Ashley to the clearing and laid him down in the back of the Mercedes. Putting the big car in gear, Gabriel headed into Tylertown and followed the signs for Walthall County General Hospital. "You're a pretty good shot with that Colt, Arnie," said Gabriel over the constant sound of Loewen crying.

"Not really. I was aiming for his heart." Arnie's reply had Ashley crying louder.

It was 2:30 Friday morning when Gabriel pulled up to the emergency entrance. "Stay with him, I'll get help," called Gabriel. He ran to the entrance and grabbed a duty nurse who was walking by. As he babbled something about a man being shot, the nurse backed away from him, not knowing what to make of a man wearing pedal pushers and six inch red, white and blue platforms. "I need help. Congressman's Rogers' aide is in the back of my car, and he's been shot."

The mention of Congressman Rogers got the nurse's attention, and she yelled to the desk that she needed orderlies and a gurney. "Tell ER, gunshot coming in."

Gabriel led the way out to the Mercedes, and the emergency room nurse checked on Loewen. Gabriel spoke to Arnie, "Stay with him to the emergency room, I'll park the car and then I'll call Ben."

Luckily there was a pay phone in the lobby outside the main doors. He called Ben's apartment, knowing that his partner would know what to do. A sleepy Ben O'Shea answered after a half dozen rings.

"Ben, it's Gabriel. I think I have that leverage for you."

"Gabriel? Forget it. The spider ran away......," he said sleepily.

"Ben don't go back to sleep. Something happened, and I need your help."

There was a pause on the line before a more alert Ben said, "Why are you calling me this early?"

Gabriel told him about the cabin, the letter, and pictures, as well as Charlie. Lastly, he told him about the confrontation with Loewen and the aide's offer to help get the killers.

"Are you saying Rogers had his wife killed?"

"I don't know that Ben. Loewen said it was all his idea and that Rogers was clueless."

"I'm coming. I'll radio Sheriff Mitchum on the way and have him go to the hospital. He's a pretty good guy. He'll get to you way before I do, so you'll have to repeat the whole story for him. Make sure Loewen doesn't go anywhere."

At the mention of Sheriff Mitchum, Gabriel wondered if the man would remember their phone conversation. He ran back into the hospital and found Arnie in the emergency room waiting room.

Nodding to the adjacent operating room door, "They brought him in there a couple of minutes ago." After a few minutes, the orderlies came out. Arnie overheard one orderly say, "Fucking pussy."

"You really need to get rid of those boots," said Arnie, looking down at Gabriel's feet. Gabriel looked around the waiting room and noticed that the half dozen people were looking at him. "Want a coffee? There's a machine." Gabriel asked.

"No thanks, Gabriel."

Just then a Walthall County Sheriff and two deputies walked into the waiting area. Taking a second look at Gabriel, a large, barrel-chested man called out, "You Gabriel Ross?"

"Yes, are you Sheriff Mitchum?" From the look on the man's face, Gabriel didn't know whether he was going to be arrested.

'You the guy that called my office a couple of weeks ago speaking gibberish?"

"Yeah, that was me."

Mitchum shook his head, "Ben O'Shea tells me that you have a little political clusterfuck."

Gabriel waived Arnie over and then suggested that they go down the hall where they wouldn't be overheard. Arnie and Gabriel took turns telling the story. When they had finished the Sheriff ran his hand across his forehead, "So the Congressman's aide has confessed to you two that he had the Congressman's wife killed?"

"Yes, and we witnessed him murdering a man at the cabin," said Arnie.

"The man who was blackmailing the Congressman with incriminating pictures?" The Sheriff asked, trying to grasp the story. Gabriel handed the stack of photos to him.

Flipping through the pictures a disgusted look washed across his face, "Ew!"

"I can show you where the cabin is," offered Arnie.

The Sheriff had them run through things a second time and then called to one of the deputies, "I want you to take this man to a cabin in the woods and secure everything as a crime scene. When you get there, you'll need to radio the county coroner for a body."

Once Arnie and the deputy had left, the Sheriff and Gabriel sat down outside the operating room and went over it again. "So this all has something to do with a cop's murder in Biloxi?"

"I think so, I think the people responsible for Mrs. Rogers' accident might have also tampered with the cops car. The Sheriff shook his head in desperation. "We had better keep this quiet until we know everything." Just then the door to the operating room opened, and a young doctor wearing green scrubs came out. Seeing the Sheriff, he said, "You here because of the gunshot, Sheriff?"

"Yeah, how's he doing?"

"He's a wimp. It was just a minor wound. I pulled out an interesting slug out of his shoulder, though," he said holding up a slug.

"It was a civil war pistol."

The doctor nodded, "That would explain it. We'll be moving him to the recovery area once the nurses have got the crying under control."

When the Doctor left, the Sheriff turned to Gabriel, "I'll need you, and later your Mr. Sims to come down to the stationhouse to make an official statement."

"Sure, how do you want to handle the Rogers angle? That's his aide, and the dead man was his housekeeper. Best to get out in front of this. Word will be getting out."

"The aide will be charged, and then I imagine the County DA will want to speak to Rogers about all this. I know you said the aide claimed it was all his idea, but he might just be protecting his boss or his girlfriend or whatever the fuck you call that."

The Sheriff looked down for a moment before giving Gabriel a solid stare. "A few days after Rogers 'accident, I got a call from the Mayor in Biloxi asking me to use my discretion in wrapping up the investigation quickly. It was not in the public interest he said. Then the County Coroner filed a report saying the accident was caused by wet roads and excessive speeds."

Chapter 74

Ben arrived at the Walthall County Sheriff's office around 6:30 a.m. He was ushered into an office where Gabriel had just finished signing his affidavit.

"First things first," Sheriff Mitchum began once they were all seated. "We have Ashley Loewen in the interview room. So far we have read him his rights and charged him based on this affidavit signed by Mr. Ross. Mr. Sims led my team out to the crime scene and has yet to return."

"Ben, something interesting came up while we were booking Mr. Loewen. His real name is Marko Dactel. He's from Lula Mississippi where he has a record of car theft. Looks like he changed his name to Loewen about 5 years ago. I expect he just made up the "3rd.""

"Dactel? Really?" Ben said looking over at Gabriel. "Mrs. Dactel told me that Terra had a brother."

"Mr. Ross here said you would be interested in that. We haven't asked him anything difficult, we wanted to talk to you first."

"Has he lawyered up?"

"Not as of yet, I understand that he made an offer to cooperate in return for protection. We're going to move pretty quickly on this. I'm expecting Congressman Rogers to walk in any minute now, nothing much happens in this County without him knowing about it. Mr. Ross has been filling me in on what has been going on and what he suspects has happened with Congressman Rogers' wife. Do you have any updates for us?"

"Just a couple of things. Terra Laity has been arrested and charged with attempted murder of her husband." Ben turned to Gabriel. "She found the listening device on her purse and jumped to the conclusion that her husband had placed it there. She went after him with a butcher knife. Everyone is alright, but she might need to visit her friend the plastic surgeon if she ever gets out of jail. Secondly, we had to kick Spider loose, there just wasn't enough at that time to hold him."

"Do you think Terra is going to talk?" asked Gabriel.

"I don't know yet. There's plenty to consider. The tapes you made, although inadmissible, have gotten everyone's attention from the Feds to the State police."

There was a knock on the door and a deputy stuck his head in. "Congressman Rogers is here and wants to have a word, Sheriff."

"Show him to the 2nd interview room and try not to let him see the prisoner." They decided to let the politician cool his jets and discussed how they wanted to handle the interview.

*****

Congressman Rogers was seated at the desk drumming his fingers impatiently when Ben and Sheriff Mitchum walked into the interview room. "Sheriff Mitchum, what the heck is going on here?"

"Thank you for the courtesy of your visit Mr. Congressman. May I introduce Detective Ben O'Shea from the Biloxi PD?" Rogers rose and shook Ben's hand.

"You the one looking into my nephew's death down there?"

"Yes sir I am, please accept my condolences."

"Please sit down Congressman, we need to discuss a few things," said Mitchum.

"Good, I would like to know what the hell is going on down in Biloxi."

"Well actually, we're here to discuss crimes that happened here in Tylertown." Ben took a seat across from Rogers.

Rogers looked from Ben to the Mitchum, "What is all this about, I was told there was some ruckus going on involving my manservant Charlie Benoit."

"Your housekeeper is dead," Ben said cutting him off.

"Excuse me?"

"I guess he was blackmailing you and well, he was shot dead. They're taking his body to the morgue as we speak."

Rogers went to say something then changed his mind. "I don't know what you're talking about. Explain yourself."

In response, Ben pulled out the set of photos from his pocket and fanned them out in front of them like playing cards.

Rogers's face turned a rainbow of colors before landing on white...pale white.

"Charlie?"

"Yeah, Charlie. It's all in the letter written by Esther Rogers before her death. It's all fascinating, but let me read you the best part...*If you're reading this, then I expect that I am dead. Killed by my husband, Emmett Rogers.*"

"That is preposterous, let me see that!"

"Sure, by all means, Congressman."

Rogers took a few minutes to read the handwritten letter. "This is bullshit," he said when he had finished. "She was out of her mind."

Ben smiled, "What about Ashley Loewen, is he crazy too?"

When Rogers didn't respond, the Sheriff broke in, "Congressman, we have Mr. Loewen in the next room. He was the one who killed Charlie in front of witnesses. He also admitted to arranging your wife's accident because ....well it's all there in the letter. Anyway, he has agreed to help the prosecution.

"That is terrible. I had no idea about any of this. Yes, I will admit to an indiscretion, and I will admit that Esther and I were having troubles, but I never, never wanted to see her hurt."

"Maybe you didn't know she had the pictures and could ruin you, but you knew she wanted a divorce which would have ruined you politically and financially. We call that a motive," said Ben.

"I knew nothing, I swear. If Loewen tells you otherwise, then he's lying."

"Congressman, do you think it might be possible that you made an offhand comment about your wife getting in the way, and that your aide might have misunderstood?" Mitchum offered.

"I don't know." Rogers seem to wilt before their eyes with the realization that this would all coming out in the newspaper. The best he could hope for was an end to his political career.

*****

Ben and Sheriff Mitchum excused themselves and went next door to speak to Loewen. He was sitting at the table his shoulder bandaged, his arm in a sling.

As soon as they entered, Loewen whined "Can you tell someone to turn down the air conditioning? I'm freezing ...I think I might be going into shock."

"Sure we can do that Ashley. Can we call you Ashley?"

When Loewen nodded, Mitchum introduced Ben as a detective on the case. "Why don't we talk for a bit first and then I'll get them to adjust the AC."

Ben didn't wait for an agreement and asked Ashley to read Gabriel's statement. When he was finished, Ben asked, "Is that pretty much what happened? "

"The man was blackmailing the Congressman and came at me with a shotgun. It was self-defense."

"It doesn't say that in the affidavit, and we are getting a second one from the other witness that will corroborate it."

"They're lying."

"Why would they lie about that? I understand that Mr. Ross was actually working for the Congressman." When Ashley shrugged his shoulders, Ben continued, "The second part of the affidavit, the part that you said in front of witnesses about arranging Esther Rogers' accident...."

"I was shot, I was delirious. I didn't know what I was saying."

"Okay, you didn't offer to provide testimony against the people who did that in return for protection? Before you answer, I should tell you we know who those people are."

Loewen's face registered surprise at first, then Ben could almost hear the gears turning as he tried to figure out how to spin the story. "I want immunity."

*****

"So where does that leave us, Ben? I can't see the DA agreeing to let him have immunity. He shot Charlie in cold blood and admitted to having Esther Rogers killed," asked Gabriel once the Sheriff and Ben had filled him in on Loewen's interview.

"How else do we get the real killer then?" Ben asked.

"What about the case against his sister?" asked the Sheriff.

"The FBI are going to be all over that. I got a message from Wil Graham, a contact at the FBI. They want to arrange for a full securities audit, maybe as soon as tomorrow."

"With a $2 million dollar embezzlement, plus arranging for Willy Parnell and trying to kill her husband, I can't see anybody offering Terra Laity immunity either," commented the Sherriff.

"I have an idea, but we need to get back to Biloxi," said Ben.

Chapter 75

Ben arranged for Morgan to be booked on fraud charges and put in the system, but not before walking him by Terra, who was sitting in the next room.

"What is he doing here?" she said as Ben and Willis walked into the interview room.

"Nice nose," commented Ben. Terra had white adhesive tape across her nose and a growing yellow and purple bruise under her right eye. Ben and Mitchum sat down, and Ben put the tape recorder on the table. "Morgan's been telling us a little story."

"He's a liar. I think he's a drug addict. I wouldn't believe a word he says."

"Still, I think you should probably listen to everything before you say anything more." Ben played the recording of her interaction with Morgan. At the conclusion, she was about to say something but Ben put up his hand. "Tut, Tut....wait." He played the next tape, with Terra and Frankie. Once again he had to tell her to be quiet before he played the last tape they had just made, of their interview with Morgan.

After hearing everything, she was stone-faced. "So what? You little perverts have me on tape having sex."

"Well, it's a little more than that. I believe you implicated yourself in Willy Parnell's murder. If that's not enough to get you life behind bars at Central Mississippi Correctional Facility,, then I think the $2 million dollars missing in the union accounts will be a nice bonus. The security people are in there as we speak. Oh, I almost forgot, we have you for trying to carve up your husband."

In a tone of voice that suggested that she had already anticipated the conversation, "If there is any money missing then it's all Morgan Armstrong's doing. He is the investment guy. As for that tape, you had no right to record my private conversations. I'm going to sue everyone here. And my fat fuck of a husband came at me with a knife."

"So you're not going to give me the names of the two creeps who you paid to murder Willy?" Ben asked with a smile.

"Fuck off."

They walked into the next interview room a little less sure of themselves. "So Ashley, or should I call you Marko? Marko Dactel from the striving metropolis of Lula, Mississippi. I guess you and your sister Terra were pretty happy to get out of that dump," said Ben.

"So big deal, lots of people change their name. Not a crime."

"No it's not a crime, but you have accumulated enough of those already haven't you?"

"I said I wanted immunity. Otherwise, I will see a lawyer."

"I can't offer you immunity Marko. Not when we have you committing murder in front of witnesses. Besides, we already made one deal already today. Your sister's in the next room singing her heart out about the Sons of Silence."

At that exact moment, the interview room opened, and a cop leading Spider in handcuffs walked in. When Spider saw Loewen at the table, there was a flash of recognition and something else. "Oh, I'm sorry, I didn't know this room was taken," said the cop.

"Try the next room over or have him cool his jets out there. We won't be long, I'm sure Mr. Dactel is anxious to make bail," said Willis.

When Spider was gone, Loewen was noticeably upset. "Alright, you win. But I want protection against that guy."

"Okay with us," said Ben. "Spill it!"

"My sister Terra and I met at a bar in Gulfport. I told her about what had happened and that the Congressman's wife was going to expose everything. Terra gave me that guy's name - he goes by Spider. I went to see him, and he took care of everything. I just had to get $10,000 for him."

"And how did you get the money?"

"I borrowed it from the campaign funds. I knew it wouldn't be missed."

Chapter 76

When they left Marko, Willis looked at Ben and. "Okay I will admit it publicly, you are the best fuckin' detective I have ever worked with." Ben thanked him for the compliment and veered back into Terra's interview room.

When they opened the door, "What the fuck do you want now? I want out of here this minute."

"She wants out of here Chief," said Ben with a look of urgency.

"Yeah? I didn't realize that prisoners were allowed to come and go as they pleased."

"Terra, your brother Marko is in the next room, and he just gave you up. You told him about Spider and how the guy can make all your problems go away."

"My brother is next door?"

"Absolutely, you might want to reconsider cooperating otherwise you'll be in prison so long no plastic surgeon is going to ever make you beautiful again."

Epilogue

A few weeks later, Ben and Gabriel were celebrating in a nice French restaurant in the Latin Quarter of New Orleans with Chevon and Rachel.

"So Ben, how did you get Spider to speak to you?" asked Rachel.

"He never did. Those 1% never talk. I showed him the affidavits signed by Marko and Terra, and he told me to shove them up my ass." Ben laughed.

"But you arrested Branko anyway," added Gabriel.

"Yeah, we ran a check on his phone line from the store, and we were able to narrow it down. It's a good thing we did, he was packing up to leave when we raided the place."

"Do you have a solid case against him?" Chevon took a sip of wine.

"We're building it. He and his brother have sheets as long as my arm, so he's not going anywhere. It'll take some work, but Willis is convinced the Lug Nut Killers have struck before."

"What about the brother and sister? asked Rachel.

"They both made a deal for their testimony against Spider. Terra agreed to testify against Frankie Fingers. But even with that, we have enough to put them both away for years."

"And then there's Justyne's husband Morgan....," said Gabriel.

"He pleaded guilty to fraud and is awaiting sentencing. He will likely be getting a few years. As for Justyne, she never heard the tape or saw that picture. She would have, had he not done the right thing and told her everything."

"Did she forgive him?" asked Chevon.

"Filed for divorce the next day."

"What about Congressman Rogers, Gabriel?" asked Rachel.

"The story about the affair and the letter will come out eventually. As I'm sure you're aware, he resigned. Said the burden of the office was proving to be too much without Esther's support. He plans to simplify his life and do some traveling far away from here...with his two very wealthy children."

"What about the Mayor, was there any evidence that he did anything wrong?" asked Gabriel.

"Yes and no. Terra told us that she had a sexual relationship with him and that she asked him to do something about the investigation. Doesn't look like there is any proof but don't be surprised if all this resurfaces during the next election campaign."

"What's next for you, Ben?" asked Chevon with a twinkle in her eye.

"I was going to hang around New Orleans for a bit and show off my new shoes." Ben lifted his foot displaying his 6 inch Independence Day platform shoes.

Everyone had a laugh then Rachel asked Gabriel whether he had another big case on the go.

"Arnie is keeping the agency afloat with more than enough cases. Ben, I thought we should hire a receptionist/associate when we move to the new offices."

"Can we afford it?"

"Absolutely," said Gabriel winking at Rachel. "I'll start looking for candidates after I come back from a short vacation up north."

*****The End*****